# A CANDLE FOR CONSUELA

A JOURNEY FROM TORTURE TO JUSTICE AND JOY

MIKE KINGSTON

To Lucy
with best wishes
Mike

Published by Mitre Publishing.

ISBN: 978-1-9168732-0-9

A Candle for Consuela is the first book in

THE OMEGA FILES QUARTET consisting of:

A CANDLE FOR CONSUELA

A FLYBLOWN SOLUTION

A BANGKOK VERDICT

A COVERT CORRUPTION

*To my family:*
*Margaret, Sarah, Mark, Miriam, Finnian and Ronnie who bring such joy and keep me whole.*

# PROLOGUE

El Salvador is the smallest country in Central America. The history of El Salvador has been characterized by significant economic inequality. In the late nineteenth century, coffee became a major cash crop for El Salvador, bringing in approximately ninety-five per-cent of the country's income. However, this income was restricted to only two per-cent of the population, sharply dividing the people between a small, powerful elite consisting of fourteen families, *'las catorce'*, and an impoverished majority.

The Salvadoran civil war was a conflict between the military-led government of El Salvador and the Farabundo Martí National Liberation Front (FMLN), a coalition - "umbrella organization" – of five left-wing guerrilla groups.

In its report covering 1981, Amnesty International identified "regular security and military units as responsible for widespread torture, mutilation and killing of non-combatant civilians from all sectors of Salvadoran society."

The report also stated that the killing of civilians by state security forces had become routine.

The civil war lasted for more than twelve years and saw extreme violence from both sides. It also included the deliberate terrorizing and targeting of civilians by death squads, the

*The purpose of torture is not getting information.*
*It's spreading fear.*

Eduardo Galeano

*The experience of falling in love is overwhelming for anyone, but especially for a priest. When love erupts in a priest's heart, he realizes everything he has worked for is put at risk – his ministry, reputation, the esteem of parishioners, other priests, his bishop and possibly family and friends.*

Dr. Aaron Milavec

# ONE

## 1994
## London

Father John Doyle lay back on his narrow bed, holding a copy of *Pastores Dabo Vobis* in his left hand, while in his right, he stroked his erect penis. The bedroom was dark; noises stilled save for an occasional shuffling of tired feet on the cold, bare, wooden floor outside his door.

*Synod, in the conviction that perfect chastity in priestly celibacy is a charism, reminds priests that celibacy is a priceless gift of God for the Church and has a prophetic value for the world today.*

He dropped the *'John Paul II Apostolic Exhortation'* on the dusty, beige, bare-carpeted floor, succumbing to the familiar combination of guilt, desire, and mortal sin.

His alarm clock rested in its usual place, the corner of a glass-topped table.

Set for five-thirty.

It was always set for five-thirty.

The clock stood next to a plastic glass, full of water.

Both standing like witnesses.

The only witnesses, besides conscience, guilt, and, although he pushed the thought away, his God.

The God who sees all knows all but ignores much, he hoped. His own guilt was burden enough; any more censure would expose the fraud that innocence and certainty had become.

A reading lamp threw shadows across the small room. An old bureau stood in one corner, papers piled neatly on its surface. Two chairs stood next to each other, one wooden and one soft, covered with dark blue upholstery.

A poster of Oscar Romero hung on the wall above the wooden chair.

He glanced briefly at papers scattered on the wooden chair. A folded map of El Salvador and a photograph of the town of Aguilares beside a copy of *The Tablet,* headlined *"The Living Spirit. The tenth anniversary of the murder of Father Rutillo Grande".*

Books lined his walls. Acquired over the years, they had become refuge and inspiration. Also, in times of darkness, hidden from sight and understanding, they were strident voices calling him to freedom.

Unfulfilled dreams and barely discerned ambition filled the shelves as often as the poems of Thomas Merton or the theology of St Augustine.

Here he was safe, hidden from the outpourings of hopeless irrelevance which distinguished his spells in the confessional booth and his patient attempts at pastoral care; but, above all else, the confusion hidden behind his smokescreen of orthodoxy.

The printed word was his sanctuary, reflecting the reality and excitement of life, the spirit of wonder capturing him as he considered the heart of creation beating so fiercely in carefully crafted sentences he loved so dearly.

He despaired at the contrast. The wonder of a life fulfilled. Creation unrestrained and expressed in words of beauty and hope but clashing with the despair of life in its sad, barren reality.

He had been trained to deny beauty and truth except for that approved in sombre words and explicit instruction. For his cowardly acquiescence, he allowed himself the luxury of despising himself. However, orgasmic excitement kept the feeling at bay for a short time until, with relief - in the tender moment following ejaculation, when his thwarted desires and fantasies spilt out in meaningless triumph - he returned to self-censure and perfection.

A pair of shuffling feet scuffled along the floor outside his room. He picked up the draft of his sermon:

*"God is not forgetful or indeed absent when you need him. The time you feel most alone is the time that God is standing beside you, hoping and waiting."*

He hoped that God had been absent for the past twenty minutes.

Walking to the window, he saw a black Mercedes limousine idling at the bottom of steps leading up to the church. Exhaust fumes trailed into the fresh, damp, morning air. The vehicle's rear windows were impenetrable. The driver's expression was dark; the scrutiny from that black-haired, stern face, bleak and intense.

Father John's sharply defined features fractured in the rain-spattered window as he stared at his own reflection in the glass while the car slowly moved away.

He felt a tremor of fear.

* * *

Senor Adolfo Guzman gazed through the water stained window of his limousine, toward St Mary Magdalene Church. His thick fingers, enclosed in heavy gold rings, opened a file containing an architect's plans. He briefly perused the plans before tossing the documents to the floor and looking at the building alongside the church.

The sign outside read "St Mary's Mission – Helping homeless people transform their lives".

Alongside the sign was a mock-up thermometer showing progress toward the three hundred-thousand pounds the church was trying to raise for expansion. They had so far raised forty-five thousand.

hand, adjusted a blue silk tie, finally touching his narrow dark moustache. Sweating from the brief walk, he wiped his head with a handkerchief. The man's face was broad, sour, and distrustful. He looked around the small reception room and then back to Sheridan.

'Is he the best there is?'

'Desmond Williams is certainly one of the very best. A Queen's Counsel.'

Approaching his solicitor, Guzman leaned down and spoke very softly. 'One of the best, Mr Sheridan? I thought I was paying for *the* best.'

The other swallowed and instinctively drew back, smiling nervously. 'There is nobody else with greater experience, expertise and personal contacts in the area of immigration. He is, of course, also a member of parliament.'

'He's also costing me a great deal of money,' said Guzman, 'and so are you. You'd both better know what you're doing!'

He moved to the reception desk and tapped a finger on the dark wooden counter. A diamond glittered from one of the three gold rings adorning his thick fingers.

His voice was harsh, breaking the concentration of the receptionist staring at a computer screen.

'We have an appointment.'

She looked up.

*'Now.'*

Before she could respond, Sheridan intervened pleadingly,

'Desmond knows we're here. He will be with us shortly.'

He felt the intensity of the man's scowl. 'Nine o'clock you told me.'

Guzman continued flatly. 'It's now five minutes past.'

The receptionist replaced a hastily raised telephone.

'Could you come this way, gentlemen?'

Guzman struggled behind, his fractured breathing punctuating the silence as they ascended two flights of stone stairs.

Desmond Williams QC, white-haired and immaculately

dressed; pinstripes, starched white shirt and waistcoat; was waiting at the top. His welcome was affable, employing manners preserved from a bygone age.

Guzman perfunctorily grasped the offered hand but did not reply to Williams's greeting. The receptionist's footsteps echoed off the stone stairwell as she headed back down.

They entered a large shadowy office. An expansive desk with green leather inlay stood in one corner, opposite a sofa and two chairs, both covered in similar green leather. The walls were lined with law books and court records, recording legal proceedings going back to the nineteenth century. A single lamp on the desk relieved the gloom.

Guzman sat himself down in the middle of the sofa. He picked at his teeth with his little finger then spoke without looking up.

'I need permanent residence, Williams. I need to be able to stay here in Britain, eventually to gain citizenship.'

Sheridan interrupted. 'The papers have already been sent to Desmond, and he is confident that if the financial arrangements can be agreed, you will be successful.'

Guzman's scrutiny was intense. He didn't take his eyes off the barrister while responding to Sheridan.

'I want guarantees, not confidence, and to hear from him. I haven't come all this way and paid out over ten thousand pounds just to hear again what you've told me already. I cannot go back there. Back to Spain.'

Williams gave a thin smile and began speaking.

'Mr Sheridan is quite right, Senor Guzman. Your chances of obtaining permanent residence are excellent if you invest, as proposed.'

The barrister settled back into his armchair. He spoke; his voice calm, authoritative; in paragraphs, not sentences, and discouraged interruption.

'I understand you intend to invest one million pounds in a venture capital company – with Daniel Cooper. That should take you into the new Tier One entrepreneurial scheme. Further, I understand you will be donating three hundred thousand pounds to a charitable trust for an inner-city community project. That will add substance to your application.'

Guzman nodded.

'Cardinal Trujillo is an acquaintance. He has already talked with Bishop Peter, who called me a few days ago. I have a preliminary meeting at ...' he pulled a scrap of paper from his trouser pocket. 'St Mary Magdalene. They have some Mission that badly needs funds. I had a look at it earlier this morning, and I'm meeting the priest in the next day or so.'

Williams looked up with interest.

'Daniel Cooper is also a trustee of The Mission. He has been extremely successful in your part of the world, I understand.'

Sheridan nodded in agreement. 'He is Chairman of Atlantic Santos Holdings and transformed their Latin American operations. We handle their corporate work.'

He looked toward Guzman.

'Perhaps you know him? I believe he was based in Sao Paulo at one time.'

Guzman grunted but made no reply.

Williams continued. 'Bishop Peter is a good man. We are representing his diocese in a planning appeal, Senor Guzman. I had arranged for you to meet the minister, but I understand he is otherwise engaged. He is sending his close adviser, Charles Mayer. Probably even better. Very well respected and well connected. I assume you will be free. Reform Club one o'clock.'

Williams stood.

'I can assure you that your investment and charitable donation will weigh significantly in the minds of those who make the decisions. I frankly cannot see any impediment to your obtaining permanent residence in the light of what you have told me. I'm sure Mr Sheridan will progress matters, and I will be available should any sensitive issues arise. Any family involved?'

Guzman shook his head and waved a hand at Sheridan.

'You were reading a copy of *The New York Times?*'

Sheridan looked surprised at this observation. He opened his briefcase and pulled out the article he had been reading. The headline read; *'How US actions helped hide Salvador Human Rights Abuses.'*

Guzman's face darkened.

'The US helped us to destroy communism. It was a war.'

He waved his hand in dismissal.

His voice was unyielding. 'You could never understand it.'

Williams appeared to dismiss the comment.

'Mr Guzman, you are doing precisely the right thing and meeting the right people, so there should be no problems.'

Guzman and Sheridan stood.

Williams gestured toward the door.

'Let me show you out.'

He turned to Sheridan.

'Jeffrey, a few moments when Senor Guzman has left if you please.'

Sheridan and Guzman proceeded down the stone steps and back through the narrow passages. When they left the building, heavy rain beat down on the silent pair.

Lopez jumped out to open a rear door as they approached the car.

Guzman turned to Sheridan. 'Money will be transferred to you from Switzerland this afternoon. Three hundred and fifty thousand to cover any extra costs. Fax me at the Tower Hotel once it's received, and confirm it's placed in an escrow account as agreed. Cooper's funds are already in place.'

He turned and fell into the rear seat before turning to Sheridan again.

'Mayer. Who is he?'

'Advisor to Defence Minister. His family have an interest in a private bank. I understand they are used to handling delicate Government transactions.'

The car door slammed.

Williams was sitting back in his office chair when Sheridan returned to the barrister's office.

her face, her presence, her smile, would come before him late at night, when all other images were absent, even the familiar icons for which he had given his existence.

Pushing his sermon to one side, he pulled himself up and kicked at the wall as he left his room. Walking along the corridor into the church, he knelt in a front pew. Looking up at the extravagantly carved statue of Christ facing down at him, he bowed his head and tried to offer his life and obedience once again to this mysterious lover.

Silent moments passed.

At first, he felt, rather than heard, that someone had moved in the pew behind him. Then a smell of tobacco came, followed by a whisper of cloth against wood and then a hacking cough. Father looked round. The frail figure was stooped, his face sharp and mobile, his skin the colour of parchment, drawn features carved from an empty skull. The eyes never stopped moving with anxiety.

'Father Doyle?'

Starting to rise, John felt a hand grasp his arm. The grip was firm. The voice was anxious.

'Stay.'

The tortured face turned toward the priest, dead eyes gazing at Father John as he looked from a deep well of desperation.

The priest dropped back to his knees, straining to hear the tormented, contemptuous voice as it continued.

'Remember your calling, Father. The spirit of the Lord is upon me because the Lord has anointed me to proclaim liberty to the captives and to proclaim the year of the Lord's favour, and the day of vengeance of our God.'

Those eyes glanced quickly, nervously, around the church again as John looked closely at the intense and troubled face. There was a pause at each random sound, even if only a slight stuttering in the middle of a sentence.

The voice continued.

'Remember your calling. He has filled the hungry with good things and the rich he has sent empty away.'

Dark eyes screwed up in suspicion.

'The rich He has sent empty away. Do you know those words, Father Doyle?'

John paused in replying. There was a passion to the tired, accented tones that defied trivial comment. He then spoke softly.

'I know the words of Christ. I know the song of Mary.'

'Then let your church live by them.'

Father John opened his mouth, ready to respond, but the hand still clutching his arm gripped tighter as he heard the voice again.

'Consuela Flores…'

John turned quickly, listening more intensely.

'Will be in danger. The bastard will come for her. So *keep her safe.*'

The priest grabbed hold of a shrivelled arm as that tired face turned toward him and spoke again.

'You will not understand. Not yet.'

He jerked his head and looked around the church before leaning close to Father.

'But you will.'

John opened his mouth to speak, but the voice continued.

'Too many tears have been shed, Father. Too much sorrow has passed her way. Try to find courage.'

He gestured dismissively toward the altar. 'Not this ersatz truth. Real courage is what you must find.'

A door slammed somewhere in the church. Father jumped and turned toward the noise as Mrs Quinn came from the door leading to the Presbytery. He turned back. The figure had gone, the door of the church slammed shut.

The Church Secretary looked perplexed.

'Father! The diary? You said you wanted to go through it with me ten minutes ago.'

Father Doyle rose without a word and walked back to his office, where Mrs Quinn began to read from a large diary.

'This morning we have the Festival Committee.'

The priest's sigh was long, and he shook his head. Mrs Quinn continued. 'And this afternoon, at five, you have Brother Roger.'

Father Doyle's face turned sharply.

His assistant said, 'He asked to meet with you.'

'More money for The Mission?'

Mrs Quinn smiled and pointed across toward the building in question.

'Did you know he took Consuela in a couple of months ago? She was living in a derelict squat.' She shook her head and smiled. 'Silly question, Of course you knew.'

Raising his eyebrows, Father Doyle turned and picked up a small, tattered briefcase. His voice brusque:

'Two o'clock, you say?'

She nodded. 'And a reminder about that message from the Bishop about Senor Guzman.'

He asked. 'Senor Guzman?'

'The message from Cardinal Trujillo's office.'

John still looked uncertain.

'Bishop Peter passed on a message from Cardinal Trujillo, asking that you embrace him,' Mrs Quinn explained. 'He's coming to see you later this week."

'Embrace him?'

'A turn of phrase. I assume.'

'Who is he?' asked Father.

'Senor Adolfo Guzman from Central America somewhere.'

'Trujillo? His reputation is, what shall I say, impressive?'

'A much-feared man my contacts tell me, but I understand Guzman comes bearing gifts. He wishes to make a donation.'

Standing and moving over to a wall lined with books, John asked, 'Can we be bought, Mrs Quinn?'

'Depends on the size of the donation, and it also might keep Brother Roger happy.'

'He's no longer a priest.'

She raised her eyebrows but didn't respond.

* * *

As he descended the steps of St Mary Magdalene, traffic was circling the roundabout in front of the church. Such animation to so little purpose: movement, speech, noise, ceaseless activity disguising the empty core of existence.

Father Doyle paused halfway down the steps wishing he could avoid this regular monthly trip to the Festival Committee. Many of his colleagues welcomed such a diversion, but he was not one of them. A lot of chatter about very little that could just as quickly be decided by a couple of telephone calls. He liked staying amongst his books and his people. He felt proprietorial toward his congregation, saints and bigots alike. There were enough of each and some who managed to be both. Father John Doyle loved them all.

He saw Consuela Flores working in the office of The Mission alongside Brother Roger. They both smiled and waved in greeting at John. He waved back.

* * *

The rain had passed. Consuela sat on the steps beside St Mary's Mission, eating a chocolate bar and drinking an afternoon cup of coffee. She would sit there and see the same faces passing by each day and remember her hometown, Aguilares, in El Salvador. It consisted of a few small shops; homes that were mostly hovels; dirt-poor sugar-cane farmers, as her father had been.

She looked across at St Mary's and remembered when the army arrived and took over the church. She had been in the main square at the time, and the sound of a machine gun blasting bullets into the altar still reverberated with her. The building was subsequently turned into army barracks. But despite the trauma of those days, Aguilares was still her birthplace and had been her childhood home. Memories were not all bad.

Pushing a black beret down a little further over deep brown eyes, she pulled her woollen scarf a little tighter, missing the heat of her beloved El Salvador.

A smile signified hope, bringing back those times of celebration and fervour, when the sunrise would dawn bright with expectancy and aspiration. Dreams could become true; darkness be touched by light, and the suffering of her country could end.

In the adjoining room, her brother Jorge played his guitar, singing softly of freedom and the end of starvation, and next to her lay Manuel. She had once believed that love like theirs existed only in someone else's imagination. On such days, hope and certainty had become naively intertwined in her heart and her dreams. The warm, gentle feel of fresh cotton on her naked body. Her hand on Manuel's shoulder, touching his soft skin. He would turn toward her, barely opening his eyes as he stretched strong arms above his head. His broad shoulders flexed, eyes closing again, fingers tracing sensuous patterns across her acquiescent flesh. Her eyes would close too, joining him in his darkness, listening and feeling an excited shiver of expectation, hardly daring to breathe for fear of disturbing the sublime sanctuary. Turning further toward him, her hands passing down his muscular back, their bodies meshed together. Clinging to each other; passion replacing and ignoring the fear that awaited when juices had dried, and kisses were no longer moist; as the light spread further through a morning mist, and the slow rhythmic marching of jackboots would replace the soft strumming of the guitar.

Consuela opened her eyes again, staring up at St Mary's, trying to brush off such memories that led nowhere. She knew what had prompted them but realised the absurdity of the feelings. He was a priest - *he was a priest* - and that path only led to despair.

Brother Roger sat down beside her, his face characterised by his usual gentle kindness, his joy of life. The smile that brought the sun. He brushed the few dark hairs left on his bare head.

'You were somewhere else,' he remarked.

Consuela smiled. 'I was, and I don't think I should tell you where.' She gestured when she spotted Father Doyle coming along the road from the DLR station.

'St Mary's is lucky to have you both.'

He nodded, offering an exaggerated bow.

'I have a meeting with him this afternoon, trying to get some more money for the hostel.'

'And he's coming over for dinner tomorrow evening. I hope you and Stuart will be in.'

Father Doyle headed over toward them.

Brother Roger shook his head.

'I'm working, and I know Stuart has a meeting.'

The priest was dressed in his familiar dark suit and clerical collar. Consuela smiled up at him. He looked lonely in returning her smile as if stranded somewhere he didn't understand. His face beautifully fashioned from cold, church marble, exquisite and precise. He was slightly taller than her brother, Jorge, who had intended to be a priest until he went to medical school, but this man was wiry where Jorge was burly, and the kind expression appeared to be prompted by intellect rather than freedom of emotions. The coolness disguised an intensity she had come to understand.

Doyle stopped, motionless, and for just a moment she saw uncertainty flash across the chiselled features.

Consuela wanted to reach out and touch him, to draw him closer to her. Instinctively she brushed at her blouse, smoothed her hair.

He smiled, 'Consuela.'

Pausing, he turned to Brother Roger.

'You're coming to my office? Don't ask for money.'

Roger frowned and then laughed.

'What other reason would I want to see you?'

Father Doyle shook his head and continued up the steps.

Consuela touched her companion's arm.

'Thank you for taking me in, Roger. Since I had to leave home, I've never been so happy.'

She looked after Father Doyle as he reached the entrance to the Presbytery.

'Or felt as safe.'

Roger followed her glance, then turned and smiled at her.

'I hope it lasts, Consuela. After everything you've seen, you deserve some happiness.'

* * *

As Father John re-entered his church, he dipped his fingers in holy water and traced the sign of the cross on his forehead. Here was *home*. He knelt before the cross, closed his eyes and prayed.

A few minutes later, he stood up, glanced at his watch, and proceeded along the corridor into his office. Dropping the small briefcase on the floor, he sat down at his desk. When he looked up again, he saw Brother Roger ascending the steps from The Mission, talking to a shaven-headed youth dressed in old, dirty jeans.

The darkening sky depressed the early evening; umbrellas rushed along the shining pavement as the city emptied itself for the night.

Looks more like a priest than most priests do, thought Doyle.

Perhaps he was.

The two figures sat themselves down on a bench situated at the top of the steps. Roger looked over towards the window and spotted John, who shrugged and smiled in return, as though slightly embarrassed.

In Roger, the poor and lonely discovered compassion rather than vague if well-meaning concern. They sensed in him a melancholy that brought him closer to them.

The truth had seemed so clear to John, five years ago, when Roger had confessed his love for Stuart. The Church, after all, had to live by doctrine and theological truth, or else it had no foundation. It was more important than one solitary priest; it had to be unchangeable in the shifting and unsettling times through which it passed. Compassion was the underpinning of the Church's truth, the expression of love passed down from Christ himself, but such love was not without demand and sacrifice. It was not weak and changing; it was all that had ever been and would be again.

If only things were as clear to him now as they had been five years ago.

At his window overlooking the steps, Father shuffled paperwork into a neat pile on the left side of his desk and rearranged three pens that were slightly asymmetrical: two ballpoints - one black, one red - and a fountain pen. He screwed on the top of the fountain pen and then walked over and opened the door. Roger came slowly along the corridor and into the office.

Father John gestured toward the sofa and sat on one of the chairs, on the arm of which rested a copy of *The Catholic Herald*.

Mrs Quinn had followed Brother Roger and stood in the doorway. Her glance passed from one to the other, beaming a broad smile at Roger, who gave her a wink, then turned, with a questioning glance, back to Father.

'Two coffees, please, Mrs Quinn.'

She came in shortly with a tray carrying two steaming cups and a plate of chocolate biscuits. Doyle eyed the biscuits, then looked at Mrs Quinn and frowned. She merely smiled at Roger, put down the tray and walked out of the door.

John began to speak. 'Is this about money? If so, you know you should see the trustees.'

'You are a trustee.'

'Merely semi-detached, they don't consult me; they tell me.'

Roger paused to finish a chocolate biscuit. Mrs Quinn had not forgotten his favourites. He smiled at John and shrugged.

'Yes, I know that. I wondered if you've had Dan Cooper over?'

Doyle shook his head.

'He's resurrected The Mission plans. You remember Bill Hamilton. The architect?'

'Of course,' he smiled. 'He worships twice a year on the date of both his and Emily's and his parent's wedding. That was nineteen thirty-nine, I think. They lived nearby.'

'Cooper's bringing Hamilton along next week. Not sure why but he wants to update the plans.'

'Can't do any harm I suppose, but we don't have the money. But then Bill Hamilton doesn't charge anything.'

'Cooper asked for a copy of the latest Mission booklet, detailing all that we offer. We redid it a few weeks ago with all the staff's photographs, and I included Consuela as she's almost full-time.'

Roger paused.

'Will there be more money? You know how stretched we are. We're *desperate.* I can help with paying the bills, the food, and so on, but the building itself is falling down, and it's tragic that we have to close the doors at night. This winter we know at least two died outside because of the cold.'

Father John's voice was understanding.

'We've started the fundraising.'

Then he looked crestfallen.

'It'll take forever. We'll have to think of some other way.'

'I know you're trying your best and what it means to you, John. The Mission will always remain your legacy.'

'Ours, Roger. *Ours.* It was the best time, working together, getting the hostel going.' He paused. 'There has been talk of a benefactor, but it's probably just that, diocesan gossip. How much are you subsidising The Mission yourself?'

'I don't know for sure, but whatever my family trust can afford.'

'The trustees still have no idea what you're doing, Roger. They should know how much you put in. What if you were to leave?'

'That was the deal, John. You agreed not to tell anyone. You've heard the rumour about a benefactor as well then?'

'Mrs Quinn is nothing if not well informed, and there's little here as sacred as gossip – you understand that.'

'Do you know anything more?' asked Roger.

'Not a thing.'

John shook his head. 'I am supposed to be a silent rubber

stamp; the real decisions are taken elsewhere, but I'll try to find out if any money is likely to be forthcoming.'

He emptied his coffee cup and looked back again at Brother Roger. 'Has the bishop contacted you?'

'About The Mission's fifth anniversary? Previous engagement I'm afraid, can't make it.' He smiled. 'I didn't expect anything different, John, since I'm a pariah to our Bishop Peter.'

Father Doyle fingered the small wooden crucifix hung around his neck. He clutched it gently in his hands and shook his head.

'The Church moves slowly.'

'I understand but move it should. The people know, and they have made up their minds. They have deserted in spirit, even if not in practice. For centuries, we sought money and power under the pretence of poverty and humility. We have consistently persecuted truth in the name of flawed and immoral *infallibility*.'

Father Doyle clasped his hands together in front of him.

'Do you regret it?'

He looked up at the ceiling and continued, carefully phrasing his words, hoping that Roger would understand his cry for help. Roger remained silent as the priest continued.

'At the time I couldn't understand how you allowed passion to destroy your vocation.'

The room was silent.

Roger eventually spoke. 'Is celibacy ever really possible, John, or just another cruel joke?' He shook his head. 'Our narrow sexual teaching is dividing the Church.'

Neither spoke for a moment.

Roger raised his head and looked closely at John.

'I am what I am. At that time, you said you didn't understand. And now?'

John looked at Roger, longing to piece together the words that might portray his battle between emotion and obedience.

The telephone rang. It was urgent – Mrs Kelly for Father Doyle.

## FOUR

Father Doyle knocked at the apartment door.

He knew the building well. It was just above the offices and home of Bishop Peter. Graffiti covered the dark brick walls; cigarette ends, wastepaper and empty cans littered the walkways.

Brigid Kelly was small, grey-haired, and nervous. She glanced over his shoulder and then beckoned him through the door.

'Thank you for coming, Father. Can I get you a cup of tea?' She led him into a neat lounge where a large crucifix sat on a cupboard with a string of rosary beads draped over it.

Doyle shook his head. 'It's all right, Brigid. There's no need.'

'Will you sit, Father?'

They sat opposite each other, in two chairs on either side of a gas fire.

'He's been picked up by the police again.'

She wrung her hands.

'Throwing a brick through a curry house window this time. Such shame, Father, but what do I do. He's a different boy now his da's gone. Well, probably, of course, you know that as well. He beat him too much. I told him not to, but he took no notice. It was the drink, of course. God, isn't it always. Sorry, Father.'

She crossed herself in silence, and then the words began to flood out again.

'He never listens to me. It's all this Nazi stuff I'm sure. In heaven's name, we were bombed by them, and now he has their rubbish all over his bedroom wall. I'll show you.'

She started to stand up but as quickly sat down again.

'In a minute, perhaps. Father, I'm worried. Really worried this time. He's got some money, about two hundred pounds, so where would he get it? It's not as if he can find work. He tries, of course. He promises that he's going to show me and everyone else. "People know me," he says, "I'm respected". What can he mean? Who would respect him? He won't explain, Father.'

'We've all failed him in some way, Brigid. It's a cold world out there, and we've lost the fight to give him - and those like him - any hope.'

Brigid Kelly stood up and led Father back along a corridor toward the front door. She took a key and opened a door leading off the hallway. A large sign on it read "STRICTLY PRIVATE".

She looked back along the corridor, anxiety creasing her worn features.

'He doesn't know I have a spare key.'

Father Doyle stared open-mouthed when the nervous woman opened the door. Walls were covered with images of Adolf Hitler, large swastikas, and Nazi SS insignia. Pamphlets lay in profusion on the bed, one of them entitled "The RESISTER" originating from the United States.

He started to read: '"Thousands of British youth are fighting back. Destroy the system that is treating you like dirt. Join us and fight ..."'

He placed it back on the bed. Two long knives lay on a bedside table, and a large hammer pushed under the bed was just visible.

Brigid Kelly pulled a sheet of paper from a shelf.

'Here, Father, this is why I asked you over.'

She handed him a leaflet headed: "SMASH THE MISSION".

He read on: '"Reclaim the streets from the scumbags, smack-heads, Pakis…".'

He looked around the room again and then turned over the leaflet. A handwritten note on the back read: "Tower Hotel" together with a phone number.

'Brigid, I remember …'

The front door banged shut against the hallway wall. Michael Kelly appeared standing behind his frightened mother. His voice shook with anger.

'What is it you remember, Father Doyle?'

'I remember when you were an altar boy—'

Kelly started shouting, his face red. Head shaved, fists clenched, eyes wide in rage, intimidating.

'I remember it too, Father Doyle. I'm not ashamed now, just disgusted, all the bullshit you gave out, all the crap.'

His mother grabbed his arm. 'Michael …'

The hand was shrugged away.

'How did he get in here?'

'I invited him.'

He leaned down, close to her face.

'You've no right. None. Not here. Not him. Not in my room.'

Turning back to Father Doyle, he stormed through the door and closed it behind him, in his mother's face, leaving her in the hallway.

'You're taking liberties, Doyle. What right do you have to be here?'

He snatched the leaflet from the Father's hand.

Doyle looked around the room.

'Why all this?'

'You wouldn't understand. Why the fuck should you? You're all the same: Yids, faggots, Pakis, you don't want to know. You bastards have destroyed this country. Well, fuck you, we're going to do something about it now. We're going to take it back.'

'No matter who gets hurt?'

'People get hurt all the time. I remember the time when my father cried because he was out of a job and knew he wouldn't get another. They closed his factory, and he left us. They drove him away. She pretends, but I know about people getting hurt.'

'I'm sorry …'

'Keep it,' he spat. 'Sorry! I don't need your fucking sorrow, Father fucking Doyle. Look at her.'

He pointed to the door. 'What have you ever done for her? I'll tell you what you've done. Kept her here in this pile of shit. God's will is it? Your God is it? Damp, paper-thin walls, Pakis everywhere. She's working for just two quid an hour. What is there for me? I was only born here. This is my fucking country. Fuck you, Doyle, and all you stand for.'

He grabbed Doyle's arm and pulled him to the window, pointing to Canary Wharf, looming over the tenement block.

'There, that's reality. Not your crap, and old men like you wearing dresses. What the fuck ...'

He pushed Doyle away.

'But there's no talking to people like you. All the Hail Mary bollocks and the rest of the rubbish. That's all you know.'

Father picked up a picture of Hitler. 'And what are you saying with this?'

'I know what it means - something your sort have never understood.'

'My sort?'

'Comfortable bastards who hide behind their crosses and statues. I've no time for you. I hate you fucking priests. All you ever do is lie and promise what isn't yours to give. Fairy stories that's what you give.'

Father pointed to the leaflet. 'Smash The Mission, what is that supposed to mean?'

'You'll find out… When we're ready!'

'For God's sake.'

'God? What God? Where is this God of yours? This is the truth.' He grabbed the picture of Hitler from Father. 'This is what I believe in: strength, purity …'

Doyle shouted across the tirade. 'And violence, hatred ...?'

'Yes! Yes! Because that's all anyone understands.'

His voice suddenly rang out, '*Sieg Heil, Sieg Heil.*'

Here the boy stood in a small room surrounded by swastikas, dominated by a large picture of Adolf Hitler. He marched on the spot, slowly at first and then picking up the tempo. Knees rising and falling.

Rhythmic, mesmerising ...'*Sieg Heil, Sieg Heil.*'

One arm jerked out in a Nazi salute ... '*Sieg Heil, Sieg Heil.*'

Father Doyle walked out. The bedroom door banged behind him. He could still hear the voice shouting, boots tramping.

'*Sieg Heil, Sieg Heil.*'

He looked around the flat for Brigid but couldn't see her anywhere, so he let himself out and closed the front door. The mocking, urgent clatter of steel-toed boots followed him as he headed slowly down the graffiti-marred stairway.

# FIVE

Father John Doyle opened his eyes and stared at the ceiling. The night roared. The clock on the church spire struck two o'clock. Sleep had come only intermittently as Michael Kelly's voice echoed and shrieked in the background.

Eventually, Doyle forced himself up to his feet to escape the stamp of boots and a dark room decorated with swastikas. He walked to the window and opened the curtains, a sharp crack of thunder filled the darkness and rattled the windowpane. Rain lashed against the glass.

He pushed down on the frame, making sure it was closed. A car passed outside, splashing along the wet road.

His bedclothes were damp from perspiration. He pulled the covers back and then redrew the curtains, just as another flash of lightning lit up the façade of the church. It looked just the same; nothing had changed.

Brake lights on a black car shone out as it made its way slowly past the church. Doyle turned away from the window and then quickly swung back again as he felt sure he recognised the profile of Michael Kelly in the passenger seat. By the time he looked again, the vehicle had gone.

He shook his head as much in sorrow as anger as he was gripped by the memory of Michael Kelly's desolation.

A stooped frail figure moved slowly away from a bus shelter situated on the other side of the roundabout.

Father Doyle frowned. It all looked the same, but everything had changed!

# SIX

Dan Cooper looked from his office window.

Canary Wharf – built on the old docks.

He knew the history of the place from his father and grandfather when they were bringing in coffee and sugar from their plants in Brazil and El Salvador. The Royal Albert and West India docks. Land on which his 20$^{th}$ floor office now stood.

He stared at the company's logos in picture frames on the wall next to the window.

Santos Coffee shops, Santos branded biscuits, cakes, confectionery, sugar, successful in the UK and across Europe. Plants still operating in South and Central America now part-owned by the employees.

A few weeks ago, he would have felt some satisfaction.

The company was safe. It had taken him ten years and cost him his marriage.

Had it been worth it? A question only asked when the storm had passed. When decisions were already taken, when choices had seemed like clouds passing by – mere decoration and ungraspable.

Satisfaction ended when he heard Guzman's voice again. A voice from a more desperate time. Instead of satisfaction, now, he felt shame.

He had to do what he should have done years ago had not cowardice prevented him from looking back at that time. The time when Guzman had entered his life. When the company had been about to collapse.

Now a price would be paid. But only this once. Never again.

He called Rosa in.

She had been with him for almost seven years after bringing her across from PileUp Records. He had rescued the one-time punk groupie from a desperately abusive relationship. After a spell at business school, financed by Dan, she was now the accomplished CEO of Atlantic Santos.

'I'm meeting Bayliss at the Reform Club tomorrow.'

'The MP?'

'About The Mission. And Guzman at the same time.'

'I thought you had done with him.'

'So did I.'

'So?'

'He wants to give money to The Mission.'

'No, he doesn't. I've only spoken with him a couple of times. There are no gifts from that man. I thought he was in Spain. What does he want?'

Dan Cooper leaned back and turned. The City of London spread out far below. He could just make out St Mary's in the distance.

He turned to Rosa.

She waited. The silence grew as Cooper turned back from the window. He gestured to the sofa against the wall and moved to a chair alongside.

He breathed deeply.

'It's not a story I'm proud of. Not something I want to talk about.'

He waved his hand in the air as if in dismissal.

'But it's fair you know some of what happened. The mid-eighties in South America was chaos. A debt crisis saw companies going bust all over. In El Salvador, there was a brutal civil war going on. My father had borrowed heavily to expand. Bad decision.'

He looked to the ceiling.

'Bad, bad decision. The company was going under. It was started in Brazil, way back, by my grandfather. Now it was finished. We'd had PileUp Records for about five years. Roisin and myself. We were just getting successful. As you know, she still runs it.'

'You still own half.'

'True but it's her gig now, and she's brilliant at it.'

'Gill, my elder brother, had disappeared. Died in eighty-two in New York. My father's health wasn't good. The pressure was too much for him. He went to the major banks they refused. We then tried some private banks, but they laughed us out of the door. One of them even tried to hoover up our assets at fire sale prices. Then father had a stroke. It was a disaster. I had no choice but to go out there. You know most of that. You came over just after the crisis.'

Rosa looked confused.

'But you survived.'

She pointed at all the companies' logos. 'Not just survived but thrived.'

'Thanks to a Brazilian banker, Carlos Silva who kept us on life support until Guzman came on the scene. I won't, can't, go into the details, but if it hadn't been for Guzman, we would have gone under.'

He gestured around the room.

'None of this would have existed.'

He stood and walked to the window.

'So, I owe him. And Guzman being Guzman has come to collect.'

He turned back to Rosa, his voice suddenly angry.

'But after this. The debt is paid. It will be finished.'

He moved across to a wall and removed an oil painting of Joe Strummer.

He opened a safe in the wall and took out a folder.

'There are seven companies in here. All based offshore, they go back to around 1984. I need them closed down, and every link to me or Atlantic Santos expunged. As soon as possible.'

Rosa took the file. 'That's it?'

He nodded. 'For now.'

# SEVEN

Adolfo Guzman waited by the porters' desk of the Reform Club in Pall Mall. His nose curled at the smell of inherited power and tradition, although a bitter resentment fostered the angry belief that he also belonged somewhere like this. The memory stayed with him of having to wait outside the country clubs in San Salvador. Only once was he invited inside and then only to drag out a drunk general who had come close to raping an American diplomat's wife.

A taxi halted.

'Senor Guzman I believe.'

The figure towered at least six inches over Guzman. Looking down at him with the distinct air of arrogance which Guzman was always alert to, even when it wasn't present. The face scraped clear of bristles, polished, primed, a faint smell of expensive cologne. Hair tightly held from a receding forehead. A bright white shirt with what Guzman thought looked like an army tie. Officers' mess of course, those soft hands had never seen action.

'My name is Charles Mayer. I'm…'

Guzman grabbed the hand that was offered. He saw the slight grimace as he tightened his grip.

'I know who you are.'

They loitered in the extravagant atrium. The smooth affability remained unruffled.

'Shall we...?' Mayer gestured smiling. The smile he had learned to switch on like a light before leaving Eton College some twenty years ago. A smile without substance or meaning. Gesture without form.

'Senor Guzman, I have heard a great deal about you from Desmond Williams,' Mayer continued.

The two figures walking through the expansive and richly decorated reception hall leading from the lobby, studded with portraits of nineteenth century reform movement heroes looked incongruous.

Mayer's rangy body contrasting with Guzman's aggressive bulk - the rapier and the blunderbuss.

They headed up a staircase and just as they came to the door of the dining room, the mâitre'd came rushing over.

'Mr Mayer, a pleasure to see you again. I have the usual table waiting.'

He inclined his head courteously toward Guzman, and then guided them through the dining room to a table next to a large window overlooking St James's Park. Mayer sat back expansively, studying the large room and its occupants. He nodded to a few acquaintances.

Mayer directed his gaze back across the table toward his guest. 'Senor Guzman, there are several matters to discuss as far as I'm aware. Of mutual interest, I believe.'

He waited for Guzman's suspicious agreement.

'I now keep the table just for pleasure. Any serious talk can wait for brandy in the smoking room. Do you agree.'

It wasn't a question, and Guzman remained silent while Mayer picked up the wine list and called over the waiter. He ordered a bottle of champagne before turning back again to Guzman.

'The right way to start lunch, Senor, yes? I understand that you have been in Madrid?'

He looked around the room and added in a stage whisper.

'Much deteriorated since Franco's death, eh?'

His subsequent laugh echoed quietly amongst the subdued conversation and understated privilege. The wine waiter poured them each a glass of Moët & Chandon as Guzman recognised that Mayer had just told him he had had him checked out.

'Your health, Senor Guzman. Now do tell me about Spain.'

Guzman managed to control his impatience during the rest of the meal. The atmosphere was somnolent, the wine and food adequate but, to Guzman's mind, tasteless.

At last, they moved across the landing to a book-lined smoking room where a few figures sat in old armchairs reading the papers or sleeping. Two large brandies on a tray were brought through by a waiter.

Mayer settled back into a large, worn, leather armchair, called for a cigar and then turned to Guzman.

'Right, firstly tell me about this project of yours. I believe it's connected with St Mary's.'

Guzman nodded.

'They run some sort of community poverty project and day centre for vagrants, and now wish to expand their overnight accommodation facilities. Preliminary meeting with priest this afternoon.'

'We call them "rough sleepers" now, or some similar nonsense, Senor Guzman.'

'The project will be financed through a charitable trust,' declared Guzman.

'Excellent, splendid gesture.'

Mayer looked at his watch, emptied his glass and gestured to a waiter, hovering near the door, for another brandy.

'Perhaps you would be willing to become one of the trustees,' suggested Guzman.

'I'd rather not.' Mayer smiled leaning back.

'Of course, the minister's wife does have wide experience in these matters. She organises an annual charity bash in the constituency and would be a splendid choice.'

'It would pay thirty thousand pounds.'

'Nothing to do with me, old man. I'll get her to call you.'

The waiter appeared with his next brandy.

'You know, of course, that I need to obtain residence rights…'

Mayer reached out quickly and gripped Guzman' arm.

'Yes, yes. No need for details. You're using Williams?'

Guzman nodded.

'Leave it to the experts, I say.'

Mayer leaned back in the chair.

'It will be done. You may not be aware, but I have an interest in a private bank Otterburn-Fuller. We provide confidential banking services to a range of invited clients. Including HMG ...'

Guzman frowned.

Mayer gave a mannered laugh.

'Her Majesty's Government! I will arrange a meeting with the CEO. My father is the chairman. My minister, as I'm sure you are aware, is head of defence procurement. We know that is the area of your expertise. You're moving your organisation from Spain. I understand?'

'I have a warehouse in Kent. Near Sandwich. Everything is relocated.'

The smile broke out again. 'Good, good. I'm sure we can work together. This country needs people of your means and experience.'

Guzman looked toward the door.

The figure standing there looked out of place. Hair over his ears, not combed, a tie which looked like it had been thrown on as an afterthought, black suit, far too stylish for this place and, as he stared toward Mayer, an expression of unfiltered anger crossed his sharp features.

He walked across and spoke to Guzman.

'What the hell is he doing here?

# EIGHT

Dan Cooper looked from the doorway.

Guzman! Colonel Adolfo Guzman.

'Cooper.'

Until now it had been all done by email and telephone. That stark bastard voice had brought back enough memories. Songs always spark memories. That was his life. Music, clashing growls of exhilaration and ecstasy.

The sound of that demanding growl sent shudders of dread coursing through his body.

It was a bloody time when he had gone to El Salvador. Dead bodies littering the streets. Soldiers swaggering through the slums, and every journey a hazard. Bodyguards that you hoped would keep you alive and hadn't been bought by one of the militias to allow kidnap for ransom.

That face brought those days and nights into rancid focus. The voice had been a disconnect, the end of a conversation. But seeing him after so long brought the reality of what had gone before. The reality of his own shame kept conveniently hidden until this moment.

He shook his shoulders as though shrugging away the memories. Time had moved on. He turned to see who was sitting with Guzman.

What Guzman brought was humiliation and that he could, would, live with because he could rationalise and excuse himself, however deceitful the effort.

This anger was impulsive. Dragged from somewhere too deep.

Raw.

Unfiltered.

Rage.

Before he could prevent himself, he saw his father lying on the floor of his hotel room. Helpless, like a child.

He had started PileUp Records in seventy-nine from his cluttered flat in Hackney. Punk had taken over and PileUp was at the forefront of the chaos. Roisin came with the label. They were struggling then, but it was the best of times, just as was marriage at Chelsea Town Hall and a party that had spilled over a weekend and more. The ride from then on was breath-taking, chaotic and exhilarating. Record releases, gigs, obsessed lunatics with guitars and egos.

He had only reluctantly agreed to accompany his father in eighty-four as he went the rounds of the banks. Over from Brazil he was trying desperately to keep the family business afloat. They needed funds to survive. It was that simple. The Latin America debt crisis was crippling them.

Each meeting was as dispiriting as the last. They knew Atlantic Santos was viable, would be profitable again, knew why it needed funds, but it was South, Central America and too big a risk.

So good luck and goodbye.

His father started to fall apart. Headaches, loss of balance when he walked.

One bank left. It looked hopeless. Dan had arranged it through Rupert Mayer. He had known him from university, and they had been to a few gigs together. He was CEO of the family bank, Otterburn-Fuller, but he was in New York so had arranged for a meeting with his father Lord Edward Mayer of Longwitton, Chairman of the bank, and his brother Charles Mayer. According to Rupert, Charles had been with Barings Bank but had left, allegedly under a cloud, but the story had been suppressed somewhere along the old boy network.

Dan remembered the words that had shattered his father.

Lord Edward Mayer it was, *'You don't feed good grain to a dead cow'.*

Then Charles Mayer's baying laugh echoed around the dining room at Otterburn-Fuller's London HQ.

They got back to the hotel.

His father slumped in his chair.

Just sat there. Eyes empty. His left arm fell to the side of the chair. He looked up at Dan and tried to speak. What eventually emerged wasn't words, but an incoherent cry for help.

Dan called for an ambulance.

As he waited, holding his father in his arms like a new-born baby, the telephone rang.

It was his father's office from Brazil.

A Colonel Guzman would like a meeting.

He looked at Guzman and Mayer.

'What the hell is he doing here,' he roared at Guzman.

He didn't wait for a reply.

Snatching the tie from his neck he thrust it at the doorman on his way out.

A cab was passing.

'Just drive,' he said, sat back and stared through the window.

# NINE

The priest stood at the door, carrying a plastic bag. He waited a few moments before knocking, feeling like a teenager on his first date. He could cope with nerves, but this was the feeling of setting out on a journey without knowing the destination, and for once, he didn't think he cared. The memory of those whispered words of warning in the church, and young Michael Kelly's threats, added confusion and tension to the pleasure. But, as he raised his hand to the door, he realised the bewildering happiness that had entered his life when he had first seen Consuela on the steps of his church.

'Hello, Father.'

For a moment, he was speechless.

John, Father, Doyle felt a blush rising as he saw a smile break out on her gentle features which could have been tenderly carved from fine-grained alabaster so soft was her silhouette. Dark hair framed a face that never seemed still, emotion touching each expression, bringing a depth which invited understanding.

She wore a black silk dress that, although loose, showed off her slim figure.

Doyle thrust away the sudden unwelcome sense of yearning.

She waved her hand in front of his face. 'Hello.'

Snapping out of his trance, he looked sheepish and sputtered, trying to cover his embarrassment.

'Sorry. I was just surprised.'

Consuela smiled. 'Because I'm not wearing jeans? This dress is the only one I own.'

She shrugged. 'And it is too old and too …' she smiled, 'travelled.'

'No.' Father sighed deeply. 'Yes, because you're wearing a dress and because you look so nice in it.'

'Is that a compliment?'

Raising his eyes, he smiled and slowly relaxed.

'Yes, it's a compliment. I didn't mean that you don't …'

Consuela grabbed his arm and pulled him into the narrow hallway. 'I know what you meant.'

She turned and looked him up and down as he followed into the kitchen.

'It's the first time I've ever seen you without your collar and the usual suit.'

He was wearing an open-necked shirt and a pair of light-coloured trousers. Something as straightforward that had cost at least thirty minutes contemplation.

'I'm a bit traditional,' he admitted.

'They suit you,' said Consuela and then adjusted one of his shirt collars which had ridden up. He swallowed at the moment of intimacy and moved quickly toward a table laid for two.

'I know you get invited out a lot, while this is the first time I've been able to cook for a long time. Anyway, I can enjoy the company and will apologise in advance if the food is terrible. 'We have papusas: corn tortillas from El Salvador.' She laughed, 'Well they are as good as I can manage.'

The sound of South American pan pipes filled the small kitchen as Consuela pressed PLAY on a cassette player. She laughed above the music.

'Roger bought this for me. Make me feel at home. What do you think of that?'

She whispered. 'He is so kind, but pan pipes ...' She pulled a face and turned the music off.

'How did you meet him?' John asked. Roger had always been defensive about disclosing exactly how he met Consuela.

She sighed.

'He helped me once when I was in trouble ...' she paused. 'When I was feeling troubled.'

She shook her head. The subject was closed.

John shyly pulled a book from his bag. 'I thought you might like this.'

Consuela frowned in surprise and examined the hardback. Her mouth fell open.

'Father! Oh. It's beautiful. *One Day of Life*. How do you know Manlio Argueta? He is so important.'

Holding the volume like a precious stone, her hands stroked the cover and then she carefully opened the pages, moving her fingers over the paper. When she looked back at Father, her eyes were moist.

'This book meant so much to us. It was banned, you know. Argueta was exiled to Costa Rica. We had to hide it away.'

She put her head in her hands and breathed in deeply before leaning forward and gently kissing his cheek.

'Father Doyle, you are a wonderful man.'

She continued to feel the pages.

'I used to read out his poetry when I was teaching. Quietly, of course, just sentences without saying who had written them.'

She continued stroking the pages.

'Some of his words were dangerous, as well as beautiful.'

She started to read: '"Why do you think they give them those big guns that look like tree branches and are larger than they themselves? To shoot, baby, to shoot. Because if they don't, that gives rise to talk that the authorities are useless, are nothing more than decoration."'

'We knew who he was talking about. We know who they were shooting at. Us. And they drove him out for saying it.'

She kissed her fingers, touched the cover of the book, and

closed her eyes for a moment. When she reopened them, they were filled with tears.

'You were a teacher?' asked Doyle, trying to fill a silence that intensified his uncertainty.

'Just for a few months in the Jesuit infants' school in Aguilares.'

She shrugged.

'Then the army burned down the school. They claimed guerrillas were hiding inside. That wasn't true. So much violence…'

The words trailing off, she shook her head vigorously, as though trying to erase the memories.

Father Doyle sat down and watched as Consuela, face suddenly covered by a broad smile, moved over to the stove.

'And now for that, I feed you. We have cheese and sausage papusas ... Oh yes, I already tell you. And we have salad.'

Pointing at an empty bowl by the sink, she frowned.

'Oh God, sorry, Father, no salad, I forget.' She opened the fridge and quickly extracted lettuce and some tomatoes.

John stood and offered to help.

Consuela merely frowned at him, opened the fridge again and pulled out a can of beer.

'You drink, I make the food. OK?'

He sat back down.

'We also have beans and rice.'

She pointed at two saucepans on the stove.

Turning to him, she said, 'Let me sip that, please. We have some more, I think.'

She drank almost all the beer. Laughing.

'Rice and beans, beans and rice, it's OK.'

Consuela finally served the food, and they sat and ate.

There were three more cans of beer, which they drank. The talk was comfortable, the food enjoyable.

John leaned back once the plates were empty and his beer finished.

'Consuela, that was wonderful.'

She smiled. 'You think so. I used to be a good cook. Not so good now, but OK.'

He thought of mentioning that strange, troubling encounter in the church, but thought better of it. Which later he regretted.

'We might have some good news about The Mission. A benefactor!'

'We certainly need money.'

'Someone from your part of the world: Central America but not sure which country.'

'Why?'

He frowned but didn't answer.

Consuela repeated the question:

'Why is somebody from Central America giving money to St Mary's?'

Father Doyle paused. He hadn't asked himself that question. Something also later regretted.

He shook his head. 'I'm meeting him tomorrow.'

Consuela asked the name.

'I think it's Guzman.'

She looked away from him. When she turned back, her face was dark. The pleasure that had illuminated the evening had gone. Her voice was flat. 'Common name.'

She got up and moved to the window, staring out in silence before coming back to the table. John reached across and touched her hand in an unconscious gesture. If he had thought about it, he would not have done it. Thought only came to him however when Consuela slowly withdrew her hand, sliding it away, already closed, like a reluctant claw. He swallowed and felt foolish.

'I'm ...' she stuttered.

He noticed her eyes. She seemed far away now, in a colder place. The joy of the evening had drifted away from them. He felt it was his fault and stood up feeling witless. They parted with immaculate formality.

Father Doyle stepped into the warm night. He didn't want to go back to his room, not yet.

A dark tremor of fear ran through him, again. Checking the time, he started walking.

* * *

Sirens echoed in the distance as he turned onto the main road, coming ever closer as a police car sped along the almost empty streets.

Two figures stood in a doorway. They eyed him carefully.

'Father? We don't see you out here very often.'

He walked to the doorway and recognised two of the regulars from The Mission.

'No. It's a bit late for me. I'm up too early.'

A pair of headlights appeared as a vehicle turned onto the road.

'Here's your man now.'

The van came down the street toward them as they stood there on the pavement. It came slowly to a halt, and Roger leaned out of a window.

'John, you've not been out here for a while.'

'Perhaps too long.'

'I'll be down the road. I can't stop here.'

Roger looked quizzically at Father. 'You want to come with me? You can serve.'

They looked up and followed the path of Concorde as it banked over London on its approach to Heathrow.

Father answered Brother Roger. 'Sure, I'll serve.'

A car pulled up behind, 'Have to move, I'll be just down the road.'

The van accelerated slowly along the street, turning into a small alley at the end and stopping. A dim light came on in the back. Figures appeared in the gloom surrounding the van. He couldn't see where they emerged from, but they slowly walked toward the light that shone in the darkness. One of the men, big, burly, bright eyes shining on his broad black face laughed as he gently ushered the knot of men into something like a queue.

Father Doyle got in the van to help. As they served the food, Roger indicated the now almost ordered line and he told Father about Ray, the large figure still laughing with and moving the chaotic group toward the kiosk.

'Ray's working almost full-time at The Mission. I've become to depend on him. I want to see if we can get him a wage.'

'What's his story?'

'Familiar, I'm afraid. Army career. Falklands. Ireland. He looked over as John cleaned a worktop.

'He tells it better himself, Father.' Roger said with a smile.

# TEN

Mrs Quinn opened the office door.

'Ray is here.'

Father Doyle frowned.

Following a morning of meetings, he had forgotten the arrangement made the previous night.

The man standing in the doorway started to walk away. His expression, on a face whose contours spoke of conflict and desperate compromise, was resigned.

'It's OK,' he muttered, embarrassed.

'Ray.'

'Ray.'

Father Doyle shouted after him.

'Come in. Coffee?' he asked as his visitor returned.

He waved Ray to one of the visitors' chairs and sat down opposite him as Mrs Quinn soon reappeared with two cups of coffees and a plate of biscuits.

'Roger told me you were in the army?'

'He's right.' Ray gave a grimacing smile. 'My profession. My career. I loved it.' He took a sip of his coffee and shot a quick glance around the room.

'I didn't have a great education as my parents split up when I was a kid. The army gave me some security.'

Father opened his arms wide.

'So why this?'

Ray hesitated.

'Are you sure? Another hard luck story? You've heard them all before, here, haven't you?'

'Everybody's story is different, Ray. We're all different, in our own ways. The Falklands, was it?'

Ray closed his eyes.

His large hands covered his face before looking closely at the priest.

'Are you really sure?' He gritted his teeth and shook his head. 'Am I sure?'

Father Doyle leaned forward, in encouragement. He sensed a story rarely told.

'I asked the question.'

Ray took a deep breath.

The voice emerged from hidden memory.

'It was three in the morning. I was cold. Soaking wet. Tired. Hungry. Surviving on willpower and training. Relying on instinct.

Father Doyle let the pauses linger.

'Star shells and tracers were going off all along the front. It was the final push for Port Stanley. We were driving for the northern sector of Wireless Ridge. The bombardment from the Harriers and Yarmouth and Ambuscade offshore, had softened the Argie defences. Many of those that were left in the area had just taken themselves off Mount Longden.

'I was on my own, almost at the top of the ridge. One of the Blues and Royals Scimitars screwed up the range. A shell blast knocked me into a shallow trench. I was out of it. I'm not sure for how long. Probably only a few seconds. When I came to, I was looking at this young Argie. Nearly shit myself; he had a submachine gun trained on my head. My own gun was lying across the other side of the trench, I looked back at him as he leaned against a rock, and then realised his stomach was a pool of blood. He just looked at me, shook his head and reached into his pocket. I jumped over and grabbed his gun, but he pulled out a cross and held it toward me.'

Ray fingered the cross around his neck.

'Spoke perfect English but kneeling beside him I could only just hear him. "It's too soon," he said. "I'd hoped for longer." At that moment I envied him, it was all so simple. I held the poor bastard's hand. How long he lasted I have no idea. Everything was suddenly silent, or so it seemed. Then his head dropped.'

Ray gripped the cross around his neck so hard his calloused knuckles shone white. He coughed to cover the emotion and blinked quickly.

Leaning forward he sipped the remains of cold coffee before resuming.

'He fell sideways.

Onto the ground.

He was dead. At that moment, a grenade exploded just behind the trench. This time I was out for three days. By the time I came round, we were in Port Stanley.'

He stood and walked to the window looking over at The Mission.

'I was OK for quite a while, a couple of years really. Then Enniskillen happened. Remembrance Day eighty-seven. Picking body parts off the road! Then the nightmares started. I started seeing that Argie kid's face. Hearing his voice. Explosions. Screaming.'

He released his grip on the cross.

'The drink helped. It dulled the senses, for a while. But the guilt kicked in. That I was alive.'

He wiped his forehead.

'That felt wrong. And his face, his voice. I withdrew from my family. From my friends. I'd wake up with the bed soaked in sweat. It was horrible.'

'Couldn't you get any kind of help?'

He frowned. 'I was a soldier. I soldiered on. You don't give in. That's just how it was.'

He sipped at the coffee and wiped his face.

'I was in a pub in April ninety-one. You remember the regiment had killed three PIRA members in Gibraltar. Some guy was mouthing off about all soldiers being murderers. I'd had mates killed in Ireland, so I smacked him around, and then two others who tried to stop me. Got sent down for three years, served two. When I got out, Julie had gone. With Tessa, she was seven.'

He paused. His head dropped.

'She'd visited me for a while, then the visits stopped. Wrote, said she was scared of me and for me. I'd kicked off on one of the visits. It wasn't good.'

'Just the one child?'

He nodded. ''We couldn't have any more. Tessa will be ten now. I haven't seen them in three years I tried to find them but...'

He shook his head.

'Julie's parents were dead, just had a brother in Doncaster. Tried a few of her old friends. Nothing.'

'Where did you live?'

'When I went inside. Aldershot. Army housing. A few mates tried to help find her but they had dropped out of sight. Of course, I was discharged. It was finished for me.'

His fists clenched.

'I couldn't hack it anymore.'

'Did you try her brother?'

'Slammed the door in my face. Can't blame him.'

'And then?'

'Ended up on the streets.'

He shrugged.

'Until this place,' he gestured across to The Mission, 'eight months ago. And your man, Brother Roger. He made me feel welcome. Treated me with respect, went out of his way to see the person and not just the problem, and that has meant so much.'

There was a noise from down the corridor. They both looked toward the door.

Mrs Quinn glanced between the pair, her expression stern and unyielding. Her tone was accusing.

'You have an appointment with a Senor Guzman?' she demanded of Father Doyle.

'Yes.'

'You're welcome to him.'

'Mrs Quinn!'

She was gone.

The door swung wide open, banging into a bookcase.

'Ray.'

Doyle raised his arms as if in in submission.

'We'll continue later.'

Guzman's face was red from the exertion of climbing the steps up into the church. He ignored Ray walking from the room.

'Father.'

The stolid sweating figure moved toward Father Doyle who, before he had time to respond, was pulled roughly toward the perspiring figure, who then knelt and kissed his hand.

Guzman rose slowly from his knees, belying the soft, malleable, flesh of his sweating hand by exerting a grip that was both intimidating and painful. With difficultly Father Doyle managed to withdraw his hand from that hard grasp.

The voice was deceitful; however, there was no correlation between those sharp, observant, cold, eyes - too small for his fat, perspiring face. Lips turned down at the edges.

Father Doyle sat himself down in the centre of the sofa, gesturing his visitor toward the smaller, wooden, easy chair.

'Senor Guzman, please sit down.'

Afterwards, on reflection, he had no idea why his instinctive reaction was to make Guzman feel uncomfortable, which he clearly was, as he tried to wedge himself into the narrow chair.

'I'm afraid I have to leave urgently within ten minutes, but I know this is only a preliminary meeting.'

Guzman's smile was an unpleasant sight, forced and artificial.

'I have heard of your work at The Mission and I wish to help.'

'That is very generous of you, Senor Guzman. We are always looking to improve our facilities.'

Guzman picked absentmindedly at his teeth. He merely nodded and looked from the window. His car was parked by the steps, a driver standing by the passenger door. Guzman already seemed bored.

Father followed his glance. He recognised the car from a few days past. In the early morning.

'Daniel Cooper told me,' Guzman continued.

'You know him?"

Guzman nodded again but did not elaborate. He turned to Father Doyle. 'How much?'

'I'm sorry.'

'Cooper said you were hoping to raise about three hundred thousand pounds.'

'That's the total amount needed. We would be grateful for anything you could contribute.'

'OK.'

Father Doyle was confused, raising his eyebrows, 'OK?'

'I'll give you three hundred thousand.'

After a shocked silence, Father expressed his surprise.

'*All* the money? Three hundred thousand pounds!'

Guzman nodded.

The rumours had been way off. John Doyle smiled. In three months, they had raised forty-five thousand pounds. Now suddenly here was an offer of over six times that amount.

Guzman looked down at his plump hands. The tone was disinterested as though he were reading from a script.

'If I can help this worthwhile project, Father, I would be honoured. I admire your work greatly.'

The priest pointed through his front window.

'Can I show you around The Mission?'

'That won't be necessary, I've already spoken to Bishop Peter and Mr Cooper and they have told me all I need to know and given me detailed information about The Mission you run.'

Father Doyle was surprised and confused, having known nothing of any such discussions or meetings. There was never a shortage of people wanting to be the bearer of good news so why not this time? He examined Senor Guzman more carefully. An expensive dark, three-piece suit hung from those wide shoulders; his facial skin was smooth and carefully tended, apart from a scar stretching from his left earlobe down into his neck. The manicured fingers were as large as sausages; thick, frightening and grotesquely decorated with gold rings. One of the latter glittered with the biggest diamond Father Doyle had ever set eyes on.

Guzman began speaking, impatient at the scrutiny.

'I will be making arrangements in the next few days. John Bayliss, who is a member of your parliament, has said that his wife is prepared to be a trustee of the charity.'

Father John knew Bayliss. He was a local MP and a minister of some sort. Never much of a friend to either the church or The Mission except when self-interest reared. His wife as a trustee? Something was wrong, he could feel it, but without being able to put his finger on anything specific.

'Will you yourself want to be involved in the operations of The Mission?'

'That won't be necessary.'

'Why St Mary's, Senor Guzman?'

'I was told it is a worthwhile project and told you need the money.'

'Indeed, we do, but this is such an unexpected and generous offer.'

'So, what's the problem?'

'Problem?' asked Doyle.

'You're hesitating,' demanded Guzman. 'Why?'

'I was not previously aware of your interest, Senor. It's not the usual way these things are handled. I understand you have no personal knowledge of St Mary's?'

'Do I need to?' Guzman's voice betrayed irritation.

'It is usual, that's all I'm saying, I believe you are acquainted with Cardinal Trujillo?'

'We occasionally played chess together, he is a good man.'

'Where was that?'

'San Salvador. when he visited our country. He went off to Rome around ninety-one.'

'What brings you to *our* country, Senor?'

Guzman remained silent. His eyes narrowed. Doyle felt the force of his scrutiny. Then Guzman bent over and picked up a pen from the tabletop between them and began to tap it on the wooden surface.

The sound was metronomic, hypnotic, and strangely frightening. All the air seemed to have been sucked from the room. Even the light lost its lustre.

Father John gripped the arm of his chair. Stray words flashed across his mind filling his apprehensive trance.

Guzman's voice was soft.

'I am here to give you money, Father Doyle. Is there any more you need to know?'

The pulsing, tapping sound didn't pause in the silence ensuing between them. Guzman's cold unblinking stare didn't move from Father John's eyes.

'I have to consult, Senor.'

Doyle swallowed, his voice cracking slightly under the sudden tension.

Guzman smiled, a twisted expression.

'Do you, Father Doyle? You have to consult?'

Father continued uncertainly. 'We must meet again. Perhaps next week?'

Guzman nodded but Doyle felt something cold and dead coming from those small, distrusting eyes.

The priest shuddered. Pictures flashed before him: blood, flesh, hair, skin, body and mind, spirit and soul crushed underfoot. Pushing aside the frightening sensation of evil he felt he had met.

Father John shook his head and turned quickly away. The moment passed.

Guzman pushed himself to his feet and walked from the room. He didn't speak or look back. Had he done so he would have seen Father John kneeling on the floor of his office, holding tight to the cross that hung round his neck. Eyes closed, hands shaking.

Doyle took a moment before he stood and looked from the window. He saw the heavy figure marching down the steps. Halfway down he suddenly stopped. He looked back at Doyle and then turned to the window of The Mission.

Doyle saw the back of his head. Beyond it, in the window of The Mission he glimpsed Consuela. Her mouth fell open. Doyle suddenly thought of Munch's *Scream.* Undiluted terror radiated from her desperate expression.

Guzman turned away before continuing down the steps. When he reached the kerb, his driver leapt out and opened a rear door. Guzman paused briefly before getting in. He scowled back at The Mission.

Doyle stared after the car as it joined the traffic.

A blue moped pulled out from the alley alongside the church and followed it. Turning away, the window of The Mission was empty. Consuela had gone.

He continued to stare across.

He only later realised that the moment changed his life. The certainties that had sustained him fell away. All that he knew was undermined, so many of the truths he had spoken tasted like grit.

He ran to the door to get across to The Mission.

As he did so Mrs Quinn called out to him. There had been a phone call from the local hospice. Their chaplain was off sick, and they needed Father John. They needed the priest urgently.

The priest was needed. He went.

The man himself wept.

To himself.

On his way out he asked Mrs Quinn, 'Do we have anybody

in the church who has lived in or knows about Central America? El Salvador in particular.'

She didn't but promised to check.

He gathered up his case and vestments. As he did so he looked again from the window and saw Brother Roger rushing after Consuela as she ran from The Mission.

# ELEVEN

Roger found Consuela sitting by the door to The Mission.

She was staring at the floor. Lifeless. He touched her shoulder. She jumped. Her face was filled with terror, quickly changing to relief when she saw it was Roger.

'Thank God. I thought it was him.'

'Who?'

'Can we get away from here? Please?'

'Shall I walk you home?'

She nodded, glanced up the steps toward the church, picked up her bag and ran from the building. Roger struggled to keep pace with her.

He escorted Consuela through the front door of the small, terraced house a five-minute silent walk from St Mary's. Slumping into a chair, she stared open-mouthed, unblinking at the wall. There was no response even when Roger tried to pass her a cup of tea. She started to shake, rubbing her hands hard, feverishly as though scouring them of dirt and grime.

'Consuela, you need to rest.'

No answer.

'Consuela, I have to get back to work.'

There was still no reply.

'Stuart will be back later. I'll drop in during the evening.'

She pointed to a slightly open window. Roger frowned, but she carried on pointing.

He strained to hear her trembling voice. 'Close it… lock it, please.'

When he turned again, her eyes had closed.

* * *

Stuart looked into her bedroom in the early evening when he returned. Consuela lay still on her narrow bed.

Roger had told Stuart, his partner, what had happened.

'I have no idea what triggered it but it was like going back to the days when I first met her, at the clinic.'

When he tried speaking to her, she didn't respond.

* * *

Consuela lay still, her eyes open again now, but seeing nothing in the small room. There was just enough space by the side of her bed. A wardrobe pushed against the end of the mattress partially obscured the window overlooking a set of traffic lights, throwing shadows across the ceiling and walls. The ceiling light was off. Silhouettes occasionally moving slowly around the room. She watched without interest, barely aware of the sounds of life outside. They seemed irrelevant.

Memory was her only companion…

*It was dark. A small, barred window cut into the top corner of an unpainted brick wall allowed light to filter through, but only reluctantly. There was no joy in this place. Here existed a new layer of fear. Previously there had been defiance and courage, born of solidarity. Here Consuela knew only the brutality of solitude: total except for the company of a spider which darted quickly between mounds of dirt scattered across the concrete floor. It stopped, cautious, frozen for a moment, before resuming its crazy path. She followed its trail. Eyes focused, hearing her own heart beating so fast - troubled, insistent, demanding - she stared down in desperation at her only companion.*

*Only two days ago she had been free. There was shared excitement then, only forty-eight hours before; a hope that something better could be achieved. But there was also sheer exhilaration and a laughing desire to show them that their control was not absolute. By handing out leaflets for a proscribed meeting, or painting the FMNL logo on a long-ignored wall.*

*There was no excitement here, not now. No hands to grip in intimacy amongst the darkness of the streets or holding each other in the back of a beaten-up lorry, carrying posters to paste on a lonely wall.*

*There had been excitement then.*

*The excitement of escape, running together; boots chasing, echoing down empty streets; windows and doors slamming, the muffled sound of bolts gently secured and shutters fastened; sounds of truth, the pulling back of the bolt of a rifle looming in front of a hard face. The urgent rhythmic clatter of steel-tipped boots on stone pavements. A harsh shout, a voice issuing orders that preceded indiscriminate pain.*

*Manuel and herself. Flying free, each footstep, each slamming of a shutter, bringing them closer together and making them feel more heroic, standing up for what was right. They both had the courage, alongside others even more heroic, to speak the unspeakable and to oppose the corrupt and omnipotent. Feet skidded from corner to corner, the only sounds filling the dark night. Pursuit was fading, for they knew the streets well; the alleys where jeeps could not follow, derelict houses which brought escape and then a falling together as exhilaration and desire mixed in orgasmic delight.*

*Fear was lost in the frenzy as they pulled at each other's clothes. There was little tenderness at first, but release there was, bodies struggling together, the laughter of liberation mixed with a roaring ecstasy. They were truly at home now as they stroked and kissed, tasting desire and fear mixed in a cocktail that transported them to another place. She rarely allowed herself to wonder whether the risk was worth it since the reward was so sweet; the blinding beauty of satisfaction and the joy of slowly, exhaustedly, drifting into sleep in Manuel's arms. His hands on her breasts, his body pushing gently against hers, both damp from exertion and passion.*

She briefly heard Brother Roger's voice in a part of her psyche that remained inaccessible.

*Feet skidded from corner to corner. They were the only sounds filling the dark night, pursuit had faded, for they knew this street well. Abruptly, heartbreakingly, they crashed to a halt looking into the barrels of at least twenty guns. Unwavering eyes were targeting them. The voice when it came, was quiet and undemanding. The game was over. They looked at each other, too scared for tears; here was the moment of dread which would colour the rest of their lives. She caught Manuel's eyes, her body shaking with terror. She reached for his hand; they gripped and held; there was silence. Waiting, watching, in the face of this swaggering certainty, they felt the scrutiny. She saw a slight movement.*

*Their grip became tighter.*

*The sound deafened her.*

*Instinctively her hands went to her ears, although she wished she had held on.*

*Did Manuel even know she released him at that moment?*

*She wanted him to know she was still with him, even to the end of time. His time.*

*The sound deafened her, and she fell to the ground. Fury, hopelessness, grief, revulsion - words came haphazardly, more for comfort than substance. Her eyes opened then clammed shut just as quickly. To erase the sight of his face.*

*Manuel's face.*

*Exploded.*

*Ruptured beyond hope.*

*After a moment, she touched the side of her head and felt warmth and cloying moistness. Her hand was darker than she expected.*

*Manuel's eyes looked directly at her; there was no smile on his lips now, but in his eyes, there was still hope, and love.*

*Or so she imagined.*

*He opened his mouth, and she strained to hear. It was no more than a whisper, no more than a single syllable -* **'I'***. At least she thought she heard that; later she didn't know. Perhaps it didn't matter.*

*His eyes held hers, his mouth fell open.*

*His eyes closed.*

*The spider stopped scurrying now; its head darted to one side and then returned quickly again. A bolt was pulled back.*

*A key turned.*

*The door opened, but still, she didn't take her eyes off the spider. She wouldn't look at what she knew was about to happen.*

*Boots hammered against stone. Thick legs, small vicious eyes too small for his face: cruelty and horror. A heavy boot hammered down on the cold, dirty, floor.*

*The spider lay crushed on a stone slab.*

*She waited and knew the pain would begin again.*

*The humiliation.*

*The betrayal.*

*Her betrayal.*

* * *

Consuela didn't immediately recognise the concerned face leaning over her. She pulled back into the safety of her small bed.

'Are you all right?'

Her voice was suspicious.

'Why?'

Stuart was tall and lean. Prematurely grey hair topped a thin, mobile face driven with nervous energy.

'You were shouting,' said Stuart, 'I was worried.'

'Oh. Stuart, I'm sorry. I didn't know who it was for a minute. Where's Roger?'

'He's doing the soup run.'

Consuela relaxed; the late-night food had often been the only meal she saw when she was squatting. Stuart now stood at the foot of the small, narrow bed, twisting his hands together.

'What can I do to help?'

She sat up and clutched her knees, eyes wandering uncertainly around the room. 'Are the doors locked? And the windows?'

He nodded.

The sound of traffic passing below gave a faint background to the small room. She looked about her surroundings and listened. A small portion of time and space was all she inhabited now. To perpetuate existence, she passed through the simple motions of reality. Slowly over the past few years, she had tried to find a sanctuary.

That was the first step: safety. Understanding and truth were too remote and unattainable; life and mere survival came first. Her wounds had almost healed except for the gravest injuries which mutilated what lived inside her wounded body. They were deeper, more painful; inaccessible and arbitrary.

The fear persisted that she would never be whole again and that never again would passion and love be embraced without also reawakening the horror that still haunted her. She had no real control and no defence against the occasional shattering blows. They would come without warning, forcing her into submission; dragging her off to a place where there was only horror, turmoil, agony.

The future was only glimpsed through a dark and menacing melancholy which shackled and confined her as she struggled to escape. But even those nights of dread and sweat-soaked waking torments had not prepared her for *this*.

His eyes; the eyes that had watched.

The voice; the voice which commanded pain; which ordered the degradation.

His hands; the hands that had turned the switch; that had ordered murder.

She shook involuntarily.

Stuart leaned across and laid a hand on her arm.

The smile she gave him was pallid and unconvincing, her voice almost inaudible.

'I'm sorry. I didn't mean to wake you.'

'What is it?' asked Stuart.

'I saw someone I haven't seen for a long time and... it brought back memories, bad memories,' said Consuela.

'Do you want to tell me?'

She looked at Stuart. 'I can't.'

Her moist eyes stared up at the ceiling. A car drove past, and she turned to him again.

'I'm sorry.'

'Shall I stay?' he asked.

She shook her head. 'I'm tired, and I think I'll be able to sleep now. Is everything locked up?'

He nodded. 'I'll check again but remember I'm only just below your room if you need me. Just shout, any time.'

'Thanks,' she said as he stood up.

Her smile was genuine as she continued.

'Tomorrow it will be different.' I hope, she thought.

Consuela lay still as Stuart returned to his bedroom. She waited another thirty minutes before getting up and dressing, throwing some clothes into a small daypack, and tiptoeing down the stairs. The night air felt fresh walking through dark and empty streets. When an occasional car sounded in the distance, she paused and listened. If it came any nearer, she jumped into a shop doorway or down an alley, huddling into a corner, hidden from sight.

Voices began spinning along the streets, and the frantic figure darted from corner to corner. A police car came by. Consuela ran into a deserted underground car park. Silence echoed around concrete as she folded herself into a tiny gap in the bare wall.

She heard the noise of a car as it slowed and then halted at the garage entrance. The electronic static of a radio echoed in the dead silence. Nothing moved. Then just a quiet rustling as something brushed against the darkened walls. Whatever it was, it was moving slowly and gently through empty spaces. A footstep echoed in the stillness. She curled up tighter against the wall as if trying to become invisible. Mental images flashed before her, bright lights on polished metal, cold eyes, depravity - black horror.

Somewhere close, a dustbin lid clattered to the ground. She slid further against the wall, mouth wide, her eyes petrified.

A voice laughed, a cat ran across the floor, the footsteps retreated. The car pulled away... all was silent again.

Eventually, after walking across Waterloo Bridge, she found the steps leading to the basement apartment and hammered on the door. A battered blue moped leaned against a wall nearby, light filtered from the end of a hallway. A stooped figure reluctantly made its way toward the door.

'Josef, it's Consuela.'

The door opened slowly. Josef Perez looked at her suspiciously and then beyond her to the steps and up to the street. When satisfied she was alone, he beckoned her through the door and led her along the hallway into a shadowy living room. Newspapers lay scattered across the floor. To one side, a battered portable typewriter sat on a large table.

A female figure stood in another doorway leading from the room, she was vague and indistinct in the gloom, but Consuela felt strength flowing from an impassive face she knew so well.

The figure came forward and drew Consuela close to her, strong arms bringing some relief from the nightmare. Eventually, she looked up into those dark eyes, her voice almost a whisper.

'I saw him again, Alejandra.'

Josef Perez sighed deeply, and Consuela looked toward him.

'Guzman... I saw him. He was at the church, at St Mary's.'

Alejandra Perez led her over to a sofa and announced that she would make tea.

Consuela turned back to the shrivelled-up figure of the man. His head kept jerking sideways as he asked. 'Lopez was driving?'

Her frown hinted at irritation. 'You knew?'

Perez muttered to himself and shrugged.

'You knew?' she insisted.

'I knew he had arrived in London. I have contacts. One day I will take revenge.'

'You knew about St Mary's?'

There was no response.

'You knew he would be there?'

'It was possible.'

Her voice rose in anger, 'But you said nothing.'

He stayed silent, gazing at her through hooded, exhausted eyes.

'Consuela nothing is ever certain.'

He frowned, his expression changed to anger. 'Ask your priest.'

Consuela was confused. 'Who?'

'Father Doyle.'

'What has he to do with it?'

Perez shook his head in irritation.

Consuela leapt to John's defence. 'What should he know?'

Perez muttered under his breath. 'He is a fool!'

Her answering tone was angry. 'He is a good priest.'

'I can't judge that. What is a good priest: someone who knows the catechism by heart, who reads the encyclicals? Is that a good priest? What do I know of these things? The priests I grew to love had to defy the Church itself to represent their truth.'

As he spoke, his voice rose in anger.

'They crawled through the mud with the people. They went hungry when the people went hungry. Then these priests asked their Bishops, Archbishops and Cardinals, the Pope, why should the people be hungry in a land of plenty, and they asked why so many lived in slums when there were palaces. They were told to keep silent by their masters in the Vatican, who then forgot El Salvador and left the people abandoned in their slums.'

He snorted in contempt. 'But they said they would pray for us.'

He held up both his hands as though in prayer before clenching them into fists.

'But some, the bloody saints, they stood by us, and many of them died. Rutillo Grande, Romero and many others. For God's sake, you knew them. You saw them get shot.'

He moved to a window and pulled aside a small corner of the curtain. Peering out in apprehension.

'Don't tell me he's a good priest, Consuela. Tell me he's a good man. Tell me he cares, and that he will stand by you when you need his help. Tell me he will do more than just pray when you are in trouble.'

Consuela's voice was soft as she looked at Josef's troubled face.

'He does care. I feel it. But he has his life. The church.'

Fierce eyes stared at her.

'He can serve the people without wearing a robe. If he cares, he will always care. If he doesn't, then putting on black vestment and white collar will not change him.'

'You don't understand ...?'

The hunched figure knelt in front of her and took both her hands in his.

'You say I don't understand? Consuela, I understand much more than you think. I know what happened to us all. We were wounded and mutilated.'

His voice took on a soft and gentle tone, as though apologising.

'I know you betrayed your friends…'

Consuela buried her face in her hands, but Perez pulled them away. She shook her head, trying to hide her closed eyes from his.

'We all betrayed our friends, Consuela; don't you realise that? There was no way you could resist. Either we whispered their names quickly out of terror, or we whispered them later from pain and exhaustion.'

He stumbled away from her, falling against furniture, grabbing at the windowsill, and again looking out into the street.

'And then we spend the rest of our lives living in the shadow of our shame. Never able to escape that feeling of guilt. Perhaps your priest may lose something precious to him, but in you, he will have found a jewel without flaw… as I have.'

The door pushed open. Alejandra Perez's voice was clear and strong. Where Josef's tone spilt over with anger, Alejandra's said simply that she had survived and would never bow the knee again.

She put the cups on a small table. 'I heard you.'

Walking across to Perez, she put her arms about him. Her voice lost none of its strength but was filled with new tenderness as she moved him gently away from the window.

'Perhaps Consuela is living for today and not yesterday.'

He bit his lip and stared at his wife as she continued:

'You can never bring Raul back.'

He looked back and forth between the two women and then stumbled from the room, clutching his leg.

'His life stopped on that day. He holds himself responsible and has never rested since.'

She handed Consuela one of the cups.

'Dear Consuela, the other day I saw you smile for the first time in years.'

Consuela pursed her lips and reluctantly nodded.

'Our holy mother church is a cruel rival,' said Alejandra.

Her heavy shoulders shrugged. 'But enough of them live a lie.'

She looked at Consuela's face.

'But, no, for you, I see that is not the answer.'

Consuela shook her head. 'What would be the purpose of that? It would diminish him and destroy me.'

'Well, you know him…'

Consuela interrupted. 'I know him little enough. Perhaps it's just that I think he protects me. He makes me feel safe, and I want to believe that is love. I've spent so many years running.'

She shook her head and fell still.

Alejandra sat impassively in the silence.

Consuela's voice when she spoke again was fearful, her eyes full of tears.

'And I don't think I can let him or any man touch me again. When I feel his hand on mine, I want him and then almost at the same time my body fills with dread. All I know is that feeling of terror. Hopeless terror and fear of intimacy. I loved so much, so strongly, I thought my heart would explode when Manuel was killed. There was no time to grieve, though. One moment I wanted to die. The next moment death was offered to me.'

She shook her head.

'I desperately fought for life.'

A silence fell on the room. Eventually, Consuela looked up.

'It's all the same mess now: love, desire, pain, sorrow. How can I distinguish them when one follows from the other, and when love may just be sorrow or pain again? How do I know any more? Yes, I feel safe with him, but is that love? I do feel desire after so long, but I know that it just brings hurt. And there's nothing but despair to come from that, Alejandra, because I can't risk rejection again. For him, there is nothing, because he would be overwhelmed by such guilt at abandoning the life he knows and loves.

'Perhaps it is just that he cares, and I've forgotten that there are decent people still in the world and it's not love I see, it's just kindness. He touched my hand the other night, and I don't think he even thought about it. It was spontaneous. A gesture made to a friend. I felt sick. But not because it was him. God, I wanted him to hold me and make me safe, but at the same time, I remembered. The memories are still too powerful.'

Consuela looked up to see tears streaming down Alejandra's face. Tears rolled down those glistening dark cheeks, from her fierce bright eyes, through the expression that typically was so proud and defiant.

They reached out to each other. Strong arms gripped as they shared the pain that memory had left in its wake. Consuela sprang from her seat, took a tissue from her pocket and wiped the tears from Alejandra's face.

'Listen to me. What am I saying? He is a priest, and I am wasting all this time dreaming. For God's sake, Alejandra, stop me. I am behaving like a fool.'

Her voice echoed around the small room.

The large woman stood and grabbed hold of Consuela's arms. She pulled her close. Consuela smelled the pungent aromas of El Salvador - papusas, beans, tacos, tortillas - on Alejandra's clothes. She was immediately back in her mother's makeshift kitchen. She heard her father playing the guitar, occasionally her mother singing along to the music. Jorge, her brother, sitting on the dirt-floor reading books he had borrowed from the church. He was always reading, and the floor was strewn with his ragged books. Whenever their mother tried to hit a high note, her voice inevitably cracked, and she would start to laugh, her father would wail in good-natured protest. Jorge would look up at Consuela, and they would raise their eyebrows together.

'Tomorrow, Consuela, we go off together to the country for a few days. Josef has a friend with a cottage that's empty at the moment. We go down there, and for one or two days, we get away from the noise. Do you have any of your things with you?'

Consuela looked up again and nodded, pointing to her backpack, resting on the floor beside the door.

'OK.'

# TWELVE

Father John Doyle saw Roger heading over from The Mission.

It was early for Roger, who didn't usually get in before ten after his late nights on the soup run.

'Consuela has gone.'

John felt suddenly helpless, stranded.

His response sounded strained.

'Gone?'

'She was feeling desperate last night and vanished this morning.'

'I don't understand.'

'It must have been Guzman. She ran when she saw him here.'

'But, I still don't understand why. Did she know him?'

'Stuart spoke with her more than I did. She said she'd seen somebody she hadn't encountered for a long time and that he brought back bad memories. Who else could it be?'

Father Doyle was silent. He recalled seeing her face at the window of The Mission together with the simultaneous sense of evil.

'What do you know of this Guzman?' asked Roger.

'Almost nothing. Just that he wants to pay for all the building work.'

Roger's voice was incredulous. 'All of it?!'

'I was going to tell you this morning. He has offered to donate three hundred thousand pounds.'

Roger's mouth fell open.

'We've struggled to raise forty-odd thousand. That means we could go ahead?'

'If we take it.'

'If?'

Roger closed his eyes and shook his head.

'We have to know more. We can't refuse this money unless we're certain it's ...' he stopped. 'I don't even know what we have to be certain about.'

'Apparently, he's already spoken with the Bishop and Cooper.'

Doyle looked out from the window.

'I'm going to speak with the Bishop and find out what's happened.'

He turned back to Roger. 'You don't have any idea where Consuela is?'

Roger shook his head. 'She just left. Took a small backpack. Left no note. Nothing. You know that I first met her at the clinic.' He paused. 'She never gave me any details about what happened to her.'

'You've mentioned a clinic before.'

Roger looked uncertain. 'She had suffered extreme trauma, and that's what she appeared to be experiencing again yesterday.'

'You've never said what sort of clinic.'

Roger hesitated, his voice when it came was uncertain.

'I feel you should know because you may be able to help. It was the torture clinic in north London. I was a volunteer there. I always remember one of the survivors saying: "They say torture is an act of killing someone without their dying. I am still alive, but inside, I feel no life. I don't know who I am anymore." I sometimes see that in Consuela too. That's why I asked her home, to try to find herself again.'

Father Doyle's eyes opened wide with a feeling of grief. He

stared through the window. He should have realised. He thought he was coming to know Consuela, but this showed just how inadequate he was. How derisory his experience of life.

The pair of them fell into an uneasy silence. They were accustomed to quiet, but now silence extended to uncertain impotence, struggling to find a way forward. The sound of traffic started to intrude.

Father Doyle looked across at Roger.

'I met him here, in this office. I also met something I'd never experienced before, an evil darkness. It took my breath away. I thought I was just being hysterical. Perhaps I was. Later, after the hospice, I spent an hour in the church trying to rid myself of that sensation.'

'What now?' asked Roger. 'About The Mission.'

Father forced his attention away from Consuela, with difficulty.

'It seems that Cooper and the Bishop have decided for us. I – we – need to know more.'

'Good luck with the Bishop. Cooper is a relatively recent trustee but he has been good for The Mission. He introduced Guzman."

Father Doyle raised his eyebrows but said nothing.

Roger smiled. 'OK. I'm allowed a little bitchiness towards Bishop Peter surely. As a non-person, in his eyes, I guess that doesn't matter much anyway. I'll phone Daniel Cooper. I am the manager, after all.'

He stood up. 'Let me know how you get on with the Bishop. If I hear anything from Consuela, I'll call you.'

'What exactly do we know about Cooper? I've always found him pretty laid back. Very helpful.'

Roger shook his head. 'I don't know him but will try to find out some more.'

John stared out through the window as Roger left.

He stood and moved to a bookcase, running his hands across the dust jackets. These books were such a part of him, so much truth he thought he had absorbed. Printed words that had illuminated his life.

Now, at this moment, when he needed help, he found none. The memory of Consuela's face passed before him, but none of these assembled words had prepared him for such anguish. They had sheltered him and protected him when in truth, neither was needed.

He glanced again through the window and saw Brother Roger moving toward The Mission, suddenly understanding the anguish that his fellow priest would have gone through when he had met Stuart. He also, shamefully, remembered the pious platitudes he had offered when all Roger had wanted - as John did now - was a small measure of understanding, acceptance, and compassion.

He called out to Mrs Quinn, 'Could you get Father Cuff along here, please? I'm going to take a few days off to sort out this Guzman business.'

'Are you sure?' She looked confused. 'You never take time off. Isn't it a bit premature anyway, you only met the man yesterday?'

Perhaps she was right, he thought, nevertheless…

She sat down in the small chair. 'In any event, not a good man. I don't think. There's something about him. Is he genuinely the benefactor I've heard about?'

Father Doyle nodded silently.

Mrs Quinn shook her head but said nothing further.

'Any luck with Central America?' he asked, changing the subject.

'Not offhand. There's one man, though, not a priest or anything like. Most unlike in fact. I'll let you know this afternoon.'

'OK, could you please get me the Bishop as well? After you've called Father Cuff.'

A retired Priest, passing some time at St Mary's after a lifetime spent in County Cork, Cuff readily agreed to take over the services and sacraments for the next few days.

When the telephone rang, the Bishop's voice was guarded. His assistant had clearly warned him of the subject of the call.

Father waited till the pleasantries were over. 'I met with Senor Guzman yesterday. I believe you have had discussions with him and Dan Cooper.'

'Cardinal Trujillo himself asks that we make him welcome. Surely it is unnecessary for further enquiries.'

Father sensed hesitation.

'I understand.' Doyle paused. He eventually offered a quiet, 'But…' leaving words unsaid.

'I think we should extend that welcome,' said Bishop Peter.

'Of course.'

The conversation was skirting around the Bishop's knowledge, whatever that might be. John knew it must touch upon it eventually, though, even if tangentially. That was the nature of their life.

Father Doyle spoke again. 'He is from Central America. El Salvador, to be precise.'

'I understand so.'

'It has been a very troubled region.'

'Indeed. Excesses no doubt.'

He had known Bishop Peter for many years, the first encounter being when John was in Rome studying. The man was a consummate politician but primarily a decent person. There was an unease in his voice that Father Doyle had rarely noticed before, as the Bishop offered,

'It is difficult for us to understand.'

Rationalisation? Doyle felt the opening – justification – meaning he knew more. He said nothing.

The Bishop continued. 'We are privileged here and cannot hope to understand their way, their culture, the pressures on all levels.'

Doyle waited again, but this time he sensed words being carefully assembled.

'As you know, I am a Jesuit. We must always be prepared to forgive.'

'Indeed.'

'Cardinal Trujillo was extravagant, voicing his appreciation of Colonel Guzman's assistance to the Church.'

'Colonel?'

There was a pause as Doyle waited.

'Of course, as I said, we have no understanding of these matters.'

The Bishop's voice had regained its composure; the subject was closed. 'Incidentally. It appears Jeremy Keswick has been taken ill. We'll be looking for a new Chair of Trustees. I've asked Daniel Cooper to step in for the moment. I know he's pretty new but very capable and has good contacts.'

The phone call ended.

Father Doyle sat back and gazed out through the window. He thought that the word had slipped out by accident. Guzman, a colonel? But that wouldn't have been the case. The Bishop had told him for a reason and reminded him he was a Jesuit. Why he had been telling Father Doyle would emerge later - much later, when it was almost too late. There was more to Senor - Colonel - Guzman than was being revealed. Perhaps Consuela knew the truth about the man. So, where was she? Where the hell was she?

He headed across to The Mission, realising the building seemed empty without her. Brother Roger sat in his office, surrounded by piles of paper.

'I didn't realise how Consuela kept this place so organised.'

'It's only been a day,' said Father Doyle.

Roger shook his head, looking down at a pile of forms.

'I just spoke with the Bishop. It seems Guzman was a Colonel.'

'Cooper wouldn't take my call. Apparently in meetings all day. What sort of Colonel? I wonder. El Salvador army?'

'I presume so. I'm not sure the Bishop knows though. Cardinal Trujillo referred him. What do you know about him? You know more of the curia than I do since your time in Rome.'

Roger laughed. 'A spell at Thomas Aquinas University hardly qualifies me as an expert.'

'More so than me, Brother,' said Father reminding Roger of his Dominican roots.

Roger snorted with laughter. 'Trujillo was, and still is, the bane of the liberal faction. Rome's enforcer. He was Archbishop of Medellin from '79 and Secretary General of the Latin American Episcopal Conference from '72 until '84. He led the establishment opposition to liberation theology and was Reagan's favourite churchman in the region. Once called Oscar Romero a "crypto-communist".'

'What about now?' asked Father Doyle.

'Heads up the Council for the Family, fighting hard for the institutions of family and marriage, and the virtues of fidelity and chastity. Once he was appointed, I knew my time was up. Use of condoms is immoral, and gay love is a perversion; therefore, I'm a perversion.'

'And he introduced Guzman to us?'

'It would seem so.'

Roger continued. 'Keenly supports the status quo in Central America. That usually means the army.'

'So, I guess Colonel Guzman *could* have crossed the Cardinal's path,' suggested Father Doyle. 'He claimed to have played chess with him.'

'It's possible ... and it answers one question but also poses many more. The reputation of the El Salvadorian army during the civil war one of brutality and terror. Eighty thousand were killed, seventy thousand by the army. Many others just disappeared. Families were destroyed. Since I met Consuela, I made it my business to find out.'

They both fell silent. Father Doyle stood up and walked from the room without another word. He left The Mission, feeling the drizzle on his head as he walked across towards the church. There he paused on the steps. A breeze blew softly on his face. He needed time to understand. Traffic poured along the main road heading towards the City. A red bus pulled into the stop. Three young schoolgirls wearing hijabs ran past laughing.

Nothing had changed.

He drifted into the presbytery and then his office, looking sceptically across the small room. So much of his life had been spent in this place. He examined the books on the walls, so much of what he thought had been bled from these works. When he was empty, their words had filled him, replacing an aching void that threatened so many times to overwhelm and leave him desperately searching to bring comfort to a crowded church, when he had almost lost hope of finding sustenance for himself.

He slumped down onto his chair.

Random words and thoughts flashed through his head as though he were in a trance. Some words and memories endured; the rest just passed on by.

*We do not have all the answers here, yet there will come a time when all questions will be resolved. There is a choice between good and evil, and it is a choice we have the right to make, and our ultimate choice is a part of this living earth. The clouds pass on by, the tides flow, snow falls, freezes, melts, and fills rivers which irrigate the land, producing food. There is balance and harmony, and we are not divorced from it. No less do our words change the universe. Each syllable that we utter enters the subconscious life of the world and is thus available for good, or evil. The words we speak are an expression of who we are, and who we are is what our world is. We cannot escape our responsibilities, not by turning away, or by merely kneeling and passing the buck to what we call our God.*

He shook his head, trying to still the cacophony, to silence the voices.

Nothing had prepared him.

He walked from his office into the empty church.

Silence crowded in on him amidst a sensation of dread, the intensity of his emotions both distracting and terrifying him. He needed a firm anchorage, a solid foundation which would not shift. There was certainty, or there was despair. Washed up now on a desolate beach, all he knew was the sand beneath his feet, slipping away as warm sea washed over peeled and bloody feet.

He whispered, to himself, as though in hope: 'I will find the courage.'

When he got back to his office, he saw a note that Mrs Quinn had left him:

"The person I was trying to remember is Gerry Keane. He was a journalist, retired now, I think. Written a couple of novels. He comes to the church occasionally but not to mass. Most days, he has lunch at The Grapes. That's the best place to find him."

# THIRTEEN

The coffee shop on the Strand was, unusually, almost empty. A few solicitors were reading quickly through files resting beside their early morning caffeine fixes before crossing the Strand to the Royal Courts of Justice.

Jeffrey Sheridan brought two black coffees across to the table where Desmond Williams QC studied a file which he immediately pushed into a battered leather briefcase lying on an adjacent seat.

'So, Jeffrey, Senor Guzman. You have more, I understand?'

'Colonel Adolfo Guzman.'

Williams raised his eyebrows but said nothing.

Sheridan continued.

'There's one firm in El Salvador which is in the same alliance as us. I spoke to their senior partner, Roberta Pineda. She certainly seems to know her way around, but I can't honestly say that she was candid. I gave her the personal details we have of Guzman, without revealing any particulars of the current situation. He was in Spain recently but left suddenly.'

'Why would she know that? Why is he of interest to her, or her firm?'

'Exactly. Unless she was acting for somebody who's been looking for him, you mean.'

'Which could put yourself in a difficult position if you have revealed his current whereabouts.'

'That's true, but you know we also have an office in Zurich and so I routed the call through there. She called me back there to confirm my identity. Fortunately, I am listed as being a partner in the Zurich office.'

Williams leaned back. 'You have reservations about this case?'

'About Guzman?'

Sheridan paused.

'I am doing a favour for another partner who handles Cooper and Atlantic Santos Holdings' corporate work. It comes in at a few million a year in fees. But, yes, he makes me uneasy.'

'The Church?'

'That's part of it.'

Williams waved a languid finger at Sheridan, raising his eyebrows, silently posing a question.

Sheridan nodded.

'Born and bred. I was brought up in the Church. Have a brother, Vincent, in holy orders.'

'And now?'

'The same.'

'And Guzman worries you?'

'He has ever since I first met him. There are questions I don't want to ask, and the quicker this is done with, the better. I just fear we may be leaving St Mary's with a problem that may backfire on them in the years ahead. Cooper had to carry out due diligence. Guzman, an ex-colonel in the army is sitting on a cash pile of over hundred and twenty million.'

Williams raised his eyebrows, looked at his watch and then across to the court building. His voice became brisk.

'We have a client, Jeffrey, and he is our responsibility. I'm sure the church can make its own decisions and look after itself. Tell me more of what ...' he looked at Sheridan's legal notebook - 'your contact Pineda said.'

'First, the background and therefore the reason for her

hesitation. Fourteen families essentially rule El Salvador. They control the corporate sector, banks, agri-business, and retail. The army has always, in effect, been their security force. So, Senora Pineda's firm relies on these families for the bulk of their business, hence the reason for her cautious discretion. However, she did give some details, and she certainly knew more about Guzman than I expected she would. Which certainly poses questions she didn't answer. He joined the army young, trained in the Gerardo Barrios Military Academy, which he later headed. Spent some time in the US and was promoted to Lieutenant in the National Guard in 1980. He had a rapid rise through the officer corps until 1984 when he was promoted to colonel and became assistant to Colonel Ponce, who was head of the National Guard.'

'She is well-informed.'

'Very! That's just what I thought, and there's more. But a quid pro quo was now on the agenda. I think she's got a client - or clients - who want to know exactly where Guzman is. She quizzed me very strongly about our interest in him.'

'And?'

'I emphasised Zurich and finance. Switzerland, banks and such. I was able to remain a touch opaque on the matter.'

'There was more you said.' Williams rechecked his watch. 'I have to be in court shortly.'

'He was made Director of the Military Academy and was a key figure in the Atlacatl Battalion, which enjoyed a chequered reputation at best. He was Ponce's go-to guy. Ponce became Chief of General Staff, and then Minister of Defence until recently. He resigned when he was named in a UN report on the Jesuit murders. There were also some hints about arms deals, which I couldn't fathom. She gave no further details.'

'Jesuit murders? I only vaguely recall…'

Sheridan looked sombre.

'Six Jesuit theologians murdered at the university in 1989.'

Williams interrupted. 'Was Guzman named in any enquiries?'

'Not as either a subject of enquiry or as being responsible. He was only named as being in the chain of command. Not that it would have mattered, an Amnesty later released those that were convicted.'

'In that case,' Williams stood up, 'our client is clean. However, if there is any further noise or he's implicated, then he will find he has no friends. I have to get to court.'

Sheridan watched the tall patrician figure walking across the Strand. He looked again at his notes – at details he hadn't told Williams. Detail that the QC would not have wanted to hear, without proof. And, as far as Sheridan knew, there was no proof. That didn't mean there wasn't truth.

* * *

Father John Doyle walked through Ropemakers Field, recently opened above the Limehouse Link Tunnel. It was a tranquil area amongst the urban sprawl, and he had started to come here often just to escape. The Limehouse Cut canal and basin sheltered beneath concrete developments gathering pace in the newly gentrified area just across the Thames and from Canary Wharf's bank of ever-expanding skyscrapers.

He had been invited to The Grapes previously for a couple of book launches. This lunchtime was quiet, with no customers in the front bar. He made his way to the small room at the rear which led out onto a terrace overlooking the Thames. The terrace tables were all occupied, but there was nobody in the room apart from someone at a small table perched just below a window looking over the terrace. A smoke haze surrounded the dark-haired figure studying him over the rim of a small glass filled almost to the brim with - he assumed - Paddy's Irish Whiskey judging from the bottle sitting on the table. A picture of Charles Dickens hung on the wall behind the pair of sharp eyes scrutinising him, and alongside was a cabinet full of Dickens novels and a small bust of the writer.

Doyle perched himself on a small wooden stool. Silence

followed. Just a nod, barely an acknowledgement, alongside undisguised suspicion. Eventually, the man spoke.

'Father John Doyle.'

The voice was quiet, a croak.

'You're not here looking for souls to convert, I hope.'

Murmurings from the terrace acted as a backdrop to their conversation.

'I'm never going to refuse that chance.'

Doyle put out his hand. 'Mr Keane?'

'I'm afraid there's no chance of any conversion here. The road to Damascus doesn't pass through this tavern. And it's Gerry.'

He took another sip and shouted across to the bar.

'Glass, if you would, please, Robbie.'

The barman, who had just come down the stairs with an armful of plates from the restaurant, brought across a small clean glass.

'What are we drinking to, Father John?' said Keane as he dribbled some whiskey into the fresh glass and moved it across the table.

'I'm looking for some help.'

Keane squinted over half-moon glasses at Doyle, his sharp features seeming to slice through the haze as he took a long drag of his cigarette before sipping from his glass.

'Help, you say?'

He leaned back against the wall.

'It's a long time since I took your sacraments, Father John.'

'You once attended the Church?'

'The family was from Dungarvan in County Waterford. I fidgeted my way through Mass over there until we reached here when I was seven. Got dragged along till I was twelve and that was that.'

'Your parents didn't insist?'

Keane took another sip.

'Killed in a car crash when I was twelve. I was in the backseat and survived. Didn't think much of their God before, and certainly not afterwards, for allowing that.'

Father Doyle sighed. 'You still come to the church occasionally.'

'That I do. Like the quiet.'

His glance grew more intense.

'I particularly like the solitude.'

'I remember.' Father recalled the time when Keane had pointedly ignored him a few months back when he had tried to engage him in conversation as Keane sat in a rear pew at St Mary's.

'Good.'

Another sip, another drag,

'Help, you said?'

'I believe you knew Central America in the eighties?'

The response, previously disinterested, turned apprehensive. Words eventually came, following a coughing fit and a long pull at his glass.

'Why would you believe that, Father?'

'The community knows much, Gerry.'

'Mrs Quinn, I guess ... amongst others.'

'You were a journalist?'

He nodded.

'Can I talk in confidence?'

Keane raised his eyebrows. 'I'm not sure. Why would you want to?'

One of the bar staff walked past and out on to the terrace, returning with two empty plates. Meanwhile, they sat in silence again.

'If I said off the record, would that work?' said Father.

There was a glimmer of a smile.

'OK. That works. What do you want, Father Doyle?'

'John, please. I need to know about El Salvador.'

Keane clenched a fist and tapped it gently on the table. 'That bastard place.'

'We have a situation.'

'We?'

'The church ...'

Keane interrupted. 'The Church in Rome do you mean, or St Mary's?'

Doyle hesitated. 'Now there's a question. St Mary's, I suppose. Someone from El Salvador wants to donate money to the church, but I am concerned about him.'

'Why do you say there's a question?'

'Because Rome has endorsed him.'

'But you're not sure about him? You say Rome, how does that work?'

John Doyle took a sip of whiskey, gave a little cough and enjoyed the warmth spreading through him.

'A Cardinal Trujillo.'

Keane snorted, his expression turning vicious.

'A fucking bastard priest that one is. Whoever he is for, I am against. He supported the bastards who sponsored death squads and tortured their way through the civil war out there.'

The words came quickly, barely scraping past the anger.

'OK, Father John, who is this person you talk of, and why are you concerned.'

He refilled his glass.

'And let me tell you I am not neutral in this.'

He breathed deeply, the words slowing. 'So perhaps I'm not the right person.'

'Why?'

'No, no. I'll not get into that … not yet. What is it you want? We can both decide later if I can help.'

He reached into his jacket pocket and took out a small notebook.

'His name is Guzman. Colonel Guzman as I believe he then was.'

Keane looked up sharply, took a long gulp of his latest drink before sitting back and looking to the ceiling. He held up his hand when Doyle started to speak. The silence lengthened before he looked across at the priest.

His voice was calm, measured as though holding back emotion.

'Tell me, why are you concerned about him?'

Doyle paused. 'Just instinct I'm afraid. I've nothing more than that at the moment.'

Keane ran his hand across his face. He looked away as he took another deep breath. Then his voice came out like a sigh.

'Colonel Adolfo Guzman.' He shook his head. 'I hope not.'

Father took a sip of whiskey and waited.

'I left in '89. My last gig. A week after a dear friend was killed out there. A week and a day after six priests had been murdered.'

He closed his eyes.

'Colonel Guzman.'

He breathed out and looked to the ceiling.

'I hope I don't know your man, Father John. Perhaps there was more than one Guzman.'

He didn't seem convinced.

He suddenly banged his glass on the table, so that whiskey spattered the bare wood. 'Dammit, you've dragged me to a place I'd left behind.'

He emptied the glass.

'I'll check back over my notes. You get as much as you can on him. Make sure we know exactly who we're talking about. We'll find out about your Colonel Guzman.'

He leaned back in the chair. 'OK. Now you're a long way from your pews, Father John. I understand you're a decent man.'

He smiled at Doyle's surprise.

'You're not the only one able to tap into the community gossip network.'

He scribbled a telephone number on a beer mat. 'Here's my number so call me if you have anything more; otherwise I'll call you.'

He waved his hand vaguely towards the door.

'Now let me get back to my lunch.'

He held up his empty glass.

The audience was over.

# FOURTEEN

Father Doyle walked up the steps towards the church. Brother Roger came rushing from The Mission, holding a piece of paper.

'This was dropped through the front door sometime this morning. I just got home and saw it. It's from Consuela, saying she's fine and there's a number in case of emergencies.'

'Any idea who left it there?'

'No. Stuart's at work. It was lying on the doormat with the morning post. I thought you should see it. I was going to call but ...'

He put his hand on John's arm. 'Perhaps you might call?'

John nodded. 'Thank you.'

Roger turned back toward The Mission.

'Let me know as soon as you have anything.'

John called the number as soon as he entered the office.

He recognised that voice: anxious, rasping, accent almost disguised.

'Yes.'

'It's Father John Doyle.'

'The message said emergencies.'

'Yes.'

'What is the emergency?'

John paused.

'No greater emergency than this. Somebody we care about. Who has been a part of our church is missing.'

He heard the scorn.

'Your church? Is that who cares?'

John clenched his fists. He had controlled any anger he ever felt for too many years. The mystery of faith, bloodless reasoning and logic had been the touchstones of his existence.

But this! This fever. Consuela had shifted the axis. Creating something unknown to him before. Something he couldn't now control.

He shouted. '*I* care.'

He paused, scrambling desperately for restraint.

'We care.'

There was silence, then Doyle continued.

'Please, I know you came to the church but what was I supposed to do? You gave me nothing. You said nothing.'

'Antonios coffee house, Wild Court, Holborn. Thirty minutes.'

The line was disconnected.

He ran out of the church, toward Limehouse station.

* * *

He recognised the suspicious anguished expression staring at him from behind a shabby copy of the morning *Guardian*.

'Would you like a coffee?' asked Father.

The other nodded.

'We have tried to help,' said John as he returned and placed a coffee in front of the stooped figure nervously rubbing his hands together.

Father held out his hand.

The appearance of frail lifelessness belied the solid clasp that gripped his hand and the sudden warning that flashed across the man's features.

'Try harder,' he barked.

'I don't know your name.'

'Josef Perez.'

He paused.

'I warned you Consuela would be in danger.'

'You were speaking in riddles. You said nothing about the danger. What was I supposed to do?'

'Keep her safe. Keep him away from her.'

'Him? Guzman?'

'Who else could it be? He comes after I warned you - from the same country. What is wrong with you?'

Father looked out from the window

'You knew he was coming?'

Perez's voice was now almost a whisper.

'I know Guzman. And so does Consuela, that's why she's in danger.'

'So why didn't you warn me properly?'

He waited. No answer.

'*Colonel* Guzman?'

Perez's face suddenly snapped with renewed energy. Doyle realised now that there was an impulse driving Perez that he couldn't yet fathom. The man was defeated and yet resolute, almost in the same instant.

'For God's sake, I want to help Consuela, not harm her. Give me that chance.'

Perez sipped his coffee in silence.

'Tell me about Guzman. I need to know more.'

Perez shot out the words too quickly for Father Doyle to make notes on the notepad he had extracted from his pocket.

'Colonel Guzman. Atlactl Battalion, Director of the Military Academy. Henchman of that bastard Ponce. Trained at the School of the Americas. Strutted, brutalised and murdered his way through my home country in the eighties.'

He leaned closer.

'A monster, Father Doyle. So, what the hell is he doing in your church? His type gives nothing for nothing.'

Perez suddenly leapt up.

'Be by the telephone in your office. This evening.'

He headed out through the café towards the bustle of Kingsway.

Father Doyle leapt from his seat. He searched the pavement and thought he had been too slow until he saw the stooping figure heading toward Aldwych.

The pavement was crowded, but he had no trouble keeping Perez in sight until eventually, he saw him enter the doors of Bush House. He checked the display on the outside. It read: "BBC World Service".

## FIFTEEN

Father Doyle headed to The Mission as soon as he arrived back from the Aldwych, and his encounter with Perez.

He caught Roger in his office just before he went home for the afternoon, readying himself for an evening on the street food run.

'I went and met up with Josef Perez. It seems he knows Consuela and I think he knows where she is. He's calling me this evening.'

'Why wouldn't he tell you where she was when you met him?'

'I don't think he has a very high opinion of the Church - or perhaps just of me.'

He paused.

'I met him a few days ago in the church. Before Guzman. He told me then that Consuela needed protection. I had no idea what he was talking about.'

'You should have told me.'

'I expect I should.'

He paused.

'Mrs Quinn thinks I'm overreacting to Guzman.'

'Is it just Guzman?'

Doyle walked over to the window without answering. He

looked across to the church to see Brigid Kelly coming down the steps. She rubbed a hand across her forehead, a faint, forced smile transformed her anxious expression as she spotted Father John. He raised a hand in greeting.

Roger continued, 'I've not known anyone look as terrified as Consuela did after she'd seen Guzman. You said yourself that you felt something malevolent.'

'Evil is the word I used.'

Roger nodded.

'We know he served as an army officer over there. The Bishop dropped that in. And the army was responsible for murder and torture.'

Father Doyle related what Perez had told him about Guzman.

Roger continued.

'It hangs together, doesn't it? Army and torture, Colonel Guzman turns up, and Consuela runs. I met her at a torture clinic. What are we involved in here?'

'Perez said Guzman's type gives nothing for nothing. So what is he getting in exchange for the £300,000?'

'I have no idea. He could have donated anonymously if he was so inclined. We wouldn't even have known he was involved.'

'That might have been better. But he didn't, so we do know. I must get back to my office as Perez will be calling me. I hope.'

'Why?'

'I said I want to help Consuela and he told me to wait by the phone.'

He shook his head.

'Gerry Keane called Cardinal Trujillo, excuse the vernacular - "that fucking priest".'

'Introducing us to Guzman looks more debased the deeper we dig.'

'That was Dan Cooper wasn't it?

'Mentioned him at a trustees meeting. No details. Possible benefactor.'

'Cooper had family interests in South America. Did you find out any more about him. Just to see if there's a connection with Guzman we should know about?'

'Still looking. Nothing much yet. I've got Stuart checking him out. The question is: do we take Guzman's money or not?'

John stood and made his way towards the door. 'Does the good the money will do allow us to ignore how it has been acquired? Does the character of its donor taint the funds?'

He paused.

'Does money have a conscience? And Consuela would never set foot here again.'

'How big an issue is that John?'

Doyle raised his eyebrows. 'I'm not answering that.'

He opened the door. 'Do you think she could be in danger?'

'Surely it's only her memories she's running from. To get away from Guzman because of what his presence reminds her of.'

'Possibly. I hope that's all. Sorry, wrong choice of words, but what if it is more than that? What if Consuela poses a threat to him even now?'

'I don't understand.'

'It was something Perez said.'

Doyle checked his watch. 'I have to go.'

* * *

A door banged. A voice raised.

Dan Cooper leaned back in his chair.

'Guzman? He said he would be coming over. He can't come quietly?' said Rosa.

'Have you made progress with those companies?'

'Just waiting for confirmation. You want me to call security.'

'It's OK. Leave him to me. Did you contact the architect about meeting at The Mission?'

'Bill Hamilton. Yes. He's calling back. Will make himself free sometime next week.'

Rosa held the door as Guzman marched in, ignoring her. He moved to the window of the forty-third floor of One Canada Square.

'Where is that bloody church? Can you see it from here?'

Cooper walked to the window.

He tried to find St Mary Magdalene through the haze shimmering over the River Thames and the surrounding inner-city clutter. He pointed in what he knew to be the general direction.

'There. Can't see it today.'

'It was you who got me involved with that bloody place.'

Cooper stayed silent as he could feel the rising anger waiting to burst out. He recognised it from many years of experience and knew better than to try and stall it.

'I met the priest.'

Guzman turned a manic glare toward Cooper.

'You said you'd given him the details.'

'No. It had to come from you. Through the Bishop.'

Guzman slumped onto a sofa positioned across the room.

'Bloody priest! I've known too many of them over the years.'

He leaned forward.

'And I've not come over here to be interrogated by another soft piece of Catholic shit.'

'Interrogated?'

'It's not the way things are handled apparently; he has to *"consult"*. What the hell is that supposed to mean? Does the church want the money or not? In any event, it's just a pointless gesture to keep some bastard politicians sweet. You've had my money, Cooper. You said it was enough and it better be.'

'Your money is still yours. Invested in your name. It will guarantee you the right to stay. You want it back, say the word. Go back to Spain.'

'You *know* why I need this. I'll not trail around the world forever looking over my shoulder. Don't assume you're immune. I go down, you go with me - remember that.'

'Then leave it to Williams.'

Guzman's eyes narrowed. His voice was contemptuous. 'Problem priests? There's always a solution to that.'

Cooper paused, a shiver of fear and remembrance running through him. He said nothing.

Guzman stood up.

'They think they want money now. The church will soon be desperate for it if this isn't resolved. So get it resolved. I will talk with Williams in the next few days when I want to hear my application has been accepted. You understand?'

'I've opened the door. That's what you asked.'

'Have you got any details of The Mission. The staff?'

Cooper opened a drawer. He pulled out a brochure entitled: "Helping the homeless transform their lives".

'This is new, only done a week or so back.'

Guzman flicked through the pages before stopping at photographs of staff including Doyle and Brother Roger. He pointed.

'Who is this?'

Cooper looked over.

'Consuela Flores. She handles administration. Grants, benefits and such like.'

Guzman looked closely at the photograph.

He muttered to himself, his voice sceptical, 'Consuela Flores.'

He took the brochure with him as he stomped from the room.

The telephone rang as soon as the door was closed.

'Yes.'

'Mr Cooper. It's Roger Maskell at The Mission.'

Cooper cursed under his breath.

'What can I do for you, Mr Maskell?'

'I was wondering why we have not been kept informed regarding Senor, excuse me, Colonel Guzman's proposed donation to The Mission.'

'You've been chasing the trustees for money to improve The Mission for a long time. The raising of funds is not your responsibility, while management of The Mission is. I suggest you focus on that. Good afternoon.'

He slammed down the telephone and cursed himself. Guzman had unsettled him. Maskell was a good man, and it was not the right way to deal with him.

* * *

John Doyle sat in his office looking out through the window. The phone stayed silent. He breathed deeply, urging the phone to ring. His computer suddenly alerted him to an email. It was the Bishop's assistant forwarding an email from Cooper. Trustees meeting next week about a substantial donation. He grabbed the internal phone, and Roger answered.

'Did you call Cooper?'

'I did. He told me to mind my own business. Not like him. He's usually pretty laid back.'

'What about a trustees meeting next week to discuss Guzman?'

'No. He said nothing.'

His external telephone finally rang. 'Must go.'

He grabbed the receiver.

Perez's strained voice didn't bother with pleasantries.

'Victoria station. Forty-five minutes. Coffee shop, first floor.'

The line was disconnected.

* * *

Father Doyle recognised those stressed features as soon as he reached the top of the escalators. Perez was nursing a half-drunk cup of coffee. He rejected a refill and gestured impatiently for Doyle to sit down. Looking carefully around the crowded concourse, his scrutiny eventually fell on Father John.

There were no preliminaries. The priest strained to hear the soft voice.

'I met Consuela in a Mexican restaurant in Shoreditch. She was working as a waitress while staying in a squat. She became friends with Alejandra as there are few enough of us over here. It took me longer to get to know her,' his eyes narrowed, 'since I don't trust anyone. But Consuela was genuine. *Is* genuine.'

He leaned back letting out a deep sigh.

'I won't tell you about Consuela's life, I don't have that right. But life in El Salvador during the civil war was something you will never experience, and I hope I never will again. I was an associate editor at *El Diario de Hoy*. A journalist who never rocked the boat. I followed orders and put out the lies the Government told us to. Then I made a mistake. It was late at night, and I was tired after working twelve hours because a colleague had gone home sick. I copied what I thought was a Government piece issued from Ponce's office. It said that Colonel Ponce had met with Schafik Handal, the communist leader and guerrilla commander.'

Father John asked, 'Ponce? The army chief of staff?'

'Yes. Anyway, I knew there had been a few secret peace talks and I assumed the Government wanted that disclosed. Perhaps to stall the FMLN.'

'FMLN?'

'*Frente Farabundo Martí para la Liberación Nacional*. The opposition. Guerrillas as the Government saw it.'

He shook his head and wiped his eyes.

'Anyway, I went to collect Raul from school the next day. I was late. The road was empty. Too empty. There was an army jeep parked by the school gates.'

His head dropped, his hands twisting together. The pain was too much.

Father John placed his hand on a sinewy arm. 'Stop.'

'No.'

He felt the anger as Perez's head rose, and he brushed aside John's hand.

'No, this is a reality you must understand. Lopez grabbed Raul by the hair. I shouted in protest. Then I saw Guzman in his body-hugging uniform. The bastard was staring at me directly. I shouted again and started to run toward Raul. Guzman just nodded. The bastard just nodded.'

Perez's head started to shake, and his fists came up against the sides of his head as tears rolled down his cheeks.

'Blood just poured out of him. I would never have thought such a little body – eight years of life – contained so much blood.'

By now, a few faces turned toward their table.

His voice came again, straining through a level of despair Father John hoped never to hear again.

'The bastard thought I was with the guerrillas, passing on their propaganda, and that was unforgivable. It was a warning to anyone else as well.'

He stopped speaking and stared at the table.

John was unable to find a response before Perez continued.

'And Consuela… she has suffered in ways you can only imagine. And, even then, *your* imagination only takes you so far. I know she had at last found a balance at your church and The Mission. With you and Brother Roger. But that was shattered when she saw Guzman.'

He sipped at the cold remains of the tea. Doyle indicated to get another cup. For a moment's respite as much as anything. Perez dismissed the offer.

'You will never understand the place the church holds for her.'

He gave a mocking smile.

'Not for me. I was privileged, or so I thought. But for the *campesinos*, the church meant hope, sanctuary and caring. The priests gave shelter and education. Their voices called for decency, the end of exploitation and corruption. For that they were murdered as well; for that the Vatican and priests like that bastard Trujillo called them terrorists.'

He grabbed Father John's arm again.

'But they found the courage. They persisted. That's what your church means to Consuela: not just a place to meet your friends on Sunday morning, but a much greater significance. Seeing Guzman there, meeting you, shattered her more than you can realise.'

He finally gestured toward the counter.

Doyle went across and ordered tea and a black coffee. He looked back at Perez, saw the man's eyes anxiously scanning the crowded space, occasionally lingering, then quickly moving on.

The rasping voice resumed as soon as Father John sat down.

'And don't tell me you understand, because you don't. You can't. Don't hurt Consuela. Don't promise what you haven't the courage to sustain through the anguish that may entail. You have a good life and are a respected man. As a priest, people look up to you.'

He mocked. 'Whether you deserve it or not.'

His eyes didn't leave Doyle as he took a sip of the coffee.

'What can Consuela give you that you don't already have? Be certain you have a proper answer before you go any further. I know you might care for her. I see that in your eyes. But is it enough? Do you know enough of life to set off down this path? There's always sacrifice, and I doubt there's been much of that in your life.'

He fell silent. Doyle stared into the sad, despairing eyes.

He had an answer. But was it enough? For Consuela. Did he have enough to give her? How could he answer that, as he had denied himself the resources that might sustain him. The Church had been his mistress, and her demands were cold and ever buttressed by bells, incense, and robes.

He looked into that uncertain, expectant, demanding face. At the fierce expression, and the reality just revealed, at such painful cost. Truth demanded more than a platitude, more than insipid reassurance. This was a moment when he had to confront his certainty and somewhere deep within; somewhere beyond the words which came too easily; beyond the feelings inhibited for too long; beyond desires which had been denied; he knew the answer.

He suddenly knew.

He nodded.

It was enough.

Perez looked at his watch. He handed over a train ticket that read Haywards Heath.

'Seven minutes. Platform fifteen. Wait at Haywards Heath station, at the entrance. Someone will come for you.'

He waved the priest away.

# SIXTEEN

The priest waited by the coffee kiosk outside the station.

Three coffees and two hours later, a car arrived.

It moved slowly, suspiciously, around the station entrance before the driver looked over at Doyle and beckoned him over.

'Father John?' he asked.

'Yes.'

He gestured for Doyle to get in the car.

They drove in total silence toward a place called Bolney, before turning on to a minor road and then a narrow lane which led to a cottage where they pulled over. Father John grabbed his bag and moved through a wooden gate, hanging half-off its hinges, and down a narrow untended path to a front door sheltering in a small porch.

A light shone dimly behind a dark curtain covering one of two small windows at the front of the building.

A shadow moved after he knocked.

The small voice was almost lost beneath the sound of leaves rustling in the breeze.

'Who is it?'

'John … Father John Doyle.'

The door opened, and Consuela stood there.

Doyle let out a sigh of relief. 'Thank God!'

She came toward him, moving gently, unselfconsciously, into his arms.

He had never known anything to compare with this feeling.

He wanted to cry out with joy, relief – and above all, hope.

'Father. John!'

Consuela suddenly, abruptly jumped back away from him, 'I'm sorry.'

'Why?'

'You know why, *Father* Doyle.'

The sound that came to his lips was of anger at himself and frustration at his reticence.

He whispered a curse under his breath.

Consuela moved back down the small hallway.

He watched her; the contours of her body; trying to control the panic ripping at sensitive nerve ends.

She called back to him.

'Close the door.'

He followed into the kitchen where steam rose from two saucepans on a hob. He stood still in the doorway, staring. She was wearing a bright red patterned shirt hanging loose over a pair of jeans.

He stood there, in silence, trying to control his emotions.

'You hungry?' she asked.

'I've had two bars of chocolate while I was waiting at the station,' he answered.

'How long?'

'About two hours?"

'Good you're hungry then."

She pointed to a chair and laughed. Her face suddenly lost its smile.

'Josef told you about Raul?'

John sat down and nodded. 'He did.'

'He rarely speaks about it anymore. But his whole life is governed by that dreadful moment.'

She shook her head. 'But whose wouldn't?'

'Guzman?'

'It's his life. Now. Revenge. Justice, he calls it and why not.'

She turned down the hob as steam filled the small kitchen.

'He had started to recover. The BBC World Service gave him a contract, and Alejandra gave him strength. Then he found out the bastard had moved here. From Spain.'

'That's what he meant when he said he would come for you. It was Guzman.'

Consuela looked confused.

'He came to the church. Told me to keep you safe. I didn't understand.'

An edge of frustration crept into her voice. 'When was this?'

Doyle appeared not to hear.

'Was it him, Guzman?' he asked. 'That brought you down here?'

She nodded, then quickly turned away and held her hands up as though in submission.

'Not now.'

She waved toward two saucepans.

'We have pasta ready.'

He asked. 'You knew I was coming?'

'Josef called. I hoped.'

She looked around, 'You like the cottage?'

'It's beautiful,' he said.

'A friend of Josef's owns it, but he's in America for a while.'

Suddenly she looked over at the saucepans still simmering.

'God, you must be so hungry.'

She turned again as though remembering something, looking directly into his eyes.

'When did Josef come to the church?' she demanded.

'Before Guzman came. I didn't know who he was. Why he had come.'

'He said I was in danger.'

Doyle nodded. 'But told me nothing.'

She shrugged, picked up a large wooden spoon and turned back to the stove. Suddenly the spoon cracked against the stove, the noise resounding around the kitchen. Consuela whirled round, her anger barely contained.

'We eat. Then we talk.'

She banged down two plates of pasta covered in tomato and basil. They ate in silence, but John felt a further blast of anger when Consuela occasionally looked toward him.

As soon as they had finished eating, she grabbed the empty plates, placed them in the sink and folded her arms.

'OK, so Josef came to see you?'

She walked over to the window and looked out.

'Why?'

Father Doyle inhaled deeply.

'As I said. He wanted to warn me that you may be in danger…'

Before he could continue, Consuela whirled round, her voice echoing around the small room.

'I may be in danger, but neither of you told me ...'

John tried to speak, but there was no pause.

'He comes to see you, the priest in his collar and suit, but not *me* ... not me who may be in danger.'

'He asked me not to tell you ...'

'Huh!'

'Because he wasn't sure about ...'

'What an absurd excuse is that for either or both of you? I tell you this, Father John Doyle, I am thirty-one years old, and I will be treated as an equal with you and with any man. You understand. You ever treat me like a child again and you'll regret it. Right? Understand?'

'I'm sorry—'

'You didn't hear me right. I didn't ask for your apology. I ask if you understand.'

'I understand.'

Consuela sat down again as John continued.

'But please tell me why you are here. Why you just left.'

'I've telephoned Roger today. It was wrong, but I had to get away from him.'

'Him?'

'Guzman.' Her face darkened as she said the name again. 'Colonel Adolfo Guzman.'

Father looked confused. 'I don't understand. What has he to do with you, Consuela?'

Her voice was soft as though trying to dissociate herself from the words she spoke. She moved to the window, looking away from John, excluding him.

'He is from El Salvador, my country. He is a torturer and a murderer. He killed my friends ...'

John's mouth fell open. He couldn't find the words.

She inhaled deeply and then sat down again, opposite him.

'You know nothing about what you've stumbled into. I mean with me and ...' she paused and closed her eyes, '... with this person, Guzman.'

Her hand briefly touched his.

'I want to tell you; you deserve that.'

She forced a smile, moving again to the window, as though she needed a distance between them.

'I was born in Aguilares, El Salvador. It's a small town; a main street, shops, stalls, a market, churches, wonderful people. My brother Jorge is three years younger than me. Father had a smallholding - a bit of corn, sugarcane - but he also worked for one of the big landowners because the land never made enough to live on. It was scrub poor. We lived in a shack. My mother died when I was twelve – pneumonia – but the community came together, they helped father. I went to a Jesuit school set up by Father Rutilio Grande. He was killed by an army death squad in 1977 when I was fourteen. Archbishop Romero was killed in 1980, in San Salvador ... you remember?'

She seemed grateful for a momentary pause and took a deep breath looking again from the window before turning back.

'Of course. I remember,' said Doyle.

'My father went to Romero's funeral and never came home. He was killed. Jorge and I survived. I helped at a school for a while, and then I became a health worker. The army didn't want that.'

'Why?'

'It was El Salvador, a civil war, a war against the people by fourteen wealthy families who felt threatened that the *campesinos* – peasants – us, might ask for a share of their wealth if we were too strong, if we were educated. The army was their private security, and if you helped the people, you were an enemy.'

Father Doyle started to ask a question.

'John, please. This is too hard. I have spent years trying to forget. Let me tell it my way.'

He nodded. His words were superfluous anyway.

'The army burned down our small health centre. They claimed we were harbouring insurgents. A lie, of course. The army was targeting the whole town. That's when I first set eyes on Guzman. He was only a captain then. There were mutilated corpses strewn all about the streets: teachers, labour organisers, health workers, students. They were the targets. I was held for three days. They threatened Jorge. That he would be killed if I didn't stop supporting the insurgents. I was beaten.'

Her scornful expression mocked the meaning of the words.

'Not too badly, just hit with sticks, burnt with cigarette ends. The cell was covered in dried blood. It wasn't too bad. I got out after just three days.'

Her head dropped. She rubbed her eyes. John touched her hand.

'No, please. I won't be able to carry on. You must know this.'

She paused and looked across at him, her eyes blurred with tears.

'No. I'm sorry you don't have to know this. You can stop me.'

He fashioned a smile and looked deep into her dark brown, misted eyes.

'Of course, I must know. We both know that.'

She looked away, her voice soft.

'I'll try, but not everything. Not now, perhaps never.'

Her sad smile ripped into his attempt at self-control.

'Jorge was studying medicine at the university. So, we moved to San Salvador, the capital. I started to travel around the San Vicente state, trying to improve health care and education again, asking government officials for more money for schools and healthcare initiatives. Inevitably some of my friends and colleagues were involved with the FMLN.'

'The rebels?'

'The government called them that.'

She paused for a deep breath.

'When they picked me up the next time, they took me to a National Guard post. I was held in a basement for two weeks. Guzman was there and controlled everything. I tried to resist. I failed.'

'What? Why…?'

He began but stopped when he saw her expression, shaking her head and imploring him, silently, not to ask too much.

'After that, I stopped work and hid away. Too ashamed to meet with my old friends. The friends I had betrayed.'

'What happened to Jorge?'

'Jorge was in his second year. Medical School. Later he disappeared. Afterwards.'

Her voice fell silent.

'Afterwards?' he asked.

Consuela shook her head. 'No. No more.'

He entered into her dejected silence, realizing now what Josef Perez had meant when he had warned him.

He walked over and looked from the window.

Consuela stayed at the table. She bit her lip, picked up a tissue and wiped her eyes. 'He killed my friends. My brother, just gone. Disappeared.'

Guzman's blank eyes arose before him: the knowledge of evil.

The horror.

He was not surprised and knew that there was more that Consuela was not telling him. But the expression on her face discouraged him from asking.

He desperately wanted to reach out and touch her hand, just to reassure and give whatever small comfort he could. But he remembered how she had pulled her hand away previously. Perhaps that was right. It had to stay like this.

He spoke quickly, trying to calm the unease that reverberated inside his body and mind, he asked.

To fill the silence.

'What is Josef Perez's story?'

'He probably told you, he was an editor at *El Diario de Hoy,* one of the largest selling newspapers in El Salvador. Got out when Raul happened. They butchered him. Left their home with nothing. Alejandra keeps him going.'

Consuela shook her head.

'It destroyed him. He can't escape from that moment.'

'What about you? Guzman?'

'Back then, afterwards, in San Salvador, I wanted to face him, to destroy him. To rid myself of the nightmares. But in time they left me. Until the other day. Now I don't know.'

Her scared expression longed for reassurance that he didn't know how to give her.

Suddenly she seemed to shrug the moment aside and to stop thinking of Guzman.

'You have to get back early tomorrow. I'll come with you. I've been here long enough. It's late now. Come on. I'll show you upstairs.'

He picked up his overnight bag, still lying in the hall and followed her. She pointed at an open doorway leading into a small bedroom.

'You sleep in here.'

Father Doyle felt the tension growing inside him. They looked into each other's eyes on the dark, musty landing. Desire bounced off the wooden walls and reverberated in their emotions and hopes. John felt weak as he looked at each curve of Consuela's body and glimpsed the soft skin he longed to touch and hold.

Those few seconds spanned a lifetime. It was exquisite

torture, delicious agony; and hopeless. He stepped across the small landing, into the room Consuela had indicated. Her soft breathing filled his consciousness, he was ready now to give up everything, just a word - one word - and she could be in his arms, and the rest could take care of itself. He entered the door and turned to her. She hadn't moved and her smile, so sad, hadn't changed.

Just one word.

His heart banged and demanded, he held on to the door frame, his legs feeling weak.

*One word, please.*

Consuela screwed up her face, turned away and shut her door. The hallway was suddenly empty and cold.

Father Doyle finally closed the door behind him.

* * *

He lay awake in the dark, silent cottage. Then suddenly he heard a low moaning. It was soft, hypnotic and, in the quiet black night, terrifying. He got out of his bed and pulled on his trousers. It was hard to work out where the strange noise originated until he realised it was coming from Consuela's room. He knocked, but there was no reply. The moaning continued. He opened the door quietly to find Consuela lying on the floor, curled up in a foetal position with her hands clenched firmly into fists. Her eyes were tightly closed; the moaning sounded shocking as if coming from a place far away. He hurried across, tenderly picking her up from the carpet, lowering her onto the bed.

His voice was quiet and gentle. 'Consuela.'

She was looking directly at him, but he realised she didn't see him. She sighed deeply, shook her head, and drifted deep into the semblance of frantic confusion.

*Memory passed down through the ages, reluctant but indifferent, bringing a vague understanding that this is not what was ever intended. Names that touch a horror contained so deep it sometimes reaches a place of turmoil, the greatest torment, the loudest scream bringing agonised confusion. Survival becomes an experience as much as death, inducing reaction as primitive - life the greatest triumph; death the final victory for those that pass over in tranquillity.*

Consuela silently recollected pictures, and scenes, taken from a vicious video filmed during a nightmare that never ends.

*Hope is all that is left at the moment of passing. Hope of the past, and hope for the future, mingled silently and surreptitiously with the uncertainty that it has all been a mistake and that we have misunderstood everything all along.*

John stayed silent as Consuela let out another huge sigh of despair.

*Some actions deserve no forgiveness. I prayed for my name to be recognised. Hoped someone would remember me one morning, as they looked out over peaceful fields and blue skies because they had heard my name. It was the mirage which I could see but never reach, yet hope was enough. Just to forget the bitterness and the emptiness of hatred; leaving me to live again, to feel again without the panic so deep it tears my guts apart.*

The voice was low, 'I want vengeance.'

Her eyes opened. She looked around the room.

'John! What's happening, where are we?'

'In the cottage.'

'Cottage?'

Her face was confused. She touched his arm, stroked his cheek, and began to weep. He put his hand onto hers, and as if his touch were electric, she recoiled from him.

His mouth fell open in dismay and confusion.

He spoke, the tone softly apologetic.

'I'm sorry.'

He stood up and backed slowly to the door.

'If you need me ...' He pointed toward his bedroom, with a smile, confused and sad.

'Through here.'

'No,' she insisted, pointing to a chair against the wall. 'Please don't leave me.'

* * *

They travelled back through an early morning mist hovering over the luxuriant Sussex landscape. Sunrise peered through low cloud over the South Downs as Father Doyle and Consuela sat in a car driven by one of Josef's contacts.

'Will you return?' he asked as they moved toward Roger and Stuart's house.

Consuela didn't reply.

'To the church. To face Guzman.'

He paused. 'With me?'

'For what reason?'

'Justice ... and truth.'

'Those would be good reasons.'

She grimaced and then smiled.

'Consuela Flores against Senor Guzman, with his money and a limousine and a suite in a luxury hotel and the Bishop; Cardinal Trujillo; members of parliament; lawyers.'

Father Doyle looked surprised.

'Yes, Roger has told me everything.'

The laugh was dragged from a well of hopelessness.

'I am just Consuela Flores.'

She paused at the sound of her own name.

'Still waiting on her asylum application. Whose justice and whose truth would it be, Father John? Not mine, I think.'

She stared from the window as they reached the house.

'I won't come back for all that. But to face him? To see if I can be whole again? Possibly. But then he will know who I am and know where I am, and perhaps only one of us will survive that.'

'I don't understand. Perez also said Guzman mustn't know you are here. Why the danger now?'

'Perhaps Josef is right, and I should hide. But perhaps it is time to stop hiding, although I have no hopes left of justice, and truth is a story the victors get to tell.'

The car stopped in front of Roger's house, and Consuela jumped out without another word.

Father Cuff was taking early morning Mass. John joined with the congregation. He knew the words so well.

Dark images dimmed, but for barely a moment.

* * *

Mrs Quinn looked worried as she waited outside his office.

'I don't know if it's important, but I saw Michael Kelly with that driver again.

Father John opened his door. 'Driver?'

'Guzman. The black car. His driver.'

'Yes.'

'I was visiting my sister in Dagenham. They were sitting huggermugger in a corner of the Eastbrook pub. Kelly had two of his skinhead friends with him, but they were outside in a battered old white van. Probably doesn't mean anything but something doesn't seem right.'

She started to walk away, then turned back.

'Oh, Gerry Keane called. Come over this evening, he said, but bring a bottle. You'll know which one.'

She gestured to his office. 'The plans for The Mission extension are in there.'

'What plans?'

'Bill Hamilton, the architect sent them over. He said he could make it next week to meet you and Dan Cooper. Rosa has arranged it.'

She frowned at Father Doyle's concerned expression.

'Why? We have the money now, don't we?'

'Who told you that?'

'Cormack. The Bishop's lad.'

'So, he did, did he?'

'Is that not the case? From that unpleasant piece of work, Guzman?'

Father eyed a pile of new papers on his desk then he glanced suspiciously through the window of his office.

'Could you please get me Rosa.'

He walked over to the documents and unfolded several of the architect's drawings featuring a proposed rebuilding of The Mission that had had to be postponed a few years back.

The telephone rang.

'Rosa. You sent plans of The Mission across to us.'

She agreed.

'Guzman's money?'

'Father John, I don't want to talk about that man. I can't understand why Dan has anything to do with him, but I suppose the money might do some good. You know Bill Hamilton? The architect.'

'Of course.'

'Well, he can come over next week if it's OK with you.'

'I'd like to speak to Dan.'

'Of course. I will get him to call. He's in Sheffield today visiting one of our factories.'

There was a pause.

'You sound concerned.'

'Guzman. He's my concern.'

There was agreement from Rosa. She said she would make sure Dan Cooper called.

# SEVENTEEN

The rest of the day passed in a blur of routine and irrelevance. As the room started to become dark, the movements outside his door decreased: just occasional slow, shuffling feet on polished, shining wood.

Father Cuff's stick tapping against the walls.

Sitting on the edge of his narrow bed, John remembered when dark solitude had been a refuge, immersing him in unspoken words that emanated from the place of mystery towards which he thought he was travelling.

Now, though, was it movement or just standing in a stagnant pool waiting for something to happen?

The words he chanted he loved no less. Words that expressed the great truths of humankind and their source was sacred:

"I was hungry and you gave me food, I was thirsty and you gave me drink, I was a stranger and you welcomed me, was naked and you clothed me, I was sick and you visited me, I was in prison and you came to me."

Words that still endured and inspired.

He had opened himself wide in devotion. It had seemed the only response.

Filled with the spirit of all he had ever loved, in the only way he had ever known to express love: words; words; words.

Thomas Merton's *New Seeds of Contemplation* lay open on the small coffee table next to the catechism of the Catholic Church.

A single cup stood empty, dried coffee stains gathered at the bottom.

Sacred words: truth, but no longer the only truth.

He read the words; "It is not we who choose to awaken ourselves, but God who chooses to awaken us", but he had lost his bearings.

He opened the catechism.

Passion: the word struck into the core of his knowledge and his sudden blinding uncertainty. *Feelings or passion are emotions or movements of the sensitive appetite that incline us to act or not to act in regard to something felt or imagined to be good or evil.*

To be good or evil? He felt empty. His chest was tight. He struggled for breath. Trying to stand, his legs felt weak - too weak. He crawled across the floor and pulled himself up into a chair. Fear, absurdity, what was past was gone, finished.

*The virtue of chastity therefore involves the integrity of the person and the integrality of the gift.* But he knew the touch of her hand, and picking the catechism from the coffee table he threw it across the room.

He looked out through the window at a threatening sky. He had eagerly read the words of life; without realising they were not a substitute for life.

Reaching across he touched the covers of his books, beginning to understand what they were saying for the first time. Familiar words he had spoken and chanted for over ten years, they had given sustenance and hope. The missal had lain open, but he did not need it because he knew the words. They were life and substance. As time passed, these incantations had become truth, not the route to truth. Meaning was irrelevant; order and habit had stripped the fervour from the comfortable chants which filled the church.

*Hail Mary ...*

*Blessed ...*

*Have pity ...*

He loved them and had given them life thousands of times, a newspaper seller shouting the late city prices, obscure in meaning but everything in understanding acquired over centuries of whispering in faithful's ear.

* * *

John Doyle held up the bottle of Paddy's Irish Whiskey like a trophy.

Gerry Keane waved him through the door and then out onto a small balcony overlooking the Limehouse Basin.

Barges moored in the Basin carried a few people sitting on their decks. Three separate couples strolled around the edge of the water.

The picture was tranquil, but Doyle felt the tension leaching out of the dark expression Keane directed at him. They sat at a small table. Two glasses and an ashtray waited, alongside a notebook and a file of documents.

Keane gestured to the glasses, and then the bottle. He stayed silent, sitting and looking over the peaceful scene while Doyle poured the whiskey.

The man's voice when it came, was soft, almost lost, as a police car sped across the bridge over the entrance to the Basin, its siren shrieking.

'I've spent a few years getting away from that place. It was the end for me. We didn't use to be targeted. In Vietnam, Cambodia, Beirut, friends and colleagues died, were killed, but that was because we were working in a dangerous environment. Central America was the first time journalists were deliberately targeted as enemies.'

He took a long sip from the glass and waved a hand at Father Doyle to give him a refill.

'El Salvador was different. Lists of reporters' names posted outside the Camino Real Hotel where we all stayed, with one word at the top, *Muerte,* meaning death. Rooms regularly trashed, tyres slashed when we went out of San Salvador. Dead bodies placed outside the hotel for us to see. The US milgroup guys played along.'

'Milgroup?'

'The US had around fifty advisers, usually ex-special forces called the Military Advisory Group. They were supposedly helping out the El Salvador army. There was generally a few of them hanging around the Embassy - always on to us to toe the government line. The US line.'

'Which was?' asked Doyle.

'That the insurgents were hardened communists looking to defeat the peace-loving democratic government of El Salvador which, if defeated, could mean the dominos would fall and Fidel Castro and the Soviet Union would be knocking at the door of the White House.'

He gave a mocking smile.

'Bullshit, of course. The peace-loving government was kept in power by an army out of control, murdering and torturing their way across the country. There were massacres, try El Mozote in eighty-one.'

He drained the glass again, demanding a refill.

'Priests were assassinated, and the basement of the National Guard Headquarters was given over to torture and death. Around seventy thousand people were murdered by the army and their militia death squads. Anyone who spoke out disappeared or their bodies were left at the roadside as a warning.'

He leaned back and took a deep breath.

'I didn't take sides. Ever. There are always saints and sinners on both sides and some who were both. The FMLN - they became the main opposition - took lives as well, just not as many. Estimated at ten thousand. Most of them a sad and tragic waste. But they weren't hardened revolutionaries. When we got out of the government clutches, we met up with a people trying to survive through poverty; no education for their kids; poor health facilities and when anyone tried to change it …' he pointed at Father Doyle's small crucifix hanging around his neck …

'including your sort, they were murdered. The military had a slogan at one time, "Be patriotic, kill a priest".'

He emptied his glass again, barely noticing that Father Doyle had not yet touched his.

'You asked about Guzman ... I'll come on to him, but you need background and context before talking of specifics. He was a product of the place, the time and the environment. I've never felt it my duty to excuse but only to explain, and then let whoever reads or listens make up their own mind.'

He pulled a packet of cigarettes from his pocket, looked at them and handed them to Doyle.

'For fuck's sake, take them.'

He pointed at his empty glass.

'The place was a shit-heap from way back. A few families own all the decent land. Coffee, sugarcane and corn are the main crops. The rest is parcelled out in small plots to families who can never grow enough to live on, so they also have to work for the large estates – for peanuts of course. If anyone raised their head to complain or tried to organise the *campesinos*, the estates always had their own security force, the army, to stamp it out.'

Doyle finally sipped at his glass. He was just a spectator here. Keane was absorbed in another time and another place. His eyes strayed across the water to the Basin, the barges, people wandering around the water's edge, but his preoccupation was elsewhere.

'That was the deal until after the Sandinistas threw out Somoza in Nicaragua in '79. Jimmy Carter was President then, and he started funnelling military and other aid to the Salvadoran regime, as I said, fearing that Central America could fall under Cuban and Soviet influence. On 2nd December 1980, between Carter's defeat and Reagan's inauguration in January '81, four Maryknoll nuns were raped and murdered. I was based in Washington at the time and went across there when that happened. I had met up with two of the nuns on an earlier trip to San Salvador. Went to the site, close to the airport, as they dug out the bodies. I talked with the US ambassador at the time, Bob

White. He'd had dinner with two of the nuns the night before their murder, and they'd stayed at the Embassy that night. He knew who had killed them. Everyone knew. The army. He was sacked by that bastard Al Haig for refusing to say that the Salvador army was carrying out a proper investigation. Which of course they weren't. They didn't need to because they'd organised the killings. The writing was on the wall once Jeanne Kirkpatrick, who Reagan later made UN ambassador, said "The nuns were not just nuns. They were political activists." Another fucking lie. One of the Colonels described them as "commie bitches". From that moment, the die was cast, the army knew they could get away with anything.'

He abruptly stood up. Father Doyle grabbed his glass before it fell off the swaying table. Keane leaned over the balcony then ran a hand over his face as he looked back at Doyle. His expression told of revulsion. He closed his eyes. Father Doyle had to strain to hear the muted sadness in the voice.

'I remember them digging up the shallow graves … pulling the bodies out. One by one. Beautiful people. Just there to help. The youngest was Jean Donovan, only twenty-seven.'

He shook his head.

'I remember thinking: what sort of people could do this?'

He gave a cynical laugh.

'But then we'll talk of your Guzman later. Of course, Oscar Romero, the Archbishop, had been murdered by a death squad in March the same year.'

He held up one hand as though in surrender.

'Give me a minute.'

He gestured toward Doyle.

'Cigarette?'

'Are you sure?'

Keane shook his head and walked back into the apartment through the balcony door. Father noticed his fists clenched tightly by his side. He turned and surveyed the Basin. The normality and tranquillity of the scene clashed with the images bouncing around in his head. He remembered Consuela's words, her anguish, and now this. A world apart. Not a report he'd read in *The Tablet,* nor a radio broadcast heard as he sat in a comfortable chair - or a television documentary; life through a screen, sheltered and safe. These words were raw; they were a truth his sheltered existence had evaded until now: and he struggled to respond. He stared at two figures standing at the water's edge watching a seagull perched on top of a barge. They laughed together. He turned away as Keane stepped back onto the balcony, sat down, and poured himself another glass of whiskey.

'Drink.'

The tone was sharp as he gestured toward Father Doyle's half-empty glass.

'I'll not do this alone. You dragged me back there.'

The glance was accusatory.

Doyle finished his drink and poured more into each of their glasses.

'Reagan transformed Carter's paranoia into foreign policy. Six billion dollars poured into El Salvador during the eighties. Most of it ended up there, although I understand a few hundred million got lost along the way - but that's another story for another time. Reagan wanted to destroy communism, and that meant the Soviet Union. Central America was just one of the proxy wars he fought to keep America safe.'

He laughed.

'Well, the truth is the Berlin Wall started to come down in 1990.'

He shrugged.

'Perhaps all the deaths were worth it. As I said, I didn't take sides although it was difficult not to in those times. I lived out there from 'eighty-six. Wanted to get out from behind a desk. Stayed until 'eighty-nine.'

Keane sat back and looked up at the sky. He poured a full glass down his throat and again held up the empty glass.

'Do I miss it? I guess it might seem that way. Not really. Do I drink too much? Sure, but that always went with the territory and despite all the bollocks about health, which I'm sure has a point, I enjoy it. Made sure I had a book deal before I packed it in and now I don't have a news editor, a proprietor, or his current wife, to keep happy. That was my last gig; El Salvador.'

He wiped his forehead and sighed.

'You asked about Guzman.'

He touched his notebook, and then the files.

'I didn't need these. As soon as you mentioned Guzman's name at The Grapes, I remembered him. First met him at the US embassy on a visit around 'eighty-three. He was a captain then, not long back from Fort Gullick in Panama, after a spell at the School of the Americas. He'd done "anti-communist counterinsurgency training" with the US Army. Graduated initially from the Capitan General Gerardo Barrios Military School in San Salvador. After he completed Gullick he hung on to the coattails of the Milgroup boss - at that time it was an old Vietnam special forces vet who was well connected. There were claims of White House meetings. Guzman made himself useful. Colonel Ponce, who was Minister of Defence until recently, saw Guzman's potential, if you could call it that, and promoted him to major, and then lieutenant colonel, putting him in charge of one of the most notorious outfits: the Atlacatl Battalion.'

He paused and took another long slug from his glass.

'The Atlacatl Battalion was *made* for him, and he carved out his empire with the aid of the US Milgroup: using their technical assets and training. Wearing their distinctive red berets, they swaggered through the whole country torturing, murdering, answering to no-one, uncontrollable. We witnessed the consequences of their activities too many times.'

He shook his head.

'They generally left their calling card, an image of a skull and a lightning flash against a red background. Massacres I don't want to think about. Look them up for yourself, and then you'll know more about Guzman. As I said before, start with the El Mozote massacre, if you must, but do it on an empty stomac

He leaned back and put both his hands on his head.

'Jesus, Father John Doyle, you're a bastard, that's for sure. Taking me back to that fucking time. Incidentally, what the hell is he about now? I think you said he wanted to give some money to the church. Blood money that would be then, and what the hell would that be for? You may believe in Damascene conversion, but it doesn't fit with me, and certainly not with Guzman.'

Keane gazed about him as though seeking an answer.

Father Doyle breathed in deeply. In his life, he had the answer. People came to him for those answers. That was his role. Or so he thought. That had been his version of himself. A version crafted in a seminary. A version of a person he doubted now, whose authenticity seemed tentative.

He shook his head, ignoring the question, and then asked.

'But surely the US with its Congress and Senate would have investigated?'

'It was a moral crusade against the communist menace. And it was far away in El Salvador. An American friend of mine, an attorney from Washington, once corrected me after I'd suggested that Americans think the world starts on the west coast of the US and finishes on the east coast. He told me I'd got it wrong. He told me, with a degree of truthful cynicism, that most Americans think the world starts at one end of Main Street and finishes at the other. El Salvador was far away, and thus a safe place for a proxy war. An assistant secretary of defence declared, to my face, that the Salvadoran military was "nothing but a bunch of murderous thugs" but they were "our thugs killing our enemies."

'OK, give me some more of that drink – and for Christ's sake have some yourself. You're a bloody Catholic priest, aren't you, not ... rse, Protestant cleric?'

... lready feeling the effect of the whiskey but ... e's glass again, merely covered the bottom of ... re coming on around the edge of the Basin. A ... the lock from the choppy waters of the

'Colonel Ponce - how that name suits the s.o.b - was made chief of the army general staff in 'eighty-eight. Guzman was by his side. He'd been made a full colonel and director of the Military Academy by then. Ponce's go-to guy. The FMLN insurgency continued through the 'eighties, but mainly in the rural areas. On 11th November '89 they attacked San Salvador itself, as well as other cities. The elite had been insulated before this assault, but now the fighting was getting close to their luxury homes in the western suburbs. Militarily the FMLN didn't gain a victory, but they gained politically. It was a desperate throw - the FMLN's Tet offensive. International support was draining away since the focus was elsewhere. The Soviet Union was collapsing, and the attack showed that despite billions poured into the country, funding the army, the war was unwinnable.'

He took a slug from his glass.

'The early morning of 16th November '89 marked the moment the war was over. Six Jesuit priests murdered in their residence in the university in San Salvador. I knew most of them ... everybody did. Smart, gentle, theologians, for Christ sakes, trying to bring both sides together. But not in the eyes of the government, the army. Ponce and his bastard crooks decided that if they weren't for them, they must be against them. Who was the guy they turned to? Colonel Adolfo Guzman. That's not the official story of course; they lined up some fall guys to take the heat. Ponce and Guzman have walked away, at least for the time being, but it'll catch up with them one day.'

'What do you mean? Was Guzman there? I read that nine members of the army were tried in 'ninety-one, but only a colonel and a lieutenant were found guilty. Sentenced to thirty years.'

'That's true, and they served their time in a hotel near the beach at La Barra de Santiago – they were then released under the amnesty. The army leadership tolerated the trial only because of pressure from the US Congress, which made successful prosecution of the killers a condition for continuing aid to El

Salvador's government. The Salvadoran military covered up any involvement of higher-ranking officers in the army command. Men such as Ponce and Guzman. The problem for Guzman was there were witnesses, at least one, who can place him at the scene.'

'That's not mentioned in any of the reports.'

'A couple was staying in one of the houses next to the priests' residence, and they saw that it was the army who carried out the murders. There was another witness who recognised and named Guzman.'

'Why didn't this emerge during the trial?'

'All the witnesses were flown to Miami and held in a hotel there by the FBI. An El Salvadorian so-called independent investigator arrived. His name was Rivas, Colonel Rivas. He was called an independent investigator, but surprise, surprise, he was a member of the Atlactl Battalion. He threatened the witnesses that they would be refused permission to stay in the US and sent back to San Salvador if they stuck with their story of army involvement. They knew they wouldn't get out of San Salvador's Comalapa airport alive. Two of them recanted - until they were safe with a US church group, and then again confirmed the story. The other witness, the one who had recognised Guzman, got out of the hotel and disappeared as soon as Rivas arrived. She knew him. Not been seen since, alleged at the time that Guzman was there and personally ordered the executions. She gave a statement naming him. Guzman searched for her. She was too dangerous to leave alive.'

'How do you know this?

'I was out at the university in the morning, after I got a call. The priests' bodies were still laid out on the lawn. Shot in the head. A terrible scene. A housekeeper and her daughter had been shot as well, and they were laid out in one of the small houses. The order had been given to leave no witnesses alive. They somehow missed the other three who stayed in hiding. The army made the feeble claim that the FMLN was responsible, but that excuse was soon blown apart. It ended the war. The disgust around the world was too extreme. The US forced the government to negotiate. Secret talks had been on and off since around 'eighty-four, and now the army was forced to take second place to the politicians. It was over.'

'And the witnesses?'

'The next day, I was with some colleagues in a suburb of San Salvador, called Mejicanos, just walking along the street. It had been held by the FMLN and just retaken by the army. We were talking to some scared young conscripts. There was one shot from behind us. A friend I had known for over twenty years dropped to the ground. He died in hospital. I wanted out of there. It was over for me. Left four days later, 23rd November, grabbed a ride on a French army plane with Bernard Kouchner, who was a French minister at the time. The three witnesses were on the same flight. They'd been given French protection after making sworn statements to a judge. The Salvadorian army had tried to get them. To eliminate them.'

'What happened to the statements?'

'I believe they were taken to army HQ and destroyed.'

He stood and leaned on the balcony before turning back.

'And that, my dear Father John Doyle, is your man, Guzman and his fucking beautiful country.'

He raised his glass and gestured a toast to his companion.

They touched glasses.

'Salud,' he suddenly shouted, and a few faces in the Basin turned toward the balcony.

Doyle noticed a tear rolling down Keane's cheek.

# EIGHTEEN

Father Doyle got back to his office.

The drink had dulled him.

Keane's words ripped into his equilibrium. He wasn't accustomed to pictures of horror and violence and death. He longed to touch Consuela and tell her of his sorrow and his shame at his pathetic attempts at reassurance.

What did he know?

What could he hope to know, hidden away behind an altar and a sanctimonious arrogance which the priesthood had bestowed on him?

The telephone rang.

Dan Cooper's tone was clipped. There were no preliminaries. It was unusual for someone Father Doyle thought he had come to know.

'Father Doyle, it's Dan Cooper.'

'I understood you were in Sheffield.'

'Just back. You spoke with Rosa. Concern about Guzman. How can I help?'

'Colonel Guzman?'

There was a pause. Barely a heartbeat, but long enough to speak of apprehension, quickly replaced by anxiety. He didn't understand why until later.

'I understand. The trustees will have to decide. But. Well. The money. It could transform The Mission. Bill Hamilton already has the plans. We need the extension.'

His voice sounded strained.

Father Doyle spoke slowly. Anger at the words of Gerry Keane and the whiskey, mixed together, but he kept a tight grip on emotions that threatened to spill over into incoherence.

'There has been no formal decision by the trustees?'

'No, of course not. You would be involved in any decision.'

Doyle felt his voice slowing down even further.

He didn't understand Cooper's apprehension.

Cooper's voice calmed. Father heard him changing a gear trying to regain control.

'There is a trustees meeting scheduled for later this week. You may have been informed. I'm hoping you will be available to meet with Bill Hamilton before the meeting.'

'Good,' said Father, pausing for a moment to wonder whether Consuela had agreed with what he was about to say, or whether he was substituting his own assessment for hers.

He continued as much in hope as confidence.

'There is a woman from Colonel Guzman's own country who would like to meet with him. She may also be able to help the trustees in their decision.'

The pause this time was longer. Doyle abruptly realised, without any words spoken that Cooper knew. He knew all that Consuela had told him. He knew everything.

'Her name, Father?'

'Consuela Flores. I believe you have met her.'

The pause lengthened. 'I have met her. I must go.'

The line was abruptly disconnected.

* * *

As Dan Cooper ended the call with John Doyle his car pulled up at the Tower Hotel. He saw Guzman's driver staring at him from the limousine parked in the non-parking zone.

Cooper told his driver to wait.

The meeting would not last long.

He didn't want the meeting at all.

Guzman's driver continued to watch as Dan Cooper walked to the hotel entrance.

He sighed deeply and went directly to the bank of lifts.

Why couldn't Guzman have stayed in Spain? Anywhere but Britain, he reflected.

The carpets were deep in Guzman's suite.

A long window overlooked Tower Bridge.

Guzman sat back with a large glass of whisky in his hand. He watched Cooper sitting uneasily on the sofa opposite.

The price had been paid in horror and deformed existence. Nothing had touched Guzman since the moment of realisation that his destiny was one of violence and mutilation. He hadn't dared to challenge it, to change it, nor in truth, the inclination.

What forgiveness could he ask for now?

What justice could he hope for but pain and bloody lacerating redemption, and why should he care? Nothing would affect him; nothing would stand in his way; it was too late for that.

'You said it was urgent,' said Cooper as he reached into his pocket, took out a handkerchief and mopped his forehead.

Guzman handed a printout to Cooper. It showed a white skull with a yellow lightning bolt behind it, across a red background.

'You recognise this?'

He paused while Cooper stared, his eyes wide.

'This is why it's urgent. Sent as an attachment to an email account I use. The attachment contained a virus that would have extracted all the information from my computer, but we scrubbed that clean. You recognise it?'

He leaned closer.

The voice lower, threatening.

'But of course you recognise it.' Cooper stared at the image. He could barely fail to remember it, the symbol "ATLACATL" written in yellow across the top of the document. He nodded. Knowledge was one thing, but the memory of the violence; the bloody, putrid, contemptible savagery was too much for him. He tried to control his breathing as his chest tightened, and he started to sweat, feeling hot and nauseous. He ran to the bathroom and vomited into the toilet bowl, trying desperately to calm the trembling in his arms. To ease the tight band clamped across his chest.

Guzman turned from watching Tower Bridge open slowly. The traffic was stationary on either side of the two towers.

His voice gave no quarter.

'It is intended for me, not you.'

Cooper barely heard the words, sipping slowly at a glass of water.

'I wondered—'

Guzman interrupted, his tone voice cruel.

'Wondered. You wondered what it meant. It's a long way from this, isn't it?'

He stood up and strolled around the room never taking his eyes from Cooper; resting his hand on the television, the items of furniture, the refrigerator, and then leaning close and touching the lapels on Cooper's Savile Row hand-tailored suit. He snatched up the printout from the table.

'You know what it means? Do you remember the Atlacatl Battalion? You should do. They – we – kept your company's estates clear of insurgents. They – we – killed Father Rutilio Grande, after he stated that the big landowners' dogs ate better than the *campesino* children whose fathers worked in your fields. Do you remember the Atlacatl Battalion? Of course, you do. They were your – and the other landowners' – private army. We accepted your orders, and we kept you and your land safe – and your investments safe. We saved you back then, and now you sit in a big office,' he waved out of the window, 'have a nice car and a driver and hundreds of coffee shops and bake your bloody cakes.'

He threw the printout into Cooper's face.

'But now, Senor Cooper, it's your turn to save *me* from them.'

Cooper let the paper fall to the floor. He tried to recover some composure.

'Why? They were your colleagues. Why do you need saving?'

'That's a question you haven't the right to ask. Just know it is time to pay your debts. I will be safe in this country. I will buy an estate, and I will have security, and I will live peacefully and forget El Salvador, and you can forget me and bake your cakes. But now ... now, you pay the price. You understand?'

Cooper's voice was reluctant. Guzman's violence was too near the surface, too accessible. Cooper was no coward but this easy recourse to brutality was alien and demoralising. His voice when it emerged was almost a whisper.

'So, pay them. Your colleagues.'

Guzman wheeled round, his eyes wide in fury. He gave no answer; instead, walking to the refrigerator he picked out a bottle of beer. Holding it loosely in one of his large hands, he bent down close to Cooper's face and suddenly smashed the bottle against the table. Beer spurted out over them both. Cooper jumped involuntarily, falling back into the chair as the towering figure bent closer.

Glinting jagged glass moved closer, almost touching Cooper's staring face.

Guzman's voice came so low it was almost a growl.

'I did all the work. They got what they deserved. They will never get any more. That is not your concern, Cooper. But now you understand what this is about.' He tossed the bottle into a waste bin. 'Life and death. Nothing less.'

He moved over to the window; the voice calm again as though this was a routine meeting between colleagues. His tone betrayed no emotion or concern.

'I'm seeing Doyle tomorrow. You said he was sound. Make sure he is. Tell your trustees to accept this money. The extension to this *Mission*,' he spat the word in contempt, 'will be my building, the Adolfo Guzman, building. And I will get my fucking passport.'

Cooper's mouth lay open, saying nothing. Eventually, he answered, looking for help, trying to find a way to disguise his disgust, knowing his words could provoke more ferocity, but also knowing that if he remained silent the consequence could be worse.

'The woman wants to meet with you.'

Guzman looked up and suddenly smiled. 'The woman?'

Cooper breathed slowly.

'The woman I mentioned previously: Consuela Flores.'

'I remember. I saw her picture. I saw her at The Mission.'

Guzman moved across the room and extracted The Mission brochure from his briefcase and located Consuela's photograph.

He mocked. 'Consuela Flores. Oh, yes, I must meet with this woman.'

'She may also ask to meet with the trustees.'

Cooper strained to hear the voice.

'That will not happen,' said Guzman as he walked back to the window. He pulled out his phone, waving his hand at Cooper to indicate he was dismissed.

He almost ran from the room.

## NINETEEN

Bishop Peter's voice sounded exasperated.

'John, you have been telling me for two years how desperately we need the hostel, the expansion to The Mission.'

'I'm concerned about Senor, Colonel Guzman. Where his money comes from, and his activities in El Salvador.'

'You've already said, but I have other voices telling me he is, what can I say - at the very least - acceptable. Voices that speak from prior knowledge of the man. Cardinal Trujillo no less. Charles Mayer, your member of parliament's advisor vouches for him. You will be aware that the Mayer family have been of great assistance to the Church.'

John Doyle had no such knowledge. He didn't even know who Charles Mayer was.

The Bishop continued, although his voice lacked conviction.

'If you are determined to refuse his money, give me something that I can hang my hat on. Money, which I must remind you, will do a great deal of good in our community.'

'I understand, Bishop. There may be further developments shortly.'

'Very well. This nonsense can't carry on much further.'

Doyle heard the exasperation in the Bishop's voice: a sense of discreet complaint finding expression.

'We cannot afford to alienate our friends, and The Mission needs their support. You know this has always been a controversial project, John. If you provide me with proof, and not just conjecture, that Senor Guzman has been involved in criminal activity, or is in some other way so undesirable that we can't accept his donation, then I will reconsider. Otherwise, I must insist that we agree to accept these funds. Give me something more than conjecture.'

Doyle replaced the receiver after the formal exchange.

* * *

He glanced at his watch: 9.35. He saw Consuela arriving at The Mission, in conversation with Ray.

Mrs Quinn knocked on the half-open door.

'Cooper's assistant again. Said that Guzman would be here tomorrow. To meet with yourself and some woman?' She looked mystified. 'Who?'

'Consuela.'

'Are you sure? He's poison, and I hope I'm not speaking ill, but she is fragile that one.'

'It was her idea,' he said, hoping he was right about that.

'Why?'

'Their home. El Salvador.'

She looked sceptical. 'That says nothing,' and walked away.

She was right.

* * *

Consuela woke slowly. Her mind searched for reassurance. She looked around and realised place and time. Here there was no fear of mutilation. The door was locked, it would not be battered down; with boots, pain and anguish following close behind.

She saw a small crack across the dusty windows, which had not been cleaned for many months before she took the room, revealing a grey morning sky through glass spattered with drops of rain, trailing down through London's grime.

She had been dragged down again to life without beauty, slashed, disfigured, loveless, scorned, reviled: with no hope; because darkness gave it no substance. Her mind was filled with revenge, desperately reflecting a heart with little room for tenderness, or the incipient passion she felt when realising Father John's confusion.

Hopeless anyway. Longing wasted, redundant, sperm ejaculated on a stained sheet.

To love a priest would bring nothing but secret heartache and public dissembling.

Anxiety reared as she looked around the featureless room.

She tried to recall the words from the cottage last night: to detach them from the emotion that had then been ripping through her.

*Guzman.*

Had she said she would meet him, confront him? She gripped her hands tightly.

A grip so fierce it hurt as she desperately tried to bring back the words spoken.

She felt safe with him, with John Doyle. Father Doyle. Such stupidity. Once away from him, feelings of vulnerability washed over her again. Bastard memories from a time she wanted to forget; more than that, though, to recover a sense of value and worth for herself. To escape the shame and guilt, to become whole again. What would facing the man bring her but more repulsion, humiliation, and blame?

Suddenly the image of the six priests lying stretched out, dead, on the lawn flashed before her: Guzman strutting through the bodies, his tight camouflage uniform clinging, menacing. She watched cowering behind a tiny window in the small house they had sheltered inside from the violence.

Pushing Jorge away from the window, stopping him looking, so as not to see what would forever make him a target.

Just as she was again now.

Just as he might have been anyway.

Her brother's face flashed before her - his dishevelled black hair sheltering the lopsided grin mocking her vigilance.

The bastards would have known he was there anyway. She had made so many efforts to find him. To find out if he was alive.

Nothing.

An empty space.

Disappeared. Like so many.

A sense of dread enveloped her.

The dread that would stay with her.

Unless she confronted him.

She understood. She either confronted him or she ran. There was no other way. No appeal. No power that could, or would, assist her.

Guzman knew she had seen him in that garden. He knew she had named him. She was a danger to him. Only one of them could survive if she stayed here, and by staying, she endangered all those around her. He would give no mercy. He didn't know the meaning of the word.

She dragged herself from the bed, uncertain, scared and confused.

* * *

Cups of tea lay scattered around the tables in The Mission. Cigarette smoke drifted toward the roof.

Bleary eyes looked toward Father John as he walked through to Roger's office.

As he looked out over the faces assembled, he noticed Consuela on her own, standing at the back of the room, leaning against a wall.

'We have to talk with Consuela,' said Roger. 'She needs our help. I don't think she realises it, but she was shouting and yelling last night while she was still asleep.'

John remembered the night in the cottage.

Roger continued. 'I've asked her to come over to the church later. We can see her in your office. See how we can help.'

* * *

She had been denied a proper farewell to her father. His body, allegedly, was never found. There were around two hundred and fifty thousand people at Archbishop Oscar Romero's funeral. She wouldn't cry after that, except in the dark privacy of their shack. The two of them, herself and Jorge, clinging together, their hearts weeping. It was cruelty: the denial of what life should be and could be. The bastards distorted all that was good. Gangsters finely dressed in a panoply of politics and power, kissing hands with unctuous insincerity, bowing before what they despised, giving allegiance to God and Country, so they could call one an ally and rape the other in a perverted attempt at morality and justification.

She had somehow survived, but always remembered words of sorrow and desperation. Tears rolling down mourning faces. Her escape was not yet complete, but it would be.

She glanced through the window at Father John walking towards the church along with Brother Roger. Perhaps a time would come when she could respond without the barriers of memory and loss coming between them. Those barriers had to be pulled down first and smashed. Destruction's siren voices called out to her, either to a future or just to join with the past, she didn't know which, only aware that continued passivity was not enough. Thoughts of vengeance captivated her. She was shrinking away from Father John, mentally, emotionally, physically. He wanted to give her all that she needed, and maybe, despite her reservations, he might be aware of the cost. That might be enough, at least for a season.

She wanted longer than that, though. She needed more, or she would be forever haunted. There were no fine words left. She needed to feel the satisfaction of vindication and vengeance.

Despite the consequences.

She stood up, almost unnoticed, and walked from the noisy, crowded room into the church. The splash of holy water on her forehead mocked the rage that had taken hold.

It didn't douse it; however, just cooled her thoughts and focused her determination.

* * *

Mrs Quinn waited at his office door. She gushed her usual welcome over Brother Roger as Father Doyle shook his head in amusement.

'You see this man most days, Mrs Quinn.'

'Only across the way,' she pointed through the window at The Mission, 'not where he belongs, in this church, Father Doyle, and that's something you should not be forgetting.'

He shook his head and followed Roger into his office.

Mrs Quinn continued, 'Your man Gerry Keane called. He said he'd see you in The Grapes at lunchtime.'

'Did he say what for?'

'I assumed you would know. It sounded as though you two had already arranged it.'

'OK. I'll make some coffee.'

Mrs Quinn frowned. 'You sure you know your way to the kitchen?'

He raised his eyebrows and moved off down the corridor.

'This Guzman has brought trouble here, Brother, that's for sure,' remarked Mrs Quinn.

Father John returned down the corridor with three coffees on a tray.

'Yours is in your office, Mrs Quinn.'

She smiled at Brother Roger. 'That's me on my way.'

'It was Cooper who introduced Guzman's name at a trustees meeting. Did you find anything more about him? I remembered he sponsored a couple of fundraisers a while back.'

'Stuart got one of his City friends to check him and the company out. Chairman of Atlantic Santos Holdings based in

Brazil and Santos UK based over here.' He pulled a small notebook from his jacket.

'Atlantic Santos is a family business, set up by his great-grandfather around 1860. The man had worked on the Madrid to Aranjuez railway in the early 1850s. Learned Spanish and found his way to Brazil and worked with Daniel Fox on the São Paulo Railway in the late 1850s. He saw the potential for coffee plantations when the line would be extended to Santos port. Borrowed big in London and then paid it all off in just five years after the line opened in 1867. Bought up land around the port of Santos as well, which they still own. His father bought into El Salvador in the thirties when Brazil's coffee business suffered problems. The father still lives in Brazil although housebound now. Dan Cooper took over after the company got over-extended and almost failed in the debt crisis of the 1980s. It only just survived. Bounced back after that and started the UK company about five years ago. Extraordinarily successful. Got almost a hundred coffee shops and four factories manufacturing cakes, confectionery, biscuits, that sort of thing. Still imports a lot of the raw material from their plants in Brazil and El Salvador. He gave half the company out there to his staff two years back. Solid outfit. Still privately owned.'

'What about his personal life?'

'You ever heard of PileUp records?'

'What do you think?'

'One of the first labels that pushed punk. He started it with his then wife Roisin back in the late seventies. She still runs it. It is very successful. They divorced a few years back. Dan was living in Brazil at the time. One son, Mat.'

'Any direct links with Guzman?'

'Nothing we could find. By the way, we're going down to Cornwall to see Stuart's parents shortly. His mother hasn't been too well. Just for the night, back tomorrow.'

Father Doyle nodded; he looked over toward The Mission, his face showing concern.

'I thought Consuela was coming over to join us. She wanted to talk about Guzman.'

'She's in the church. Wanted some time alone.

* * *

Consuela knelt and gazed towards the altar. It was different here than at home, at Aguilares. There, it represented sanctuary and hope; here it was not the same. There wasn't the constant clamour of savagery outside the church door, the relentless dread that coloured the very act of being alive. Here, instead, there was a quiet shelter, or so it had seemed until a few days ago.

She made her way over to the bank of votive candles and knelt after lighting one for her brother, Jorge. She had tried so hard to protect him. He was lost now, *disappeared,* just another vacant space which love should occupy.

Another cry for vengeance.

* * *

There was a knock at the door.

Father Doyle looked up suddenly, expectantly. It opened, and Mrs Quinn stood in the doorway, her expression flashing a warning at John as Consuela appeared behind her and made her way into the room. Her expression was dark, distant.

Their eyes met in a moment of intimacy and ambiguity.

Roger's presence unnerved John. He remembered again when the man had confirmed his love for Stuart and his own pious, blinkered, and inadequate response. How narrow-minded that seemed now, as he watched Consuela's glance taking in the room as if examining his life, before quickly plunging back into her memories.

Those memories, which until yesterday, had been secreted in a place reserved for lonely nights and grateful remembrance, but now overwhelming her.

'Thank you for coming.' John Doyle's voice sounded trite, the words irrelevant.

Roger looked over at Mrs Quinn, who remained in the doorway. He frowned.

They both shrugged.

John looked across at Consuela.

She sat.

Her skin was olive, pure, like the first pressing. She seemed all expression and instinct. He wasn't sure if he saw fear or fury, but it was life. Her eyes were deep brown, matching her thick long hair, and watchful. There was a furious calm about her, that offered a contrast to his own composed artifice.

He touched her hand, unconsciously.

She hesitated to offer a smile. Her eyes, deep, scrutinising; give me pause, he thought. The examination was so fierce - or affectionate - the thought plunged like a knife into the turmoil of his nervousness.

John looked at Roger and opened his mouth to speak.

'Coffee?'

Consuela indicated the three cups already on the table.

'Senor Guzman,' began Roger.

'He's coming here tomorrow,' replied Doyle.

Consuela let out a sigh, and they both turned toward her noticing her eyes were closed. Doyle looked back at Roger; his expression concerned as if asking a question, though neither wanted to break a silence which had become suddenly overwhelming.

'I have known brave men who gave everything to stop his barbarities; men who wore the same cloth as you. He should *not* be here.'

She looked down at the floor, the words painful.

'Brave men,' she continued.

She paused.

They waited.

'More than that. Their bravery was just the finality, the consequence of everything they believed in.'

She shook her head as the words and thoughts, came stuttering out.

'They did not need to be where they chose to be. It was our life, our future. They usually came from far away and could have rested safely amongst their books, incense and bells.'

Father Doyle glanced at the bookshelves, feeling reproach.

She carried on. 'There was no expectation. They lived with our sorrow and pain and, in the end, they lost because *we* lost; they suffered as *we* suffered. The cloth they wore meant nothing to Guzman and his kind.'

She stopped. Father Doyle opened his mouth to speak, but Consuela held up her hand to stop him as she stood.

'He shouldn't be here. Not here. Not anywhere where life has any dignity. But I will meet with him.'

She stood, glanced around the room.

'Here, in this place.'

She looked directly at Father Doyle, her expression intimidating as she walked from the room. 'With you.'

He felt exhilaration. He felt terrified.

* * *

Doyle walked along Narrow Lane. The Grapes at lunchtime. He didn't drink at lunchtime. He rarely drank at all. He grabbed the glass Gerry Keane held up as he flopped down at the same small wooden table as before. The doorway to the terrace was open.

The Thames growled a choppy path as he gazed at it before closing the door and taking a generous taste of Irish whiskey.

'You look like you needed a drink. Is it that bad?' said Keane.

Father John closed his eyes and gave a poignant smile. 'I wish I knew.'

'I thought that was your job: to know.'

Father John laughed but said nothing. He leaned back against the wall before eventually breaking the silence.

'You called me.'

He looked around the empty bar.

Gerry Keane tapped his fingers on the table.

'Last time we spoke, I explained that a few million dollars diverted from the money the US gave El Salvador in the eighties was not connected with Guzman. I checked out some old notebooks and made a few calls. I was wrong.'

He shouted toward the bar.

'Robbie, a bottle if you please.'

The barman emerged from the front bar and placed a bottle of Paddy's whiskey on the table.

Keane filled their glasses and then lit a cigarette blowing smoke into the air, toward the small bust of Charles Dickens.

'The eighties, remember them? Not too long ago and, even amongst all the encyclicals and papal bullshit, you must have noticed them in passing.'

He took another drag on the cigarette as John failed to rise to his taunting.

'OK. So Ronald Reagan, Iran-Contra, ring any bells? Iran-Iraq war started in September 1980 and continued through to August 1987. Around half a million soldiers from both sides killed and about the same number of civilians. Reagan and his bunch of crooks wade in, providing arms to Iran in '85 and '86 to get hostages released, and then they divert some of the arms money to the contras allegedly fighting the Sandinistas in Nicaragua.'

He took another swig and pointed to Father John's glass.

'I hate drinking alone, makes me feel neglected.' He laughed. 'Doyle? Derived from Ó Dubhghaill, the dark stranger, are you a paddy as well?'

'Dalmuir. Scotland.'

'Clydebank?'

'Correct. My father worked at Faslane.'

Keane raised his glass and offered a toast to 'The Celts'. Father touched his glass to his companions.

He continued, 'Of course Reagan didn't want the Iranians to defeat Iraq - that was unacceptable - but a stalemate was good for business, for a while, and kept a bloody impasse in Middle-Eastern politics. So, Iraq was kept well stocked with weapons. It was an arms dealers' bonanza. Every spiv and chancer who could lay their hand on ordnance was out there. The army in El Salvador spotted a chance to make some money for themselves. Iraq had made a five-billion-dollar loan deal with an Italian bank, the Banca Nazionale del Lavoro. Plenty of kickbacks along the way and around nine hundred million of it ended up in San Salvador when five consignments of cluster bombs and one-fifty-five artillery shells landed in Iraq's Umm Qsar Port over a twenty-four-month period from around 1986. The US Milgroup in San Salvador just looked the other way.'

Doyle listened in astonishment. 'Are you sure about this?'

'Nothing I could print as the lawyers wouldn't let it through. But is it true? You bet your life it's true.'

'Guzman was involved?'

'Nothing I can prove. But if it was the army, and it was, Guzman was in the mix. That's for sure. It wasn't any big deal at the time. Billions of dollars were sloshing around. It was a bonanza for a whole pile of crooked scumbags. There were plenty of dealers to handle the shipping and the bent documentation details. The army also had somebody who controlled all the commercial shit: banking, setting up offshore companies, money transfers, pay-offs.'

'Who was that?'

'Never found out. But where there's money, there's a way, and there's always somebody around to smooth the way.'

Keane emptied his glass.

'You said he was donating to the church?'

Father Doyle nodded.

'Well, there's a good chance you now know where the money came from. He's still in the arms business. One of his companies was named in a UN report on Angola. Of course, he's here because he wasn't welcome any longer in Spain.'

Father John eyed the intense figure staring back through the cigarette smoke.

'You didn't know?'

John shook his head.

'He was there for three years. Then the outrage built about the Jesuit murders. Five of the priests were Spanish. Anyone connected to the El Salvador army isn't made to feel comfortable. That applies to Guzman more than most. An ambitious magistrate was on his tail.'

Doyle closed his eyes.

The words cut too deeply.

Keane was unrelenting. He leaned across the table and grabbed the priest's arm.

'You and your church are being used as cover. Guzman doesn't want to be hiding away in some shithole of a country. He wants civilisation. Sophistication. Spain was good, and he speaks Spanish after all. Now England the same, US too close to home for some reason. So, he wants somewhere he can buy himself a decent lifestyle and have protection from any attempts to implicate him in the events of the civil war, including the Jesuits. That's why Mayer, the MP, the Bishop, the Cardinal, your church, are all important as buffers, to protect him. You take his money; you wash him clean. Give him free passage. That's why the money is important. It gives him credibility. You understand that.'

'Why would anyone want him here?'

Keane laughed and emptied his glass.

'Why? The Guzmans of this world have their allies. Either because they share common values, such as they are, or they are useful, or they pay their way. Take your choice. You said Charles Mayer was involved, well Guzman would tick all the boxes for him. Of course, if any proof emerges. Then he's got no friends. He'd be on his own.'

Doyle got up to leave. Keane gripped his hand

'Be careful, Father Doyle.'

* * *

He needed some respite.

He didn't get it.

A blue moped was leaning up against the wall alongside the church. There was a figure concealed inside an abandoned doorway halfway along the same wall. It was Josef Perez.

Father Doyle sighed in exasperation.

The man's voice was soft, the grip on Doyle's arm fierce. 'You're seeing him tomorrow.'

'Guzman?' asked Doyle, wondering why he was whispering.

'Of course.'

'And the trustees meet later in the week.'

*How did he know that?* Doyle remained silent.

Perez ignored him. 'Meet me before you see the trustees after you've seen Guzman. I'll be here.'

He went over to his moped, kicked it into life and pulled out into the traffic heading along Commercial Road. Father Doyle gazed after him in bewilderment.

Mrs Quinn waited by his office door.

He held up his hand. 'I need some peace. One hour.'

He closed the door behind him and stretched out on the couch.

# TWENTY

Mrs Quinn banged on his door.

He sighed. Thirty minutes peace was all she had allowed him.

Gerry Keane's warning still resounded with him. The words came out as instruction, not request.

'Call Brigid Kelly. She sounds desperate.'

The woman did sound desperate. Father John promised to go straight over.

Music and marching boots resounded, even as he stood on the doorstep.

Mrs Kelly's voice was worried and weary as she opened the door.

'He's been like this all today since early morning.'

German marching songs interspersed with taped extracts from Hitler's speeches blared out from Michael Kelly's room.

'Can you try to speak with him?' she begged. 'He takes no notice of me.'

'I'll try, Brigid, but I think he stopped listening to me many years ago.'

He banged on the son's door and shouted above the clamour coming from inside the room.

Suddenly the door swung open to reveal Michael Kelly

dressed in a black shirt with a swastika band on one arm. His face was triumphant. He spat out his greeting.

'Well, well, Father John Doyle. And what can I do for you, Father fucking Doyle?'

'Oh God.'

His mother's voice was tearful as she hurried through the apartment away from the sight of her son. Doyle stood stock still, unable to react.

One arm shot out in a salute. His hand wearing a black leather glove '*Sieg Heil*.'

His eyes were laughing in a smile of victory, an expression of taunting exhilaration. He repeated. '*Sieg Heil*.'

It was a challenge, an arrogant statement of triumph. Their eyes met. Father groped around amidst this dark freak show, searching for a response as he realised the bloody victory that young Kelly was proclaiming.

Once again, '*Sieg Heil*.'

In retrospect, Father Doyle's subsequent actions marked a turning point. Releasing him from a lifetime of learned, premeditated behaviour; they led to the actions which changed his life. He had no control left that allowed for pause or contemplation. The restraint which had always held him too close to caution suddenly left him. Kelly was irrelevant. He was just the convenient catalyst that focused all Doyle's frustrations as he ripped away at barriers which kept him from the truth about his emotions.

Later he would feel some shame that Kelly was the target of the strident reactions, but above all, he felt released from a straitjacket.

Michael Kelly's arm shot out again. Father grabbed hold of it and pushed the black-shirted figure back into his room. He slipped. Father leapt over him and swept his hand across the bookshelves scattering prized volumes of hate and Nazi memorabilia. He jumped across to the tape player now spewing out an SS marching song – "Marschiert in Feindesland".

Doyle lifted the player above his head. He looked at Kelly

scrambling around the floor. 'The devil's song,' he said. 'How appropriate.'

Kelly voice screamed, 'NO!'

The priest laughed and hurled it to the floor.

The skinhead leapt to his feet, expression black, scowling, fists clenched by his side. Father Doyle's hand stretched out and pushed him out of his path as he continued to the door.

'You're fucking next, Doyle.'

Father Doyle swung around, thrusting his face next to Kelly's.

'Next?'

Kelly looked away and then snapped his head back again. His screaming mouth spat at Doyle.

'Next, I said. First, the whore,' he laughed and put his tongue out and licked his lips in a sordid gesture.

'Then the fucking priests!'

He turned away again and started to collect several of the books from the floor. As he did so, Father instinctively wrenched them from his hands and began to rip the pages away from the spines. He kicked at the relics as he turned and left the room.

Brigid Kelly stood outside. She looked shocked staring at the priest.

'I'm sorry, Brigid.'

'If only you knew how many times I've wanted to do just that.'

She continued with him along the walkway.

'I'll give him the money to replace the cassette player,' promised Doyle.

'Perhaps in a week or so, Father. A rest from hearing that din will be as good as a change.'

He made his way out of the apartment block.

* * *

Consuela smiled when she saw John on the doorstep in the early evening. They stood in silence before realising the incongruous picture they made, standing, gazing at each other while unexpectedly feeling massive relief and delight at being together again.

She stood aside, and he continued into the kitchen while Consuela glanced along the street.

'I wanted to check if you are still willing to meet with Guzman?' he asked when they sat at the kitchen table.

Consuela's voice was resigned. 'What are the choices? No not really choices. One choice. I stay or I go.'

'Why would you go?'

She leaned across the table and placed her hand on his.

'You've been seeing a journalist who knows El Salvador. He was there during the civil war.'

He nodded. 'His name's Gerry Keane.'

'I know. He was honest. We left on the same plane. He knew Guzman, didn't he?'

'He did.'

'So he knows why Guzman is here. Because he ran from Spain and he's looking for somewhere safe. He fears one day justice will catch up with him and he wants a refuge. Somewhere he thinks he will be protected.'

'Gerry Keane did say that.'

'And now Guzman knows I'm here.'

'How?' He tightened his grip on her hand. 'How would he know? Nobody would have said anything.'

'John. Father Doyle. He knows.'

She stopped, drew her hand away and stood back by the kitchen sink. 'It's about survival now.'

Consuela's voice chilled him.

'What do you mean?' he asked anxiously.

'He either destroys or is destroyed. There is no other way.'

'What do you mean when you say *destroyed?*'

'How many more people will he disfigure while we stand by and watch?'

'There's nothing you can do – not here, not now. Whatever he did happened too far away.'

'Not far enough.'

She looked away as she carried on speaking. 'I once imagined there was another way, but there isn't. He knows nothing else now; it's become a part of him.'

'There's nothing you can do,' he repeated. 'Turning the other cheek is maybe the hardest thing to do, but what else can end the cycle of violence?'

'You think I want it to be like this. War and torture disfigures and corrupts everyone. Both the tortured and the torturer. We both end up the same. Scarred. Damaged.'

She fell silent, the quiet of the evening, broken only by occasional cars passing the glass-panelled front door, enveloping them. They both felt a longing they could not express. It was uncharted territory for him, and he was part of the fear that life had become for Consuela. She had shed too many tears and wouldn't risk losing out again, and especially not to a rapacious church that demanded all John was, leaving nothing of him but a shell to be picked over.

Her voice eventually broke the spell. 'But you may be right.'

The words were a lie. He realised that. He could say nothing without delving deep into her heart and risking his innocence. He would remain impotent unless willing to jeopardise what was sacred. He stood up to leave. They strained to prevent their hands touching, or even to let a glance of intimacy sneak between them, knowing instinctively that such release would rip apart the careful barriers they had both erected.

Consuela's voice followed him from the kitchen as he started to walk along the hallway. He turned. She was still sitting at the kitchen table. He moved hesitantly back to her.

'You talk of vengeance as if it is merely a theological notion. I know the words:

*"Do not resist one who is evil. If anyone strikes you on the right cheek, turn to him the other also"*. I had friends who believed that violence achieved nothing. They died just the same.'

There followed a silence. She swallowed deeply, trying to

control emotions clashing. As her heart beat faster, she clenched her fingers together, knuckles turning white.

She spoke again as he sat back down.

'Revenge is flesh and blood; it's not an abstract concept. It's this.'

She held out her trembling hands. He took hold of them.

'Feel, this is revenge; this is fear.'

'You didn't tell me everything?'

'About Guzman?'

He nodded.

She looked at their hands. 'Are you sure you want to know?'

'Of course.'

'There is no, *of course.* There is what we decide. Whatever that is, the future changes. Why would I relive such pain? Why would you want to hear of my sorrow?'

'You *know* why.'

'I can't tell you, not everything. Not even now. Perhaps never.'

'Then whatever you *can* talk about.'

Her gaze was intense yet uncertain.

'They killed my lover, Manuel, the man I cared for beyond everything. Shot him when he had his hand in mine.'

Looking at their hands held tight together, the voice continued as her eyes met John's.

'I watched his eyes close as he died. The Atlactl Battalion it was.'

Releasing her grasp, a hand went to her forehead as she slumped back into the chair. John moved toward her, but she held up her other hand to stop him.

'No, you asked me to tell you. I'm trying, but don't think I have any forgiveness. I remember his cold eyes, the hard floor. I prayed and prayed but felt nothing. I was alone. The terror began!'

She shuddered.

'Alone, in the dark. In a cell, pitch-black. Alone.'

Pausing to reach for a glass of water from the scratched

wooden tabletop, Consuela continued in a low painful voice.

'They tied my hands in front of me and hoisted me up on a pulley until I was just above the ground. They just watched. The "aeroplane" it was called. It was agony. I was wearing jeans and a red T-shirt. I remember it all so clearly. Eventually, one of them came close to me and stroked a knife across my face and down my body. Cut my blouse away, then my jeans. They hoisted the pulley a bit more, and two of them grabbed my legs and held them apart. The blade cut away my remaining clothes, slowly, painstakingly, until I was naked. There were about seven of them. There was something that looked like a truncheon. It had wires attached, one of them stroked it up and down my legs, pushed it inside me. It was hard, cold, disgusting. I was sick. I hope I never know such pain again. My body exploded with a thousand shocks. I shook, screamed, lost all control. I was nowhere. No sensation except pure terror, and horrendous agony, but words can't even begin to convey what happened to me.'

Her eyes remained closed.

'Guzman watched ... and all the time the music. Elvis Presley. I can't hear that voice now without remembering, without feeling sick.'

She started shaking. 'No more.'

Doyle stood and put his arm around her. In his grasp, she felt small and wasted, lost somewhere in her memories, unable to return.

'You know now why I want revenge. He hasn't changed. There is no remorse - you only need to look at him. That's why I'm scared, and because he knows I'm a danger to him. I can destroy him.'

John remembered the soft feel of Guzman's handshake – strong, damp. The pleading voice: *"Father, I am a sinful man. I ask for forgiveness. Father forgive me. I am a humble man."*

Consuela was drifting away into a strange, dark place to which he had no access. He tried to push away the picture of her tortured body. Hope and love; ripped into shreds of heartless agony. God help me to love her, he thought, gazing at her face. God help me, is this pain or passion?

'I can't understand,' he said in a stumbling voice while feeling nothing but inadequacy. But would any attempt at understanding only consign her to desperate memory? Was understanding even possible?

She turned away from his gaze.

'I can't understand, but I will help you through this,' he persevered.

Her expression gave him his answer. Leaning against the sink, she glanced outside through the window.

'I'm tired. You must leave me now. Go back to your church, Father John.'

She pushed her hair away from her face.

A notebook lay open on the table, and she shook her head even as Doyle started to speak again.

'No. I won't let you destroy your life, Father. There are too many souvenirs of my cowardice already. No more, Father. I can't let you be hurt.'

She leaned over and touched his cheek.

'Go home, Father John. I'm tired now. Please.'

'But you're on your own here.'

Smiling sadly, she walked along the hallway to the front door.

'It will be all right. I'll lock the doors.'

'When will Stuart and Roger be back?'

'Tomorrow afternoon.'

'One thing I don't understand, Consuela. Why did you say you're a danger *now*?'

She shook her head. 'Please.'

He walked reluctantly down the path. Consuela was still standing at the doorway when he looked back at her as he crossed the road slowly. He moved in front of a white van and headed toward St Mary's. He was too preoccupied to notice the vehicle itself or the black car sheltering in a side road, until much later, and then almost too late.

# TWENTY-ONE

Consuela went through the small, terraced house, testing all the window and door locks. Eventually satisfied she went into the kitchen pulling the curtain on the black night that had come in. She opened a drawer. Hesitating at the sight of three sharp knives, she slowly took out two large, serrated blades before climbing the stairs. Her small bedroom was stuffy. She placed the two knives on the small bedside table.

After pulling off her jeans, she lay down on the bed wearing just a T-shirt and white briefs. Yawning, she pulled her arms tight about herself and lay there perfectly still for almost half an hour. Her eyes remained closed as she felt warm air resting gently on her skin, listening to the quiet night as it drifted by. She kept forcing her mind to reject black thoughts and memories of the past day.

Eventually, she felt strong enough.

She moved aside the knives and picked up the small notebook which sat beside *One Day of Life*, on her bedside cabinet. It opened at the list of names: killed or disappeared. They were all gone now but never forgotten. Each one a small memory left behind, yet eventually changing the way things were. Brave, resolute and impetuous they had plunged into terror and there discovered their ultimate triumph, but they were still lost. Empty chairs at tables, silent smiles where there had once been laughter. They were gone, and now the repulsive creature who had robbed them of life was here. She had never forgotten and had never been able to erase their faces from her mind. Each day plunged her deeper into the feeling of desperate shame she had spent so many years trying to escape.

Suddenly there was a noise.

Scratching.

She lowered the notebook and listened.

It came from somewhere at the back of the house.

Consuela sat up and waited, to hear more, but all was silent again.

She rose, her head tilted to one side, focusing.

Glass.

Glass scratched.

Where was it coming from? She couldn't locate the source.

All fell silent again.

Perhaps it was her imagination.

She touched the two knives.

Looking at the notebook, at the names of people she had loved, of lives destroyed, she felt no fear.

What she did know was anger.

Fury.

She would not be intimidated.

She lay down again, closed her eyes and waited, and listened.

A whisper came, so soft it was almost inaudible. The bed shuddered.

Consuela shot upright. She moved over to the door and touched the handle. Started slowly, silently, to open it.

Her heart was beating too fast, too loud.

It was the kitchen door. It had a slight, but distinctive squeak.

It was not her imagination.

She opened the bedroom door a crack.

Footsteps, so soft she barely heard, but she was sure.

There was no way out. The muffled sounds were so near, right inside her head along with the screeching resonance of memory. Breathing quietly, she strained desperately to catch any new sound. She opened the door a little more. A streetlight threw faint shadows through a window at the bottom of the stairs.

Empty.

Then a shadow moved.

A footstep certainly. But so quiet, only silence distinguished it. She closed the bedroom door again.

The landline was down in the hall.

She had a mobile but no money to load it, and she had left it at The Mission anyway.

A creaking sound echoed through the empty hallway – from the bottom stair. She gently pushed at her bed, trying to move it across the doorway. Something fell, a soft voice cursed, she moved the bed a little more and succeeded in pushing it across the doorway and then sat on the floor pushing her feet against the end of the bed forcing it into the door. It wouldn't last long.

She picked up the knives, holding one in each hand.

If there was blood, it would not only be hers that was spilt.

She felt fear, but also anticipation fuelled with rage.

The handle turned as the door nudged against the bed. She pushed harder, but the bed moved a little more as pressure increased, and the door started to open a little more.

A black-leather gloved hand gripped the side of the doorframe and pushed at the narrow gap.

She leaned forward and raised one of the knives.

# TWENTY-TWO

When John Doyle entered the presbytery, he heard the telephone ringing inside his office.

It was Roger.

'John. As you know, we've come down here to visit my parents. We're staying the night. I've been trying to get hold of Consuela, just to check up on everything, but I can't get an answer from her mobile, and the landline is unobtainable.'

'It's OK. I'll go round.'

He stopped and looked out through the window of his office. The drivers of two cars parked outside were arguing. One of the cars was a black Mercedes. He suddenly realised what he had been trying to recall.

'Roger, I must go.'

He ran from the room and down the steps.

When he reached the house, he was panting from exertion. The black Mercedes was parked along the road. He spotted Lopez sat in the front smoking. A battered white van was parked right behind.

The front door of the house was closed. He hammered his fist against the wooden frame, shouting Consuela's name.

There was no answer. The building was in darkness.

'John!'

Consuela's voice suddenly screamed from an upstairs window. He banged fiercely again and then ran across the next-door garden and to the rear of the house. The kitchen door was open, one of its panes of glass was broken. Glass crunched under his feet as he hurtled through the door and along the narrow hallway.

A hand grabbed his hair. He smashed against a wall. The figure was wearing a ski mask, he bent down and grabbed John's throat with one hand as John struggled for breath and flung out his fist, which connected with the concealed face. Not hard, but enough. He was pushed violently against the wall.

Footsteps came clattering down the stairs.

Two shadowy figures receded through the kitchen and into the darkness.

He ran up the stairs.

'Consuela,' his voice bounced off the stairwell.

As he peered round the door, he saw Consuela kneeling at the end of her bed.

'Thank God it's you,' she said, turning, and placing two long kitchen knives on her bedside table.

He pushed at the door, simultaneously heaving the bed out of the way, moving next to Consuela.

'My God, what happened.'

When she fell against him, his arm went around her and held her tight. They remained silent for another moment until she turned to him.

'Where the hell were you, Doyle? You almost left it too late.'

He stroked her arm. 'What if I hadn't come?'

Consuela shivered. She didn't reply.

'Did you recognise who it was?' he asked.

'You got closer than me. Thank goodness.' She laughed and touched a graze on his cheek. 'I didn't quite mean that. It's Guzman, isn't it? He's behind it. Who else is that interested in me?'

'Lopez's car is parked outside.'

'Of course it is. Why did you come?'

'Roger phoned. Then I suddenly remembered seeing Guzman's car as I left earlier.'

She stretched up and softly kissed his cheek.

His face suddenly betrayed every emotion: longing mixed with apprehension, shock still reverberating from the attack. A bruise was starting to flare on his forehead.

He had never felt so alive as he did now, at this moment. Every sense realising new experience, all was strange and exciting. He could smell a slight trace of perfume as her hair stroked his cheek, feeling so gentle and soft, her skin so smooth. Fingers traced crazy longings that danced in a part of his psyche that had never been touched before.

Consuela's voice broke into the dark, expectant silence. 'Where did you say Roger has gone?'

'To his parents in Cornwall.'

'Of course. I remember now. He told me.'

In his head, their two voices seemed so far away as feelings he had never known before came to life and overwhelmed him.

'Cornwall?'

'Yes.'

They spoke, but the words were irrelevant. The barrier between reserve and spontaneity was swept aside in the helpless relief of safety and longing. Consuela flexed her shoulders against him. He leaned down; their lips touched. There was a moment, a split second when they both knew from blind instinct that beyond this moment lay two diverging routes.

Consuela pulled away.

Father John stiffened.

'John, I'm not worth the sacrifice.'

Her voice was so close now.

Still, he held her, but she gently pulled away.

'We'd better go downstairs.'

He knew that these words represented either a pause or an ending. There would be time to decide which, but now was not that time.

'Let's go and get a drink.' She eyed his face. 'You'll have a black eye. I'll get a wet cloth.'

She paused. 'Will you stay tonight? You can sleep on the settee.'

They headed down the stairs. He did not need to answer.

## TWENTY-THREE

There was one call Father Doyle needed to make before he got back to the church. He knew Brigid Kelly would be out at one of her early morning cleaning jobs.

The lift still wasn't working.

Cans, empty bottles, and drug debris filled the stairwell accompanied by the overpowering smell of dried urine.

The balcony was empty.

He knocked on the door.

He waited and knocked again.

Eventually, a figure moved beyond the frosted glass.

Michael Kelly stood in the doorway. There was a fleeting moment, but Father saw it clearly – fear! It passed quickly, as though ashamed of its existence.

'Doyle, what the fuck do you want? Come to pay up for the damage, you bastard?'

His hand went to a small bruise at the side of his chin.

'I will pay, of course.'

He paused.

'Michael, I know it was you.'

A sneer fell across the angry face. He laughed.

Father Doyle spoke quickly, before the avalanche of abuse began, as he knew it would. 'Michael, I *know,* but that's not why

I'm here. I know we failed you. In some way, we failed you, and I regret that, but that's not why I'm here either.'

Kelly feigned a yawn but continued to listen.

'Be careful, Michael. The man you are working with has seen more violence than you can imagine. He has inflicted more pain - in more ways than you can imagine. That's what I came to say.'

Kelly leaned toward him. 'It's not over, Doyle. Hardly started.'

'Be careful, Michael.'

The door slammed in his face.

* * *

Father Doyle got back to his office just as the rush hour built up on the roads leading toward the City. He had barely sat down at his desk when the telephone rang.

'Is that Father Doyle … Father John Doyle?'

The voice was quiet, conspiratorial.

'It is.'

'Father, my name is Vincent Sheridan. I'm the dean of St Barnabas Cathedral and priest at St Augustine's in Nottingham. I have a delicate matter I wish to discuss. You may want to call me back to be certain of my identity.'

He read out his number, and Father Doyle agreed to call him back. He then checked his directory to verify the number. The telephone was answered at the first ring.

'Father Sheridan, how can I help?'

'As I said, it's a delicate matter, and I am embarrassed that I'm unable to tell you the source of the information I'm about to offer you, but I can assure you that it is reliable. It is regarding a person called Senor Guzman, who I understand, is preparing to offer a gift to St Mary's, your church - or rather a pastoral facility that your church supports.'

'You are well informed, Father. Are you sure you cannot tell me more about the source of your information?'

There was a pause and the voice when it returned sounded nervous.

'As I said, I feel embarrassed, but am just a messenger - and a slightly uneasy messenger at that.'

'I suppose we all find ourselves in strange circumstances on occasion. It comes with our vocation.'

'Thank you for your understanding. I am told that Senor Guzman was specifically named in the notorious tragedy of the six Jesuits murdered in San Salvador in 1989. You recall the tragedy?'

'Of course, but there was a trial and some convictions in 1991. Guzman was neither named nor charged.'

'That is true. Neither were any senior army officers, despite information that the orders came from the top of the army's general staff. However, it is understood a witness stated that she saw Colonel Guzman, as he then was, and gave statements to a judge in San Salvador and the FBI in Miami. It is understood that these statements were subsequently taken to army headquarters in San Salvador and destroyed. Colonel Guzman was deemed untouchable because of his close links to the army chief of staff, the minister of defence and, possibly, the president. It is alleged that Colonel Guzman was present at the scene of the shootings at the university, gave the orders, and directly participated in those murders even as the Fathers were lying defenceless on the lawn outside their residence.'

Father Doyle remembered Gerry Keane's words, his revulsion at the mental image was intensified by his dread at what might be the answer to the next question. 'Does your informant know the name of the witness who provided those statements?'

There was a shuffling of paper, 'A woman named as Coretta Delgado.'

Father John felt a tremendous sense of relief.

'As you might imagine, it appears that Senor Guzman would like to ensure that the witness does not have the opportunity to confirm her testimony.'

'I'm not sure I understand.'

'I can help you no further on that matter. I assume you don't know Coretta Delgado.'

He responded with some uncertainty.

'I'm afraid not.'

'Another matter which may concern you. Senor Guzman, it appears, is now wanted by his previous colleagues in El Salvador.'

'Wanted? I don't understand.'

'Some of his ex-army colleagues appear to be seeking him, with some urgency. I'm afraid I have few more details except to say that it is claimed his life would be in danger were he ever to return to his country.'

'And there is no chance you could give me any more details as to your source on this matter?'

'You must understand, Father. I can say no more.'

The confessional, perhaps?

'Thank you ... I think. I appreciate the call, if not the content.'

The line disconnected.

He looked out through the window. Just then, the black limousine pulled up at the foot of the steps. Adolfo Guzman pulled himself out once his driver opened the rear door.

## TWENTY-FOUR

Father John Doyle peered from his window as Guzman hauled himself from the limousine. The bulky figure shrugged away the assistance offered by his driver, who then pulled a cigarette from his pocket and leaned himself against the bonnet of the car, his harsh gaze directed toward the church.

Ray Lancaster, whose voluntary help had become a great support to The Mission, looked from the steps toward Father Doyle's office. Father gestured urgently from the window for him to come over. He almost filled the doorway as Doyle turned from the window, the priest paused for a moment as he suddenly realised the assurance that now filled the man's presence.

Since they had spoken it seemed a switch had been thrown. He asked the ex-soldier for his help.

When Ray had left, he turned back to the window.

Doyle felt a pair of eyes turn toward him. The gaze that swept over him was disdainful, uncompromising. Contempt mixed with glowering antagonism seemed to smash against the glass.

He almost fell away from the window. Then, in the same moment, Consuela's face flashed before him, and he determined to confront his absurd vacuous anxiety.

He moved closer to the glass and met the loathing, the scorn. A cigarette was thrown onto the steps of the church. Guzman turned and gestured irritably toward the car, the driver got back into the vehicle.

Guzman nodded toward Father Doyle and resumed moving slowly up the steps.

Doyle stayed by the window, but his gaze encompassed different views. Views that were not his own but had worked their way into his life and had changed him. Changed not only what he knew of the world but how he understood the world. All had been simulated before, but that had been his way of life. Cut off from authentic experience, now he wanted, *needed*, more.

He envisaged dry blood spattered on bare walls, swaggering shining boots marching to a different song. Bound figures hanging from ceilings. He heard screams of pain; threatening voices; the weeping despair of humiliation and guilt. He felt the loneliness of terror. Smelled the sweating fragrance of dread, of horror.

But he knew none of this as reality. It was not part of his life.

A few days ago, it would have been words on a page, voices heard through a screen, through the mist and comfort of comprehension but never the authenticity of involvement; because his calling had led him away from involvement and into contemplation.

These past few days had shattered that tranquil serenity.

He suddenly felt alive as never before.

The telephone rang. Mrs Quinn.

Guzman was waiting. She also mentioned that someone had called asking for Ray Lancaster. She had told them nothing.

He asked her to keep Guzman for a few moments.

He phoned Consuela. There was no answer.

* * *

Adolfo Guzman stared through the window at the priest. This meeting was a waste of time. Only undertaken to appease

Cooper - and he had little enough reason for that; only done for this moment and the next few days. Cooper wouldn't be where he was; big office, staff kissing his backside, if Guzman hadn't saved him and his company. He would need reminding of that yet again; very soon. Cooper could destroy him, of course, but they both realised that if he did, there would be two graves. The destruction would be mutual; he knew that, and so did Cooper.

Guzman kept control by demonstrating his indifference to his fate and his willingness to self-destruct if the game demanded it.

Cooper's attempts to make amends for the actions he had taken to enable his company to survive – and to assuage his pathetic angst – were pitiful. Cooper could now look back at what he had achieved, and weep crocodile tears at the cost to others of that achievement. But it was a level of hypocrisy Guzman wouldn't stomach.

But in truth, he wanted to set eyes on Coretta Delgado again. The last time had been in Miami when he had studied her being interviewed by the FBI while he watched on a monitor in an adjoining room. He had put a search out for the brother, Jorge, who was found, eventually, on the border with Honduras. He pulled the cedula from his pocket and flicked open the cardboard identity document. *Jorge Delgado - cédula de identidad personal* - had he been found in time, she would have capitulated and recanted her statement, but it was only after she had fled that Jorge had been dealt with.

She hadn't resisted the FBI's questions, but just referred them to the statement she had given to the bloody judge in San Salvador and remained silent. The statement should have been destroyed but a copy had found its way into the hands of the FBI. How long that would remain secure he didn't know, the bureau leaked like a sieve, but without the witness it was of little consequence.

If Coretta had been dealt with, he would have felt secure, even if for other reasons it was time to get out of the country. Unfortunately, when Colonel Rivas had arrived, she had taken flight. She had hidden well.

Only now had he found her – and then by chance. This was the first time he would have met her directly since the basement of the National Guard HQ. Was she still a threat? Perhaps he could merely discount her, and let her statement accusing him blow in the wind because she would be too weak and vulnerable to stand by her words.

He needed to see if she were still the desperate figure skulking away from Miami in panic, or could she face up to him. Had Lopez and his thugs managed to scare her off? She couldn't be allowed to speak with the trustees; he had come too far now to risk being thrown out of the country. That was a hazard he wasn't prepared to face.

* * *

Consuela sat in the kitchen and waited. She wanted the time to pass. Now she had decided: she *needed* to look once again at that fat squirming face. This time it would be without his henchmen protecting him, without the paraphernalia of torture to sustain his 'power'. Last night she had survived yet again. She had been terrified. But she was going to survive. Even in her terror, she knew she would endure. The failed attack was a bizarre acknowledgement that Guzman was scared. He was afraid of *her*. He knew who she was, and he was scared. She smiled to herself. He should be.

When she had heard Father John's voice shouting, it was the priest she had been scared for, not herself.

She moved across and placed the two knives into a kitchen drawer. They wouldn't be needed, not now. Guzman would lose. Her years of running were over. It was his turn now, although he might not run far or for long. She had no qualms left, no internal debate or moral scruple to battle with.

He would be destroyed.

The game had started.

Her mobile rang. John had used his bank card to put in some credit. He was calling now. She ignored it.

She waited. Father John. John Doyle. Another unanswered question that would be waiting for her.

Guzman would be there - she looked up at the clock - in one minute. He was always punctual, she remembered. The prison ran like clockwork whenever he was there. Torture was inflicted to a timetable. There was no waiting for pain, humiliation and degradation. It always arrived on time.

She waited patiently. Years had passed. She could wait a bit longer. Guzman would wait, too, because he knew she was here and that she could destroy him.

The phone rang again.

Perez's voice gave no emotion.

'It is arranged. I've been in touch with San Salvador. Billy will be at the church, All Hallows by the Tower, everything you need will be in the daypack. He will recognise you. I will meet you when you call. The moped is waiting behind St Mary's when you're ready. They leave San Salvador in two days. The hotel has been booked in the name Ava Rivera.'

He paused. 'Are you sure, Consuela?'

She waited and looked up at the clock. He would be waiting. He would always be waiting now he knew where she was. There would never be security, or peace. That much was certain.

'I'm sure,' she said and closed the phone.

* * *

Guzman was shown into Father John Doyle's office.

He held out his hand. Father John looked down. Thick fingers, two of them with large gold rings. Although a part of him whispered protest, he placed his hand inside the man's strong, enveloping grasp.

What had these fingers done?

What pain had they inflicted?

He drew back and glanced up into the deep, brown eyes.

What had they witnessed? Whose sorrow had they spat out onto cold stone floors? All the instincts of forgiveness that had been drilled into him flashed before him, but they found no resting place.

He tried to grab onto some of the words he knew so well:

*There is no-one, however wicked and guilty, who may not confidently hope for forgiveness.*

The words didn't reassure, but just as suddenly he remembered the next words – *provided his repentance is honest.*

Father Doyle remained silent, watching closely as Guzman battled to control the perpetual impatient fury inside him, forever struggling to emerge. He understood Consuela's fear now: the incipient hiss of anger and terror that accompanied her reluctant memories. He had seen her attempt to live her life while still in the shadow of this man, who had taken lives and mutilated them, who had taken bodies, disfigured, and destroyed them. Remembering her words, he suddenly comprehended the dread that emanated around Guzman.

Here Doyle was safe, yet he still felt a beating drum of horror and turmoil.

He was sheltered, yet nothing sacred could survive. Holy words became mangled in the face of the sweating countenance opposite him; tender thoughts bringing joy and sustenance were ripped apart to careless shreds.

*"Then they tied my hands in front of me and hoisted me up on a pulley until I was just above the ground. They just watched. The "aeroplane" they called it. It was agony."*

As Guzman's eyes narrowed, Father Doyle felt the power of the man envelop him, sucking him into all-pervading darkness.

Guzman spoke.

'I come before you as a penitent sinner and wish to give something to the Church that has sustained me through all the years.'

'Sinner?'

'We are all sinners ... I know I am no different.'

'But is your repentance honest, Colonel Guzman?'

Guzman's eyes rested on Father for what seemed a lifetime of silence. An occasional car passed outside the net-curtained window, but here, in this room, they were, it appeared, a world apart from the normality that existed just an arm's length away.

The face hadn't seen a smile for too long, his expressionless eyes just empty balls floating in inert liquid. Guzman stood up, turned a wooden chair round, and sat down on it, facing Father Doyle, his thick legs planted aggressively either side of the chair.

'I'm a good Catholic, Father. I go to Mass each day and regular confession. My last church has a new health centre which I paid for myself, and a school for orphaned children.'

He shrugged.

'And we prevented bombs being thrown into the churches, and we protected you and your fellow priests' - he thrust a thick finger toward Father – 'from destruction at the hands of communists and subversives.'

He stood up and wheeled round to face the window.

'It was another era then. You can't judge by today's standards. We had no choice. It was a war.'

Father John brushed down his clothing as if to sweep away the dankness hanging in the air. The room seemed to have no life. It had been sucked out, dismembered, and tossed aside on a rotting pile of bodies left beside a road that nobody would hazard travelling. His chest felt tight, and he tried to breathe in deeply, but his throat felt too constricted.

Guzman sat back down in the chair, which seemed crushed under his overflowing body.

Doyle repeated.

'Is your repentance genuine, Colonel Guzman?'

The man's face offered what could have been a smile. His eyes narrowed.

'Genuine?'

*"All he did was smile. I hope I never know such pain again, my body exploded, a thousand shocks. I shook, screamed, and lost all control. I was nowhere, no sensation except pure terror, and horrendous agony, but words can't even begin to convey what happened."*

'As I said, I want to repay some of the debts I still have.'

'Debts?'

'What I owe to the Church.' Guzman looked at his watch.

'What's the rate, Senor?'

'Rate. What is this?'

'You want to repay but do you think that three hundred thousand pounds is sufficient?'

Guzman leapt from his chair with surprising agility.

Father John recoiled in shock, but he willed himself to stay calm and waited a moment to gain control of the tension in his voice.

'You are no different.'

He smiled at Guzman.

'You said that yourself, I think.'

Guzman snorted. The smile on Father Doyle's face drove him to greater fury.

'I have heard all the sins of the world here, Senor Guzman. The confessional is a tour of humankind's failings. You, well, you are just another man.'

The squat, bulky figure got up and stomped around the room, listening impatiently to the priest. In the small office he was like an animal in too narrow a cage, crashing up against the bars before having to turn and retrace his steps. After a few moments, he reluctantly sat down again, irritated by his inability to discover any space.

Father John pulled his chair nearer to Guzman. His eyes never left that face straining to hold back the hostility that charged the atmosphere around him.

Father Doyle spoke again.

'Just a man, Senor, like us all - no different?'

He opened the Bible on the small table beside him.

'May I, Senor Guzman, a few words? Such penitence as yours …' he smiled at him. 'Where else should we go?'

Guzman eyed his watch again. 'Is the woman coming?'

The priest ignored him.

'The final judgement: "*He shall separate them one from another as a shepherd separates the sheep from the goats and he will place the sheep on his right hand and the goats on his left. Then the King will say to those at his right hand, 'Come, O blessed of my Father, inherit the Kingdom prepared for you from the foundation of the world; for I was hungry and you gave me food, I was thirsty and you gave me drink, I was a stranger and you welcomed me, I was naked and you clothed me, I was sick and you visited me, I was in prison and you came to me.'''*

His voice gained strength.

'They are words that make us humble, Senor.'

He turned back to the Bible still holding it in front of him. '''*In prison you visited me.*'''

Looking at Guzman, he asked, 'You visited people in prison, Colonel?'

His eyes didn't flinch from Guzman's glare which spoke of fury, and threat. In them, Father saw the pain that had been inflicted on so many innocent lives.

Guzman brushed the Bible aside. His voice was as unyielding as granite.

'I will make the donation.'

'And a plaque for you, as benefactor, on a wall, displaying name and date? To commemorate when you visited the hungry and the naked. The prisoner, of course, you already knew.'

Father stopped suddenly. 'Shall I take your confession now, Senor?'

'The Bishop is ready to accept my donation.'

'And then you can free your soul from the screams that echoed through your prisons? You can wash away the blood of your victims?'

Guzman turned white-faced. He stood up and strode to the window. Father John moved alongside him. Consuela stood outside on the steps. She laughed as Guzman's driver came toward her, then looked toward the office.

Guzman's voice mocked; 'You're no different, you priests! What do you know of her? You know nothing. Nothing of our lives.'

He touched Father Doyle's robe.

'Nobody will believe her, and for this, for her, you would deprive your community, your church, the people who find support and comfort here? Remember your own words, *"I was hungry and you gave me food, I was thirsty and you gave me drink"*. You said them as an accusation, but for what reason would you deny them?'

He pointed over at The Mission.

'Perhaps you're right, though. Perhaps there are more deserving recipients of my charity.'

There was a quiet knock at the door.

* * *

Consuela saw the car as soon as she arrived at The Mission. Slipping through a side door, she nodded to a few of the regulars and smiled and greeted Ray who was screwing a new bulb into a light fitting.

He came closer. 'I heard about last night. How are you?'

She frowned.

He laughed. 'Nothing stays secret for long around here.'

'I'm fine,' she said.

'Any ideas who might have been behind it?'

'Perhaps someone thought the place was empty, with Roger and Stuart being away in Cornwall.'

He looked sceptical. 'When are they due back?'

'This afternoon. Roger will be out again tonight.'

She pointed toward the church. 'I have a meeting over there now. Father was very brave.'

'I heard.'

She shook her head. They both looked down toward the road. Lopez leaned against the bonnet, smoking yet another cigarette.

She smiled, touched Ray's arm and made her way out through the door.

Lopez was now just a few feet away from her. She felt his disdain, and she recognised the contemptuous derision from years ago. Nothing had changed here but the location. And that was everything.

She smiled at him, but he hadn't grasped that this wasn't El Salvador and his intimidation was just window-dressing here. He was just a wretched thug who couldn't accept his impotence.

Her smile seemed to enrage him, and he started toward her.

She felt elated as he approached and then stopped and waited for him.

He loomed over her.

She laughed.

It was the first time she had felt this way, had felt this power. No longer weak, no longer desperate, no longer having to cower away or to hide from bastards like Lopez. Like Guzman.

Her laughter enraged him even more. He came closer.

'You OK, Consuela?'

Ray eased alongside. He folded his arms. He looked imposing, unbreakable. The stern gaze halted Lopez.

'I'm OK, Ray. Very much so.'

'Is he causing you a problem?'

She looked toward Father Doyle's office and saw Guzman observing her from the window. Father John moved alongside the man. She smiled towards them and then back to Lopez.

'Oh no, Ray. He's no problem, not anymore.'

She felt such a release. The years of anguish rolled away.

She made her way toward the office.

* * *

She knocked at the office door.

Father John opened it.

Guzman had sat down again, silent and imposing. Consuela had discarded her fear but still had to quell the gut feeling of anxiety.

Guzman looked toward her as Father John began to speak.

'Senor, Consuela comes from your country.'

Instant disdain passed quickly over Guzman's face when John gave the name.

He sneered.

'Consuela!'

Father said, 'You may have known each other, I believe.'

Guzman shrugged in contempt, 'I had wide-ranging responsibilities. I saw many people, but even so, I am sure I would have remembered.'

It was a moment before Father John spoke again.

'Senor Guzman, as I said, there are a few matters still to resolve before we make the arrangements for your donation to The Mission.'

Guzman looked over Consuela. He laughed, his voice scornful.

'And she is one of the matters?'

Consuela closed her eyes. His voice, his words, that accent, brought back the smell of frangipani, the sound of Torogoz birds croaking, with their blue plumage, hopping from branch to branch. Consuela heard a rhythm drumming in her head, the sound of magic and passion, the face of her homeland swirling before her. Here was the murderer recalling, in his arrogance, the murdered. He brought the smell and sound of the place he sought to destroy.

A link to love, passion, magic, and horror.

She detested him. Swaggering through her life, brutally grinding everything beneath highly polished boots, sneering even as the screams reverberated through foul prison corridors. Screams that echoed anger, resistance, but ultimately loss.

She had followed too many empty coffins in a charade of remembrance. Guzman and his thugs watching a haphazard cortege, checking faces, photographing for their files. Everything in place, boots shining, tight uniforms immaculate, hair trimmed, faces shaved, guns cocked.

Consuela glanced across at that sneering expression, mouth opening and closing. She momentarily shrank back, even as she remembered her resolve. She touched Father John's clerical gown, which she knew he had put on especially for this encounter.

Guzman's eyes rested on Father Doyle for what seemed a

lifetime of silence. An occasional car passed outside the net-curtained window, but here, in this place, now, was a world apart. He waited, looking back and forth between Consuela and the priest with an ironic expression.

Consuela's voice, when it came, was almost lost amid the sound of traffic filtering through the window.

'How dare you set foot in any church?'

Guzman's expression went from contempt to fury in a frightening change so sudden it could easily have been missed. Then the smile was restored.

'I was able to assist my last church, in San Salvador, to build a new health centre which saved many young lives. The Archbishop himself opened it.'

Consuela nodded, then began to speak.

'I remember it, just by the Jardin Botanico la Laguna.'

The words came hesitantly at first, then more confident as she realised that these were the first words she had spoken to Guzman that hadn't been dragged out of her by torture. She touched Father's Doyle's black robe again and inhaled deeply before continuing. Her voice grew louder as anger began to find expression.

Looking back at Doyle she explained,

'It's a big park in an old volcanic crater.'

She turned again toward Guzman and steeled herself to face his challenge.

'Two young children of some friends of mine were snatched from there by your thugs. They were never seen again, just disappeared.'

She looked back toward Father Doyle.

'That's what often happened to many of the children of those who opposed him and his kind. As a warning to others.'

'He also supported a school for orphaned children,' said Father Doyle.

'That is also true. The military supported many such schools.'

She moved closer to Guzman until Doyle feared he would strike her.

'Those schools, orphanages … how many children did you steal? How many parents have never seen their children again?'

Guzman said nothing.

Consuela turned to Doyle.

'They abducted those children. Some they kept in orphanages, military families adopted some, others were sold to childless American couples. Thousands are only just now starting to be reunited. It was a warning to insurgents about the price they would pay if they opposed him and his type.'

Father John searched for images to accompany these words. He felt suddenly empty; a moment of alarm flickered through him as he realised the exclusive, albeit brutal, companionship and knowledge, these two felt.

'No, no.'

Guzman's voice had dropped so low they had trouble hearing him,

'You are wrong.'

'Imagine taking a child from their mother. As a punishment. Babies ripped from the breast.' Consuela pointed in Guzman's face. 'That's who this person is.'

Doyle opened his mouth to speak, then he felt a touch of a hand on his leg and saw Consuela shaking her head at him, so he remained silent as her voice issued clear and suddenly proud, word after word shaking off the years of torment.

'And the Atlactl Battalion, El Mozote, the disappeared, the murdered, the tortured, all the blood and tears. Was the world mistaken?'

Guzman sprang to his feet, now face flushed with anger.

'Do I need to endure this, Father Doyle? I come in peace and generosity. I come with the blessing of your Bishop. And you feel you have the right to allow me to be interrogated and abused in this way. No, Father, you do not have that right. You have not earned that right.'

Father John started to speak, but Guzman continued. He pointed at Consuela.

'For the sake of this person, whose real name you do not even know. Isn't that pathetic, Father Doyle?'

Father John looked at Consuela. She glared back at Guzman defiantly.

'Coretta Delgado,' declared Father Doyle.

Consuela's eyes opened wide in disbelief.

Doyle continued. 'Is it any surprise that she changed her name to escape from you. I know the statements she gave were supposedly destroyed. I know why you've pursued her. I know exactly where you were on 16th November 1989 - in the garden of the Jesuit's residence in San Salvador.'

He stood up and faced Guzman. 'I know who you are, Colonel Guzman, and your money will not be welcome here.' He paused. 'I will see you are not welcome here.'

Consuela stared at John. She felt released. All the years of skulking in self-imposed exile, of sheltering in any available sanctuary, fell away. She jumped toward Guzman, shouting in his face.

'You murdered. You tortured. You destroyed people's lives. You shouldn't be here.'

Guzman lost control. He swayed and came toward her.

Consuela didn't flinch.

Father John leapt between them. The obese figure stopped but didn't retreat. Neither did Consuela. Guzman exhaled loudly and then suddenly turned for the door. He wiped an arm across his sweating face. A calm fury now possessed him as he grabbed his briefcase and threw some documents onto the floor. Father Doyle recognised them as copies of the plans drawn up for the Hostel.

'You'll need my money soon, you'll beg for it.'

Guzman fell silent, and another layer of menace came slowly into those small vicious eyes. His voice when it came was soft and chilling.

'Don't let her speak with the trustees, Doyle. Persuade them to accept the money and then walk away.'

'Take your money. It will not come here.'

'Persuade them, Father. Walk away and let it come to an end. Violence can stop. *You* can stop it.'

Father shook his head.

'The Bishop ...' stated Guzman.

The priest shouted as much out of relief as hostility. 'No!'

Guzman waited by the door. He pulled the *cédula* from his pocket and threw it on the table.

He laughed, turned, and marched out.

The front door smashed closed against its frame, the sound echoing along the corridor. Mrs Quinn ran into the office.

Consuela lifted the small cardboard document from the table.

'Mrs Quinn, would you please get me the Bishop?' said Doyle.

Consuela screamed. 'No. No. No.'

She fell to the floor and wept.

Mrs Quinn ran into the office as the phone rang. She knelt and put her arms about Consuela.

Doyle spoke with the Bishop's assistant, Father Cormack, requesting an urgent meeting.

A meeting was arranged for the evening, but only reluctantly, as the Bishop would not be back from Birmingham until late.

Consuela hadn't moved. Eventually, she grasped the *cédula* close to her breast and stood. Father John moved toward her. He wanted to hold her.

She turned, her face creased with tears. An expression of desolation stared toward him as she held up the document.

'Jorge.' She shook her head as the tears flowed again.

As he moved toward her. She shook her head. 'No. No.'

She staggered from the room.

Mrs Quinn held her arm. She looked back, accusingly toward Doyle.

* * *

As Doyle watched Consuela walking slowly to The Mission, he saw Ray sweeping the steps. He beckoned him to the office.

They talked briefly, and Ray agreed to keep an even closer wa
on Consuela than before.

'Quietly, please,' said John. 'She mustn't know.'

As Ray started to leave Doyle said, 'I'm sorry, I almost forgot. Someone phoned earlier asking whether you were here. Mrs Quinn didn't tell them anything. They didn't leave a name. Said they would try again.'

Father Doyle looked at Ray. The ex-soldier seemed transfixed.

## TWENTY-FIVE

Consuela sat on the side of her bed.

Jorge. Hope snuffed out. However insignificant the possibility it had sustained her through the dark days. Now to have it snatched away, thrown away like a bargaining chip. She stroked her fingers across the *cédula.* Just a piece of cardboard. But if you don't have one in El Salvador, you don't exist. Jorge had ceased to exist.

She knew what Guzman intended. To destroy her.

She stared, *Cédula Identidad, SAN SALVADOR.*

They took them from the bodies of their victims.

She turned the page. A photograph, a fingerprint. Another page the name; *Jorge Delgado.* She looked closer in the top corner of an inside page a drop of blood.

Her brother's blood.

She closed her eyes. Jorge's face so hard to recapture; she felt guilty at her failure to recover the expressions that had kept her company through the years. She looked again at the photograph. It was an image, but it was not Jorge. The life had gone. That time was past.

Memories flooded in again, abruptly, harshly. Uninvited but overwhelming.

She was dragged from that cold, hard cell again, pulled along the corridor by her hair. Screaming and shouting at her, voices she couldn't understand, mouths opening and closing, necks bulging with thick veins, eyes wide with contempt. An iron door slammed shut. Her clothes ripped off. Waiting in the centre of a small, cold, grime-encrusted tiled room, a metal frame bed standing in one corner. Seven men staring at her, as though she was an animal in a zoo. She stood naked in a puddle of her urine. They laughed as the liquid ran down her leg, then suddenly, as though reacting to a command, they shoved her onto the bed, tying her down. A gag was forced into her mouth.

Electric shocks emanated from the wide band strapped to her chest. They didn't even ask questions, just watched impassively as the power was increased. It went on for about thirty minutes, although time had ceased to have meaning. It stopped, at last, and the strap was released. She tried to get up. Nobody came toward her. She fell onto the cold, hard, floor and was left lying there.

They walked out, one by one, ignoring her, leaving her alone.

Alone and utterly desperate.

Guzman came in soon afterwards. She remembered him from before. He was smiling this time.

Perhaps she was wrong.

Perhaps he represented hope.

Perhaps he had only been watching the last time, the *aeroplane*, to try to stop them.

The smile he wore looked concerned, even understanding. She was relieved by that.

Perhaps it was all over.

Perhaps they realised it had been a mistake.

Just perhaps.

He handed her a gown. Two trails of blood ran down the front of it and on the right side.

'Coretta, how did you get involved in this?'

Even the voice sounded sympathetic. He walked toward her carrying two chairs.

'Here.'

He lifted her to her feet and held her as she stumbled to sit on one of the chairs. The grip was soft, she clung to him as though he was a lifeline.

His voice betrayed disquiet. 'Help them Coretta, and this will stop.' He touched her arm gently. 'I will make them stop.'

The words comforted her in the chill air. She remembered now, with fury, how she had been taken in. So little had seemed so much. A word, a smile. She clung to them in desperation, not seeing the deceptive distortions behind the words, behind the smile, because she hadn't wanted to see them. She had felt hope, and that was enough.

'Anything. But how can I help? I have no information or knowledge.'

He looked to the floor and sighed deeply.

'I do want to help, please,' he held out his hands as though in supplication, 'I can only do so much.'

She nodded as if assenting, but her mind was empty, apart from the pain. The remnants of the love and loyalty that had given her life still clung to her, guided her, more by instinct than intention.

'Manuel ... how well did you know him? His friends, associates. You knew them?'

How well did she know her lover? How well did she know the person whose presence had lightened each moment? How well did she recall his shattered body as he fell to the dusty road? Who was she if she now betrayed the love that sustained her?

She stared at his face. Searching for compassion.

Hoping.

'He told me nothing. I didn't know him well. Not well.'

His face changed, almost too subtle to notice. The smile became fixed. The softness disappeared. His eyes suddenly flashed. She was sucked into them, unable to look away; hoping he would answer her unspoken cries for mercy.

'You were with him when he died.'

'He was murdered.'

'You know his friends - who he met, where they lived?'

She shook her head.

'Can I have a drink?'

The pretence had ended; his voice was harsh and uncompromising. 'Not after the electricity. Now just tell me of his friends.'

She shook her head.

He stood up and kicked at the door. They were waiting outside. He jerked his head toward Coretta. Then he came over and pulled at the gown she was wearing. She tried desperately to hold on to it. He smiled, pulling harder while they stood around laughing. He tugged while she continued to hold on. Suddenly he jerked it savagely toward him. She twisted and fell. Naked again. The floor was icy stone-cold. Struggle and fear had exhausted her. Two of them lifted her on to the bed again. The bindings were tighter this time, the metal frame digging into her skin. They attached an electrode to her vagina.

He smiled as his eyes roamed over her body. Then he turned the dial.

This time it was different, voices screaming the questions at her from all sides.

They put a gag in her mouth and told her to lift her hand when she wanted to answer. There was no strength, though, she couldn't raise her hand. The pain was too much.

She was about to die. There was no way of ending it. It was over.

The pain suddenly stopped.

'Now talk,' came his voice.

She had nothing left – no resources to oppose this torment.

She told them everything.

Everything they wanted to know.

They dragged her off the bed, hauling her along the floor. She couldn't stand, couldn't walk. He threw the gown at her and then gestured for them to take her outside. Blindfolded, certain she was about to be shot.

'His friends. Take us to their houses,' he demanded.

They took her to a van, slid open a side door, pushed her inside onto the metal floor.

The blindfold came off outside Soraya's house.

He didn't even look round. She had already told him the addresses, but it wasn't enough. The car drove to each one of the addresses she had revealed. He made notes at each one. Consuela wished they had shot her. The pain had now passed. She wanted to deny what she had done.

It didn't end there. It never ends. She still felt shame.

Hearing Stuart playing the guitar down the stairs, she stared toward the window and looked down at her bag. She was packed and ready. Wardrobe empty. Drawers cleared.

An inevitable ending. She had no forgiveness, only vengeance, inevitable vengeance. What else could there be?

Finality creeping toward her like a welcome, bastard scream.

It was inevitable from the moment she stared from the dusty window in the early morning and saw those six figures spread-eagled on the lawn in front of the priests' residence. Guzman swaggering amongst them, his boots were shining in the pale patches of light flowing from the house. She could still hear, in nightmares, Martin Baro, Padre Nacho, shouting *'injustice'* before a bullet blew his brains onto the grass. Guzman smiled and then Ignacio Ellacura was next looking up in sorrow before the bullet silenced his stillborn protest.

Then she escaped – after appearing before a judge and swearing that statement which was alleged to have been destroyed in the offices of the National Guard.

Guzman had found her again, and this inevitability could be deferred no longer.

Her life was leading to this. From the moment she crept silently through the kitchen of the Radisson Hotel in Miami, after Colonel Rivas appeared, announced as an investigator by the FBI, but in reality, as Consuela knew, an officer in the Atlactl Battalion. Then she moved, quietly, treading softly and warily, through Alabama, Canada, France, finally to London - and then eventually to St Mary's.

Voices broke into her consciousness. She heard John. Pushing the small bag containing all her possessions under the bed, she made her way downstairs.

* * *

A light shone through the front window of the small, terraced house. As Father Doyle came closer, he heard a guitar filtering out onto the empty street. When he looked through the window, he saw Stuart playing the music while Roger sat on a wooden rocking chair, occasionally making notes on a writing pad.

Doyle seated himself on a low brick wall. The scene before him was filled with contentment.

He felt guilty recalling his words of condemnation to Roger five years ago. 'In the name of love' he had said at the time. Was it love or just intolerant judgement? Nothing was clear now, and in any event, who had given him the privilege of judgement anyway? It had seemed so easy to follow the Church's strictures, but the condemnation delivered was disproportionate to the biblical texts he had just reread before leaving his office. It was all about theologians falling on inconsistent texts, tossing rare bloodless meat in the air for as long as they could suck nourishment through their sharpened teeth.

The dead hand of vacuous purity; what benighted roads it had beckoned him down.

He moved uncertainly to the doorway and pressed the bell.

Roger raised his eyebrows and smiled as he opened the door. He turned and gestured Father Doyle along the narrow hallway into the front room.

Stuart looked up.

'Father, you're becoming a regular.'

Roger didn't hide his smile at John's unease. 'Coffee?'

Stuart stood up. 'I'll get it.'

John looked around the neat room and back to Roger, who cleared a chair and gestured for him to sit.

Stuart came back with a tray of coffee.

John looked up. His words were clumsy. He had to ask, but was afraid to admit the consequences, especially to himself.

'How did you survive away from the Church?'

Roger frowned. 'What do you mean survive? Lived? Got through the days? Like we all do, why shouldn't I? Look around you, you see a roof, food in the fridge, a bed for Stuart and me to share. I now know what love is. I know satisfaction, I know fulfilment. *Survival* is the wrong word.'

John confessed, 'I have never known any other way.'

Stuart looked from one to the other. 'What's changed then, Father?'

They heard the stairs creak.

John stood up, expectantly. He looked at both Roger and Stuart. 'Could I speak to Consuela alone for a minute and then I have to get to see the Bishop? I've already ordered a cab for,' he looked at his watch, 'fifteen minutes.'

'I'm out to The Mission,' said Roger.

'And I have some files to update,' added Stuart as they both left the room and headed for the kitchen. Consuela frowned as they passed her in the doorway.

'I'm sorry about this morning,' he said.

Consuela frowned but said nothing.

'I mean Guzman.'

'I know. You've no reason to be sorry,' replied Consuela.

'I didn't realise.'

'Why should you? It's a different life, a different time and I don't ask you to understand, I don't want you, or anyone else, to understand. That only comes with experience, and I wouldn't wish that on anyone.'

'I'm going to speak to the Bishop now.'

'John, why are you doing this? The money offered will do good; I know that more than most. The Mission needs it so badly.'

Doyle was confused. 'We can't take his money.'

'I never said that, so are you doing it for me? Taking sides. You'll end up being disappointed since there are no sides.

There's no winning or losing, and I'm not worth it.
good and evil; it's much more complicated than that.'

'I heard what he said,' Father John reminded her.
told me what he did.'

'I don't want to be responsible for stopping the hostel
built.' Her sudden intense scrutiny unnerved him as she continued, 'It's not just about Guzman though is it?'

John looked out the window, 'I've just been talking with Roger and Stuart.' He turned back to her. 'No, you're right. Of course, it is about more than Guzman.'

Consuela leaned forward.

'I know who you are, Father John Doyle. I'm not asking anything of you. You and Roger and Stuart have all given me so much already, don't torture yourself and don't sacrifice what you are for something or somebody who can never repay what you deserve. Don't worry about me, John. I've become strong over the past years. I've had to. I don't break easily.'

John was confused. 'What do you mean, deserve?'

'To be able to give you what you deserve ...' Consuela left the sentence unfinished.

Her face was bright with a longing that she tried to disguise, but he felt his desperate desire too acutely not to see through the beautiful mask.

He paused and closed his eyes but found no words to break into the desperate longing that engulfed him again.

Consuela continued, 'Whatever you do, be sure that you believe it's the right thing. Don't do it for me or think that you can wipe away my memories - or even ease them - by standing up against Guzman. Only I can do that. I *have* to do that.'

She gently lifted his trembling hand to her lips. 'But thank you, John.'

His body was shaking with tension and excitement.

The front doorbell rang.

Roger shouted from the kitchen, 'John, your taxi's here.'

Consuela ran up the stairs.

Father Doyle walked quickly from the room and along to the

ıtchen where Roger was opening a box packed with tins of soup.' He smiled. 'Good luck with the Bishop.'

'Thanks. Are you out tonight?' asked John.

'In about half an hour. To The Mission and then,' he laughed, pointing to the cans, 'the soup run.'

'I'll see you tomorrow then, thanks for ...' Father John shrugged and looked slightly embarrassed. 'I'll see myself out.' Roger came to the front door anyway as John walked down the path.

## TWENTY-SIX

The taxi turned off the East India Dock Road and stopped in front of the Bishop's Lodge. It was a small house standing in the shadow of the dark tenement block where Michael Kelly lived. The high-rise offices of Canary Wharf were lit up like grandiose Christmas decorations, dwarfing both buildings.

Father Paul Cormack opened the door. It was a disruption to his routine to demand a meeting and then ignore his polite attempt at refusal. Things were not done that way.

'Father.' Cormack's face was set in stony disapproval. 'Please come this way.'

Doyle followed him down a short, narrow hallway. Pictures of Popes John Paul II and John XXIII hung on the walls. They turned into the Bishop's office. The walls were lined with more photographs of Peter Hopwood taken during his fifteen years in Ohio and Chicago. Pride of place went to one of the Bishop with President Jimmy Carter.

'His Excellency will be with you shortly. As you know, he has just arrived back from Birmingham; nevertheless, he will see you.'

Doyle understood the formality was intended as a further rebuke. After he left, the priest gazed at a photograph of a lake surrounded by three volcanoes. The door had barely closed before it reopened and the Bishop himself came in. His squat, overweight figure straining against a dark suit, his white shirt collar undone. Contrary to Cormack's complaints, he exuded energy as he grabbed Father John's hand.

The eyes were laughing. 'Well, you've surely disrupted the routine here, John, I wouldn't hope for special dispensation from Father Cormack for some time if I were you.'

Together they looked at the photograph.

'Lake Atitlan in Guatemala, one of the most beautiful spots in the world. Aldous Huxley once said it "went beyond the limit of the permissibly picturesque". I spent a month on retreat at nearby Chichicastenango when I was still based in Chicago. Fascinating place. There is still plenty of Mayan influence.'

He walked across to his desk, took out a packet of cigarettes and offered it to Father, who shook his head.

'Did you drive here?'

'No. Taxi.'

'You'll take a drink then. I certainly need one.'

He fetched a bottle of whisky from a filing cabinet and poured two large glasses before turning back to Father Doyle.

'Are you sure? I thought you didn't.'

Father accepted one of the glasses. 'Occasionally.'

'It's been a day, finance and accountants, what a mixture.' The Bishop collapsed back onto a large, battered armchair, gesturing for his visitor to sit down.

Hopwood took a long pull at the cigarette before sipping from his glass.

'It's the Guzman thing, is it?' Untying his laces, he slipped off his shoes and looked at a hole in a sock.

'I understand your concern, John, don't think I don't. Do you know the expression "full-court press" from American basketball? Well, it's happening now, with Guzman. I've got Cardinal Trujillo's office, Charles Mayer, Desmond Williams QC, and the Right Honourable John Bayliss MP, all contacting me. Mayer's taking a high moral tone of course, although I suspect there's a deal more to his advocacy of this fellow than meets the eye. He's never been one for altruism.'

He took another draw on the cigarette. 'Daniel Cooper's been quiet. I expected him to weigh in; after all, he did introduce the man. But, well, there we have it, the curia in full hue and cry and I have nothing to say about Senor Adolfo Guzman except - *thank you very much, I'll have your money.*'

He paused and poked at the hole in his sock, before turning his gaze back to Doyle.

'However, John.'

His expression was intense as he took another sip of whisky and looked closely at Father Doyle.

'You tell me we mustn't touch this man or his money, but you don't say why. So, let's get down to business. You've met him a couple of times I believe?'

Father Doyle nodded. 'I saw him last week and again today.'

The Bishop spoke again. 'You know his background obviously?'

Doyle nodded.

'But there's nothing there, nothing that I can put up against the Cardinal's endorsement. So, what is this all about John? You're usually solid and pragmatic in these things, and I've always trusted your judgement.'

'About thirteen weeks ago, a young Salvadorian refugee, Consuela Flores, started helping out at The Mission as a volunteer. She escaped from El Salvador about four years ago, after she gave a statement naming Colonel Guzman as being involved in the murder of the Jesuit priests in San Salvador, back in '89. She claims she had also been imprisoned and tortured. By Guzman.'

The Bishop had been listening intently. He now spoke as he finished off his whisky. His expression had turned sombre.

'I asked Cormack. He said he had heard something of this, without any names of course, from one of his Jesuit colleagues. Go on.'

Father Doyle recounted the meetings with Consuela and

Guzman and then fell silent. The Bishop looked up at the ceiling as he lit another cigarette.

'I understand your concern. If true, we can't go near him. Is she credible, John? Does her evidence hang together, or is this a political vendetta? There was a civil war, brutality from both sides.'

'I have no doubts about her.'

'OK, John. I said I would reconsider. Will Miss Flores see me? I need to meet with her.'

'I'll ask her about that. I'm also trying to persuade her to speak with the trustees. She's extremely nervous, though.'

'Understandably. Good idea, though.' The Bishop waved a hand in irritation.

'If what Miss Flores is saying is right, it puts the trust in a terrible position.'

'I agree. Unacceptable. The money would certainly be useful, but not if what Miss Flores is saying is correct, and I hear what you say about her integrity. We'll see, John. We'll see.'

He looked at his watch. 'I have to leave you now. Call me when you've arranged things with Miss Flores. I'll speak with Daniel Cooper tonight about not accepting funds from Guzman until we've resolved the matter of Miss Flores. He's been talking about an urgent meeting to sort this out. Desperate for the money, of course.'

Father Doyle decided to walk back to St Mary's.

Forty minutes later as he turned off Commercial Road, he saw blue lights flashing outside The Mission.

Police cars and an ambulance were blocking the road.

# TWENTY-SEVEN

Father John sat with Stuart and Consuela in the hospital waiting room.

Stuart rubbed his hand across his forehead. His eyes were full of tears.

'He's such a fool,' said Stuart. 'What did he think he could do? Four of them, apparently, with baseball bats. Thank God, it's just a broken arm and a fractured skull. They say there's no brain damage.'

He shook his head. 'I try to understand his commitment. He cares too much.' His eyes closed. 'That sounded wrong. Of course, I understand, but I can't share the passion. He makes me feel inadequate.'

He suddenly turned to John, a flash of anger in his eyes. 'And you. The church. So cruel. To cut him loose like you did.' He put his hand on John's arm. 'Sorry. Not the time is it.'

Consuela leaned across 'I'm sure he thought he was only doing the right thing.'

'He looks a terrible mess. Have you seen The Mission?' Stuart asked Father John.

Doyle nodded. 'It'll be a while before we're able to open again. They smashed everything.'

'C18 all over the walls,' interjected Stuart.

Consuela looked confused. 'What is that?'

Doyle answered, 'Right-wing fascist group. The one and eight stand for A and H: Adolf Hitler's initials.'

Father John recognised Dr Selverajah as soon as she came into the room.

'We've put a cast on his arm and dressed his head. It's not as bad as it looks. We'd like to keep him overnight, for observation, just as a precaution. You can see him now. The police are just finishing up.'

Doyle glanced at Consuela. She turned to Stuart.

'You go ahead; we'll be along in a few minutes.'

Stuart rushed through the door.

'He was fortunate,' continued Dr Selverajah. 'The blow to the head could have killed him. He said that he slipped, so the blow just glanced off him. Otherwise …' She shook her head. 'Apparently, he called the police but didn't wait for them to arrive. Just went in to try to stop the destruction.'

'They haven't caught anyone yet,' said Father John.

'These thugs have been very active around here recently. We've treated some of the consequences,'

She shook her head. 'Vicious.'

Her text-pager went off. 'I have to go.' She smiled. 'He'll be OK.'

'Let's go and see him now,' said John and took Consuela's hand.

A uniformed police officer came along the corridor, accompanied by a dark-haired woman studying a notebook. Her eyes brightened when she saw Doyle.

'Father Doyle,' she said, holding out her hand. 'It's been a while.'

'Emily, nasty business.'

He turned to Consuela. 'This is Consuela Flores, helps out at The Mission. Detective Inspector Hamilton.'

Hamilton nodded and turned to the uniformed officer. 'PC Jukes was first on the scene. Luckily, he was close by, and the paramedics were just behind him. Roger was lucky.'

Jukes nodded. 'We responded to an emergency call and found Mr Burnett in a doorway. It looked bad. I feared the worse at first. Then he came round. He was only concerned about The Mission. It was a mess.'

'We're struggling with this stuff at the moment. A bookshop was burned out a week or so back,' said Hamilton. 'We have to get back. I'll keep you informed as soon as we have anything. I think Bill was coming over soon in any event. He mentioned about a development at The Mission.'

'Possibly,' said Doyle as they left.

He turned to Consuela. 'Bill Hamilton, her husband, is an architect. He designed The Mission originally. Let's go and see Roger.'

He took her hand as they walked along the corridor.

* * *

Desmond Williams QC sat upright behind his desk. He looked at Guzman and Jeffrey Sheridan seated facing him.

'I understand we may have a problem with a fellow countrywoman of yours, Senor Guzman? A touch hysterical, I understand.'

'I saw her with Doyle.' Guzman leaned forward. 'He's clearly taken with her, and there's no truth in this nonsense. I have no memory of her. It's more to do with Doyle than me, I think.' His tone became agitated. 'What is happening about my application?'

Williams answered him. 'The investments are in place, I understand, through Daniel Cooper. The investment route is straightforward, and your request for an appropriate visa is being processed even as we speak. Citizenship may follow in the normal course, in a few years.'

He tapped on the desktop with his pen.

'Senor Guzman, of course you are aware that if there are any adverse matters revealed which may detract from your application ... well, you were a politician, of sorts, yourself, then difficulties could arise.' His smile disappeared. 'You understand what I am saying. There will be great embarrassment for several people, including myself if there is any bad publicity. We rely on contacts ...'

He looked hard at Guzman. His voice was cold. 'Nobody likes their contacts burned. You understand me?'

Guzman leaned forward against William's desk. His tone was contemptuous.

'I've followed your advice and paid your price, so don't talk to me about embarrassment.' He turned away and shook his head. The subject was closed.

Williams laid his pen on the desk, a broad insincere smile breaking out again on his wizened face. 'Of course, Senor Guzman.'

The audience was over. 'I have to be in court very shortly, gentlemen.'

He gestured towards the door. 'Jeffrey, stay a moment.'

Guzman stomped from the room.

Williams waited until Guzman's footsteps had faded away on the stone steps outside the office.

'The politicians will drop him like a brick – a very *heavy* brick. Be aware of that. He's on dangerous ground.'

He picked up his briefcase. 'Could you have a quick word with my clerk?'

Williams's clerk was Harry Essex, who had been in the job for twenty-five years and got a cut of every fee the QC received. He gestured Sheridan to a chair, speaking in a brusque cockney accent. 'Jeffrey, your man is a bit of a wild card ... could cost us some friends if he messes up, so I'm issuing a fee note for fifteen thousand. You in funds?'

Sheridan nodded.

Essex continued, 'Get it over today, could you? I reckon he could do a bunk any time, your Senor Guzman. We don't want to lose out, Jeffrey.'

Sheridan raised his eyebrows. 'Be the first time if that happened.'

'Fifteen thousand today, eh?'

Sheridan nodded and left the office.

The solicitor saw Guzman's limousine waiting at the kerbside. Guzman was in the rear seat gesticulating angrily at his driver who sat staring through the windscreen, nodding occasionally.

* * *

Consuela paused at the hospital exit and spoke with Ray, who was waiting outside. He had come to the hospital, after hearing about the incident with Roger, while visiting some friends at a squat a couple of miles away from The Mission. There was nothing to be done at The Mission anyway, it was a crime scene, and a forensics unit was all over it. He knew Consuela would be at the hospital. Since Father John had asked him to "keep an eye on her" he was discreetly shadowing Consuela, without, he hoped, her noticing.

Consuela told him about Roger and then began to make her way toward the house. Ray waited and then followed. As she approached the house, he looked along the narrow road and saw Guzman's car parked around the next corner, its bonnet just showing.

A white van suddenly passed Ray and came alongside Consuela, slowing down beside her. A side door slid open. A pair of figures wearing ski-masks jumped out and grabbed her. She tried to run. Two hands gripped her arms, bundling her through the sliding door. She opened her mouth, but nothing came. Not the scream she expected, or even a whimper of protest.

Just the same as before: *they took her to a van and pushed her inside, onto the metal floor.*

She grabbed the side of the door.

A third figure screamed at her from inside the van. She couldn't make out the words.

Ray Lancaster sprinted toward the van. He had almost

reached the door as the vehicle started to pull away even as Consuela hung on trying to escape the harsh grip hauling her inside, frantically scratching at their arms. Finding her voice, she began screaming, shouting at them to let her go.

There was a screech of brakes.

The moving vehicle shuddered to a halt. She was thrown forward onto the road with one of the figures still hanging onto her.

Glass shattered. Consuela saw the windscreen disintegrate and the driver falling momentarily onto the steering wheel, the hooter screaming out.

She saw Ray Lancaster reaching for her, but before he could grasp her leg, there was a flash of movement, and her arms fell free. One of the attackers fell to the pavement only to be dragged back inside the van as it suddenly accelerated along the road. The van's tyres were squealing as it rounded a corner.

Guzman's car moved out slowly from the side road and drove past. The driver didn't glance toward them; they saw nothing through the opaque rear windows. Consuela watched the car carefully. She then turned to the figure standing between the vehicle and herself and then flopped on a wall, inhaling deeply, trying to take some deep breaths.

He was a stranger - short dark hair, wiry, intimidating. A calm ferocity featured as he watched the two vehicles disappear. She turned to thank him as he held his hand out to help Ray Lancaster to his feet.

Lancaster was smiling. 'Hello, Sarge. What the fuck are you doing here?

* * *

Mrs Quinn was waiting at the door to Father John's office.

She called after him, 'Mr Perez is here. He said he's expected. I'll bring him through.'

Father Doyle had forgotten.

Perez entered the office clutching a plastic carrier bag.

Without a word, he walked over to the window and peered out before perching on the edge of a chair.

'Father, you didn't listen before.'

Doyle ignored the allegation as accusing eyes focused on him. The voice spat bitterness across the room.

'I kept my job through patronage, and my life by acquiescing. That's the nature of El Salvador. Then Raul happened.'

He walked to the window again, peered down the steps of St Mary's, then turned back and returned to the chair.

'I had to get out of there. I knew that.'

His eyes blinked violently, distorting his tortured face as he clenched and unclenched his fists.

'We arrived here with nothing. Since then, I have lived day and night with the knowledge that I cost my child his life, and my family their home.'

Father John tried to interrupt. He knew these words. Perez gestured him to silence.

'No, no. I don't need any pious words from you, Father John Doyle. I thought I had escaped from that bastard. That at least I had rid myself of his stench. It wasn't the way of it, though. He wasn't welcome in Spain.'

Father John simply nodded.

Perez continued. 'An investigating magistrate there requested to question him about the murder of the Jesuits. Five of them were Spanish. He got out of there quickly. Even though he had to abandon his business.'

'Business?'

'Arms, weapons. He'll bring it over here. But then he'll be welcome here. This country survives on arms sales.'

'But there's an amnesty now. Whatever he's done, he could go back to El Salvador.'

'I thought that as well.'

He held up the plastic carrier bag.

'When I heard he was here, I made it my business to find out what he was up to. To find out why he couldn't return home. I still have contacts in El Salvador and a few around the world.

Twenty years of being a reporter helped. I know you've been meeting up with Gerry Keane. He was one of the best. Didn't fall for the bullshit, unlike me,' he gave a humourless laugh. 'Anyway, he *can't* go back. I found out why in the last few days.'

He held up the bag again.

'It's all in here. You need to see Cooper before the trustees meeting. Demand he gives you time.'

'He's not so keen on talking to me at the moment.'

'I expect not.'

He pulled out a single page from the voluminous documentation contained in the bag, threw it on Father's desk, and held up the bag.

John looked at the page. A document about artillery shells!

'It's all in here,' said Perez. 'He'll see you.'

He leapt to his feet, thrusting the carrier bag at Father John.

'Here take this and use it. His time is coming. I want him friendless and desperate when that happens. Just like he visited on so many people back home.'

'His time is coming. What does that mean?'

Perez glanced through the window again. He turned back to the priest.

'Some people live and have to face the consequences of their lives. Others trade life for a package of slogans. You have chosen your way. Don't ask to understand a world that doesn't fit with your arcane dogma.'

He then left without another word.

Doyle waited to see the man descend the steps. Minutes passed, but he didn't appear.

He summoned Mrs Quinn from her office.

'Where is Perez?'

'He insisted on leaving through the back door of the presbytery.'

He called Consuela on her mobile as soon as he sat back down at his desk. There was no answer. Then his telephone rang. It was from Stuart.

'Do you know where Consuela is?'

'With you, I hope,' said John.

'She's gone. All her clothes. Everything.'

'When?'

'She wasn't here when I got back from the hospital.'

'Did she leave any note? Is there anything to say where she might have gone?'

'Nothing.'

'I'll call you back later, Stuart. If you hear anything, please let me know.'

As he replaced the phone, he looked through the window and saw Ray Lancaster sitting on the wall opposite the office and talking to another person. Lancaster looked elated. It was as though a weight had been taken from him. John had never seen such genuine pleasure in the man before. The presence of his companion had brought new life to the ex-soldier. The other person was tall, short dark hair, the expression was benign but also severe, as though the concepts could co-exist while a balance was achieved. Which would prevail in more extreme conditions John didn't want to find out. Eyes passed across the window, momentarily focusing on the priest who felt intense scrutiny before the examination passed over him and continued a review of the area surrounding the church.

Ray Lancaster, normally so taciturn, had not stopped talking. He eventually looked over. Father Doyle gestured him into the office.

Lancaster came in. He stood taller than before.

'Father Doyle, this is Tony Tavinor. He was in the army with me.'

'Mr Tavinor—'

The voice that interrupted was assured. 'It's Tony, please.'

'Tony, it certainly looks like you've put a spring in Ray's step.'

Lancaster continued, 'Sarah got a message to Tony. She's been looking for me. I'm going up to meet her. And Tessa. She's ten years old now.'

'You're going home.'

'I'm not counting any chickens. But it's a step. They're away in Scotland at the moment. Visiting a friend.'

He rubbed his hands together.

'Not possible without you and Roger. Saved my life, Father.'

'Doyle turned to Tavinor. 'How did you find him?'

'I was overseas when Sarah left a message. When I heard she was looking, I put the word out. There's a grapevine. When I heard he might be here, I came back. I'm Tessa's godfather, so I want the family back together.'

'Where were you?'

'I was in Angola originally when Sarah left the message. Got the good news about Ray when I was in Langkawi, Malaysia. I came straight over.'

He turned to Lancaster and gave him a soft punch on his arm. 'Had to come back and find him.'

Lancaster intervened. 'There is more though, Father. Not good either. About Consuela. Someone tried to snatch her. We only just stopped them. If it wasn't for Tony showing up things could have gone bad.'

He explained what had happened.

John Doyle listened with revulsion. 'Have you called the police?'

'She insisted I didn't.'

'She is still scared of authority, Even here. Where did she go?'

'I waited outside the house. She told me she was OK and that I could leave.'

He paused, 'I didn't though, not after what happened and after you asked me to stick with her. About thirty minutes later, she came out, with a backpack and took off on a moped which was standing in the garden. I'm afraid I didn't have a chance to follow her.'

John glanced down at the documents Perez had thrown on his desk.

'You told me about your time in the army.'

Ray answered cautiously. 'A time I've tried to forget.'

Father John held up his hand as though in apology. 'I don't

want to take you back there but wonder if you know anything about arms dealing, arms deals – specifically Iraq?'

He passed the single document Perez had given him and then picked up the bag. 'I need some help understanding what's in here.'

Ray raised his eyebrows as he read the document. 'A consignment of one-fifty-five howitzer shells from Setubal in Portugal to Umm Qasr Port in Iraq, delivered in 1986.'

He looked intrigued and handed it to Tavinor.

'Do you mind if I work with Tony? He's more current on this stuff than I am. We were both seconded to a specialist unit for a few months in '86. Tracking Iran and Iraq's arms purchases. We can look through it all this evening.'

'Where are you staying?'

'Small guest house with Tony. Aldgate. The mission is still closed. It should be possible to get back in tomorrow. We'll give a hand clearing up before we go up north. Sarah's back later this week.'

Tavinor interrupted, 'I haven't told her yet. I'll go back up with Ray and then make myself scarce.'

'Could you come over and see me in the morning. There's a trustees meeting in the afternoon, and these documents may be important.'

'Nine o'clock?'

'Thanks.'

## TWENTY-EIGHT

Tower Bridge and the Tower of London itself loomed ahead as Consuela turned into the door of the Church of All Hallows by the Tower. Sunlight shone brightly capturing the elegant colours filtering through beautiful stained-glass windows.

She sat down in the second row from the back on the left side of the nave, beneath a window emblazoned with the motto *Ich Dien* under the Arms of *"Edward Prince of Wales"*.

There was only one other person in the church. He was standing in front of an effigy of "Philip Mark Byard Clayton 1885–1972". The man was carrying a small black daypack and looked away from the effigy and around the empty church before his glance fell briefly on Consuela. He moved between the pews and then along the aisle next to her.

As he passed her, he placed the daypack on the floor and then headed out of the church.

She knelt and drew the pack towards her. What was about to happen was right, but if there were another way, she would take it. She prayed, keeping her eyes tight shut, her mouth moving soundlessly, asking forgiveness even as she prayed for Guzman's soul.

* * *

Consuela filled in the registration form at the Tower Hotel reception desk. Perez had given her false documents, if required, in the name Ava Rivera. As it happened, they were not needed. She extracted an envelope from the daypack. It was unusual for a guest to pay in cash, but she explained she had lost all her cards and left a deposit of five hundred pounds, saying she would only be making local telephone calls and not using the mini-bar. She explained that her room had to overlook Tower Bridge, as had been confirmed when the booking was made. She told the receptionist that the view was her reason for her two-night stay.

The window of her room also had a perfect view of a small hotel car park. One space was empty. It had a "NO PARKING – RESERVED" sign obstructing its use. Consuela watched from behind the white net curtains as evening fell across the idyllic vista of Tower Bridge, the River Thames flowing gently by in the balmy evening.

After what seemed like an age a security guard trotted over and removed the "NO PARKING" sign. Lopez slowly drove the car into the space and passed something through the window to the security guard who then opened the back door to allow Guzman to step down and make his way into the hotel.

# TWENTY-NINE

John called Stuart to check if Consuela had returned. She hadn't.

Mrs Quinn stepped into the open doorway. As she appeared, he looked over to The Mission and saw Ray striding across clasping a new red lever-arch file. Tony Tavinor was alongside him. The couple looked imposing. Shoulders back as they marched across to the church. Tavinor appeared to have brought the parade ground with him, and Ray had found a purpose he had mislaid some time ago.

'Just a reminder the trustees meeting is at two this afternoon,' said Mrs Quinn. 'It's at Daniel Cooper's office this time. Canary Wharf.'

There was a gentle knock on the open door. Ray Lancaster and Tony Tavinor waited.

'Ray, Tony. Come in. Have a seat. Coffee?' They declined.

Lancaster laid the file on the desktop. John picked it up and flicked through it. The bag of jumbled papers Perez had given him were now tabbed and methodically catalogued.

'How did you get this done so quickly?' asked Father John shaking his head. 'It's amazing.'

Ray smiled ironically.

'We weren't busy.'

'So, what does it say?'

'Daniel Cooper is a trustee of The Mission. He also heads up Atlantic Santos, a very successful outfit these days. But this tells a pretty wild story. If you don't mind me asking, where did these documents originate?'

'Through Perez, a friend of Consuela's and one-time journalist in El Salvador.'

'Then he must still have good contacts out there. It evidences a series of illegal arms deals between Iraq and the Ministry of Defence in El Salvador in the mid-late eighties.'

He picked up the file, leaned back in his chair and proceeded to give John the details. The hesitation that had characterised Lancaster's character had gone. He was brisk, authoritative, and confident. John Doyle marvelled at the change. Throughout the explanation, Tavinor assisted by passing documents and very occasional pointing up items that Ray would then emphasise.

The unspoken respect between them was inspiring.

When Lancaster finished, having spoken without any notes for almost thirty minutes, John sat back in amazement.

'I can't believe it. This changes everything. Thank you so much. Both of you. It would have taken me days if ever, to work it out. We don't want to lose you, Ray, but you're too good for the work you're doing for us.'

'I appreciate you saying that, Father, but I remember when I got here. So no, I'm honoured to do any work that helps.'

* * *

The priest took the train to Canary Wharf.

The lift shot up to the forty-eighth floor of One Canada Square and he entered the Atlantic Santos Holdings reception area. There was an hour before the trustees meeting began.

He waited in the large reception area and spent his time studying the logos scattered around the walls of some of Cooper's companies. Atlantic Santos Holdings, Santos Sugar, Sao Paulo Coffee Growers, Banco du Santos, Café Santos, Yorkshire Natural Foods, Café Laris, AS Index.

A receptionist eventually escorted him into Cooper's mahogany-lined, deep-carpeted, office. The view over London and the River Thames was extravagant through a floor-to-ceiling plate-glass window.

Sitting behind a massive glass-topped desk, Daniel Cooper didn't bother to get up.

'We haven't much time, Father, so perhaps you could come to the point. You already have the agenda.'

Father Doyle ignored the comment. He was taken aback by Cooper's formality and evident anxiety; he had always been relaxed and approachable in the past.

'Daniel, this is not easy. What I have is not directly relevant to the agenda. Not directly but certainly relevant. I would be obliged if you would look at these documents.'

He extracted the Perez file from his briefcase and carefully placed it on Cooper's desk.

Cooper looked up sharply.

'What is this? There's no time.'

'It's probably best if you make time. I could, of course, take it to the trustees, but you should decide.'

Cooper pushed his hair back from his forehead as he started looking at the documents. Doyle felt the uncertainty when the eyes strayed from the papers and looked up at him. Then Cooper looked away again and back to his desk.

'I can take you through what I believe they say, Daniel. Of course, I'm sure you will understand them better than I do, but I'll do my best.'

Doyle walked over to the window, looked across the river and carried on speaking.

'These documents show details of an arms deal in October 1986 between a British Virgin Islands company Foss Holdings Limited, and the Ministry of Defence, El Salvador. The contract appears to be for one-fifty-five artillery rounds manufactured by Noricum of Austria. Foss Holdings paid Noricum ninety million dollars for those shells, but actual ownership never passed to the Ministry of Defence. That fiction was just for the end-user certificate. Foss subsequently sold the shells on to the Iraqi National Guard.'

Cooper didn't look up. He merely took a deep breath and continued turning the pages of the file in front of him. His concentration appeared erratic; he already knew what was in those files.

There was a pause until Father Doyle, still standing, looked down at Cooper's bowed head and spoke again.

'Foss Holdings is one of Atlantic Santos Holdings' subsidiaries, isn't it?'

Behind his large desk, Cooper stayed silent, still not looking up.

Doyle continued. 'El Salvador doesn't possess artillery that uses those one-fifty-five shells.'

He wandered to the large window overlooking the River Thames.

'Foss Holdings Limited is in turn owned by Natural Island Incorporated of the Cook Islands. That company paid an amount of sixty million dollars to a Swiss company called Purina S.A. of Zurich in November 1986 to their account at Union Bank in Zurich?'

The telephone rang. Cooper snatched it up, and shouted, 'Not now,' before slamming down the receiver.

Father Doyle came from the window. He sat down and leaned on the edge of the desk opposite Cooper

'There were five identical contracts over two years.'

He lifted one document. 'Here's a bill of lading, the first delivery, the first contract, described as pallets of agricultural equipment and loaded at Setubal, Portugal. The port of destination is shown as, not El Salvador, but Umm Qasr. That's in Iraq. The value on the manifest is one hundred and eighty million dollars. There were all kinds of controls, sanctions and arms embargoes imposed against both Iraq and Iran at the time. Purina was Guzman's company; he was henchman to Colonel Ponce, the then Army Chief of Staff in El Salvador at the time. He appeared to divide the sixty million between three other companies and himself. I don't know whose companies they were, but you may.'

He pointed down at three British Virgin Island companies.

'These I suspect were Guzman's colleagues' companies. Foss and Natural Island were both owned by Atlantic Santos Holdings, and controlled from your office in Rio de Janeiro.'

He pointed to the file. 'This was all a lie to get around the sanctions, and the various embargoes and Guzman is threatening to reveal everything, isn't he? That's why you're helping him.'

Cooper looked up. His voice was resigned, distressed. 'Where did you get these?'

Father Doyle raised his eyebrows but didn't respond.

Cooper pursed his lips, sighed, and leaned back in his chair looking to the ceiling. He protested, but it was only for form. His eyes closed, and he breathed out slowly.

Doyle abruptly recognised the need to confess a burden that had been carried too long, and that the desire to acknowledge culpability was suddenly too strong. A cathartic moment had been reached.

The voice came from another place, as though disconnected, taking Cooper to a time and reality he had tried to erase but failed. His eyes were still closed, and he leaned back in his chair.

'Latin America in the eighties. The debt crisis - it was a bloodbath. There was no investment and negative growth. Then in '82 Mexico defaulted. It was a disaster, and things only eventually started to recover around '89. We were going under.'

He loosened his tie but continued staring at the ceiling. Father Doyle was just a spectator in this confessional.

'As you said, the company and my father were based in Rio, it was scorched earth there at the time, so many established businesses were disappearing. I was still in London running PileUp Records with Roisin. We were having a ball. It was the most fantastic, bizarre time.'

He looked over toward Doyle. His eyes were wet. He brushed his hand across his face before continuing.

'Then my father had a stroke when I was with him in London trying to raise finance to get the company through. I had to go over there and help. There were extensive landholdings both in Brazil and in El Salvador, mostly sugar and coffee. The money America was pumping in certainly helped, but it wasn't enough, we were effectively finished because we were over-extended and there was no liquidity to bail us out. Three generations of the family business going down the tube. Then Guzman was introduced.'

He shook his head and looked at Doyle.

'He'd done his research. He knew our position. The families who run the country had accumulated overseas holdings, mostly in the US and so they could ride the storm.'

He pointed at the file.

'They didn't want to get involved with this deal.'

'But we were exposed. Guzman knew that. He came with a plan - fully formed. Contracts, shipping, end-users. Everything was set. All we had to do was create the offshore companies, process the documentation, transfer the funds. It was so easy. Too easy. Of course, I checked him out, who he was, and more important who was behind him.'

Father asked, 'You knew what you were doing? Selling arms. Breaking embargoes, sanctions.'

There was a flash of anger, soon replaced by resignation.

'Of course. But I checked first with some American officials I knew at the Embassy in San Salvador. They just looked the other way. Some for political reasons, as Reagan was anxious for the stalemate between Iran and Iraq to continue. Some for more mercenary reasons, and after all the money came from the US. Saddam was cash-strapped after years of conflict. The funds came through a loan to Iraq from an Italian bank based in Atlanta. The American Department of Agriculture backed it: almost five billion dollars. In the scheme of things, we were small-change.'

'Five deliveries. Around nine-hundred-million dollars of small change.'

Cooper nodded. 'We survived because of it.'

He paused and looked at Father Doyle - his voice contemptuous.

'We ended up with around one hundred and fifty million dollars.'

'And Guzman?'

'He was Salvador's point man. Sixty million dollars on each contract. He paid off the three others.'

'Who?'

'Not certain. The current Minister of Defence General Ponce certainly, he was Chief of Staff at the time. Probably also the then Minister of Defence and the President I would guess.'

Cooper rose and walked to the window, looking at the sky and then down to the ground forty-eight floors below.

'And he has threatened to expose you. That's why you're helping him?'

'I've no choice. We wouldn't survive an investigation. If there ever is one of course. I suspect nobody cares anymore. But the company's name would be ruined.'

'But why St Mary's?'

'He's taking steps to stay here in the UK. The donation will help him get residency. He must find a country where he feels safe. He's currently finalising the purchase of an estate in Sussex. He can then install his security and feel safe there.'

'Why does he need security? Safe from what?'

Cooper raised his eyebrows.

Father Doyle suddenly understood although he had only got there slowly. 'The last sixty million he kept for himself. That's why he can't go back. I was warned that he was being pursued.'

Cooper's agreement came quietly. 'There are people who want revenge, and they are searching for him. That's why he wants - and needs - security. How did you know? Who told you?'

'I'm not sure who sent the warning. It came through a strange route,' he said, remembering the priest from Nottingham.

The telephone rang. Cooper answered it, 'Could you apologise and let the trustees know I will be with them shortly?'

He turned to Father Doyle. 'I'm ashamed of what I did. I had to stay over there. It broke up my marriage. Roisin couldn't accept what happened. But the damage those weapons caused lives with me to this day.'

He picked up the papers. 'With respect, John. I don't think you arrived at this information without help?'

'I had assistance. Two ex-army guys. One of them, Ray Lancaster, you may have come across at The Mission.'

'Impressive.'

Doyle nodded. 'We can't take his money.'

Cooper nodded. 'I know. But we do need it. Especially now.'

* * *

John found Roger sitting up in bed, head swathed in bandages, a plaster cast on his arm, his mood indomitable. Stuart sat in a chair beside him, immediately John walked in Roger started with questions about The Mission.

Stuart rolled his eyes and got up, 'I'm just off to get a coffee.' He kissed Roger on the cheek and left the small ward.

'The trustees meeting?' inquired Roger suddenly more serious. 'What happened this afternoon?'

'As you know Jeremy Keswick has resigned. Dan Cooper stood in as interim chair. Guzman's offer has been rejected. It seems Guzman did not pick St Mary's for any philanthropic reason. He had a history with Cooper and is desperate to stay in the UK. The donation to St Mary's was intended to help him gain residency. A fig leaf of respectability and integrity to protect some political decision makers. After a short discussion, it was decided that it would not be in the church's interests to accept his money. Cooper was instrumental in the rejection.'

He paused. 'The trustees have also asked me to request that you become the new chair of trustees.'

Roger's mouth fell open. He was momentarily too astonished to speak.

John continued, 'I insisted there was nobody better equipped to carry forward the hopes and dreams for The Mission and the new hostel. Cooper backed me up strongly.'

'What about the Bishop? You know how he feels.'

'You misjudge him. He cautioned that some of our more traditional parishioners might be offended. But he agreed we couldn't find anyone as committed. It was unanimous.'

Roger paused. 'I'm no sort of administrator. You know that John.'

'There is nobody who could do this better, Roger, surely you see that?'

'We all see other people clearer than ourselves.'

As the words hung in the air, Father Doyle stroked his clerical collar, knowing their meaning but avoiding the understanding.

'John, I have to think about it.' Roger frowned, 'That presupposes there will be a Mission after the attack. Currently, we've only a broken building. The insurance won't cover everything. I've been on to the brokers, and we were under-insured. And without Guzman's money, tainted though it is ...' He shook his head.

'The Mission will be sponsored and financed by AS Index. The same amount Guzman would have donated, and all the building repair costs.'

'What is AS Index?'

'It's Cooper's company, based at Canary Wharf, so it is local. Financial voodoo of some sort.'

'That's fantastic.' Roger fell back on his pillows. 'You know I'll do it. And thanks for sorting out whatever you've sorted out.'

He frowned again. 'Now the details, please. Why did Cooper do this?'

Father Doyle shook his head. 'That was and will remain part of the deal. I can't say any more.'

Roger laughed. 'I probably wouldn't understand it anyway.'

He paused. 'Is Consuela still missing?'

John nodded

'Find her, John.' He closed his eyes. 'Find her.'

He fell asleep in seconds.

* * *

Mrs Quinn called out when he got back to his office.

'Father, there's a call from a Monseigneur Flavio Bianchi.'

John's face lightened. He smiled at his memories of Rome when a student - standing on the rails at Capannelle racecourse with Flavio who rarely won but lost with gusto. Just as the Salesian Brother lived the rest of his life. Eating, drinking, praying, debating, and singing. His hope one day was to sing at his beloved La Scala in Milan. There was no pause button, his big heart was forever worn on his sleeve, and his friendship was a bottomless pit bounded with joy, laughter, and ever-present compassion. They had kept in touch as Flavio rose through the Catholic bureaucracy.

'John. I'm in London. I have two hours before I meet the Archbishop. Canterbury that is. He's delayed on a train somewhere. Can I come over? We haven't seen each other for too long.'

'Where are you?'

'Outside your church.'

John laughed. It was so typical. He made his way to the church door and looked down the steps. Flavio was just over five feet tall and as broad. His bald head glistened from the morning sun as he staggered toward the church shaking his head and hauling a thick battered briefcase. Flavio dropped the briefcase and hugged John before pushing him away and frowning.

John saw Mrs Quinn looking from the office window.

'Where is the smile, John?' He grabbed his briefcase and pulled John's arm toward the church. John sat down in a pew at the rear of the church. He felt his ever-present unease wash over him again before touching Flavio's arm.

'First, Monseigneur? When was this?'

Flavio's laugh echoed around the building.'

'Rome, John. Rome. I stayed long enough and didn't run naked through St Peters. The triumph of mediocrity.'

John looked sceptical and raised his eyebrows. He knew Flavio's theological articles were much admired and he had contributed to several encyclicals.

'You're seeing the Archbishop?'

'I'm with the Council for Promoting Christian Unity. At present, anyway. For a little bit longer.'

'And then ...?'

'Away from Rome. I've been there too long. It bores me now. Even talking about it bores me. But you.' His gesture took in the church, the building. 'Here.' He turned back to John. 'You are troubled. I know you, John. Tell me.'

They moved to John's office. John spoke softly.

'Flavio, do you come as a friend or a member of the curia?'

'A friend, I hope. Always a friend, John. Why would it be otherwise?'

'Cardinal Trujillo seeks to influence us. I wondered ...?'

He left the sentence unfinished.

'Trujillo runs his empire in his own cruel way. We do not all agree with the path he has chosen. I assure you I know nothing of this.'

John closed his eyes, leaned across and touched Flavio's arm. 'Forgive me, my friend.'

'I think there is more,' said Flavio and then sat back and listened. He was eventually more than two hours late for the Archbishop of Canterbury. He called and claimed he was held up, while he heard John tell him of Consuela, Guzman, Jorge, the Jesuit priests, Cardinal Trujillo. It poured out as though a pipe had burst. Flavio was someone who listened without judgement, whose silence was enough as John emptied out his joy and his anguish.

Flavio took a handkerchief from his pocket and wiped his forehead. His voice was sombre.

'Those murders still cause such sorrow. They were outstanding priests, gentle souls, and it was a tragedy and an unforgivable sin. I do not excuse that crime. I'm sorry you believe I could. But there is more, John? You are troubled.'

The afternoon passed.

Flavio eventually left.

John sat back, exhausted. The very act of speaking had released a weight he had been carrying for too long.

* * *

Dan Cooper closed the door to his Stanhope Gate apartment in Mayfair. The day had been a bastard. He had visited times he'd long wanted to forget, As he slumped down in a chair and looked through the full length window overlooking Hyde Park his mobile rang. The caller was Carlos Oliveira, Atlantic Santos's banker in Rio.

Somebody was running. Heavy beathing, traffic noise. Shouts.

A fractured voice came, 'Daniel …' More heavy breathing running. Cooper could feel the panic. 'Daniel. I am so sorry. I couldn't …' He stopped and there was silence. There was more running. Then a moment of stillness. He jumped as a shot rang out. The phone sounded like it clattered to the ground. A moment later the line was disconnected.

He called back.

Not available.

He held his head in his hands. Carlos was a friend and had given Dan great support over the years. He called his own office in Rio and asked them to find out if they could contact Oliveira's bank and check out if he was OK.

It was three in the morning when his office called and told him Carlos's body had been dumped in Santa Marta. He had been tortured.

# THIRTY

Cooper put the phone down.

Rosa had reported that all traces of the Panamanian and British Virgin Island companies and their bank accounts had been removed. If someone were determined, they might follow a trail but who would bother? It was over.

Guzman's threats were empty. He should have done this before but had tried to lock that time away. In a safe and inaccessible place.

Guzman had been trying to get hold of him again, but he had refused all the man's calls. The blast of anger and irrational ferocity was more than he was prepared to face, at the moment. He knew there would be no choice in that, shortly, but it could wait.

He looked out from the window of his office. St Mary's lay somewhere beneath, amid the urban sprawl now hidden from view although never far from his thoughts.

Father John's intervention had forced him to confront memories kept hidden even from himself. He had carefully constructed an existence that deleted the wreckage through which he had waded to save the company.

A history so painstakingly assembled that he had almost become to believe it himself.

Only the unexpected arrival of Guzman from Spain had splintered the screen through which he was content to view, dispassionately, the time that shamed him.

The screen had shattered as Father John carefully elaborated a truth he had worked so hard to forget. There had been nowhere to hide, and nothing but shame to keep him company throughout the subsequent night spent in his London apartment. He needed to reconcile himself to the truth now confronting him, the truth he had to face for the first time in many years.

The call from Carlos and his murder was almost too much. The man had been a true friend. A friendship carved in desperate times when the Brazilian had put his own bank at risk by supporting Dan and Atlantic Santos. He had spoken with Carlos only two days ago about meeting up in Paris in two weeks when Oliveira was coming to Europe with his wife for their wedding anniversary.

He had called Roisin, still his best friend, and spoken with Mat, his son. Their voices had reassured him and provided a sense of decency. It was little enough but it brought some relief.

The phone rang again, although he had asked for all calls to be held.

He snatched up the receiver.

His secretary explained, 'I'm sorry, but it's from San Salvador. He said it is important and mentioned Senor Guzman. I thought you would want to know.'

He leaned back in his chair. 'Put him through.'

Rosa came into his office.

'Yes.'

He recognised the accent from his time in Central America: rhythmic but brusque. A voice unaccustomed to being interrupted, the flow certain, arrogant.

'Don't bother asking my name, Mr Cooper. That's not relevant. Just know that I represent various influential people here in El Salvador. We are aware that you are working with Colonel Guzman. We know exactly where he is. We know the hotel he is staying in. Listen carefully. As you know, there is a debt to pay.'

Cooper started to speak, but he was overridden.

'Don't interrupt.' It was a military command. Cooper fell silent.

'Guzman was our colleague. He was a trusted colleague. He betrayed our trust – that is not something we forgive.'

'We? Who are we?'

'Selective memory, Mr Cooper. You know the answer. The same people who did your bidding before decommissioning in 1992. We still exist. We do not accept betrayal. Atlacatl was a philosophy, not just a battalion, Guzman is our problem, we know where he is staying, and he will be dealt with shortly.'

Cooper stayed silent. Blood, murder, torture - a philosophy! It was a distorted world. But then perhaps he had encouraged it by his own sins of omission.

'The money, that is your problem Mr Cooper. We know how much you made from dealing with us. You might have paid Guzman, we don't care, you owe us our money and you will pay.'

'I owe nothing.'

The voice continued as though he hadn't spoken.

'As I said Guzman is our concern. His fate is settled, yours is a matter for you. Pay what you owe, and your life continues. Refuse and your life will change. Your family's life will change. Your business here will be destroyed. The Battalion has been discontinued but it still carries on. You understand me? That is your decision. Call me on this number when you are ready to pay.' He read out a number.

'I owe you nothing. Whatever was owed is paid ...' The line had disconnected.

Rosa was listening.

'What the hell?'

'I was out there. The Atlactl Battalion was made up of psychopaths. Their massacres were horrible. Guzman was in charge of most of them. They will kill him for this.'

'How much?'

'Forty-five million US dollars.'

'Where the hell do we find that?'

'It's possible with a lot of pain.'

'Guzman owes it, not you.'

'They're going to kill him. There's no doubt of that. That's why he's planning all the security and needs to find somewhere he can get himself safe.'

Pause.

'They must be on their way now.'

'How did they find out all the details of your involvement?'

'Carlos Oliveira. It must have been. Tortured! Because of me.'

'How would they find Guzman's whereabouts so precisely?'

'I don't know.'

'If we can get to him. We have to make him pay the money. He must still have it.'

'And more. He's sitting on a pot of over 120 million.'

'Then he has to pay. Get to him before they do and persuade him.'

'I'm going to call Doyle. See if those two soldiers are still around. They may be able to help.'

* * *

Consuela stared out of the window. Lopez had left for the evening, wandering off a few minutes ago. Guzman's car was still in the non-parking area.

He was going nowhere tonight.

Josef Perez had called. They were on their way from El Salvador and arriving early tomorrow. Three of them. When they arrived, they would go to the embassy and wait for Perez to tell them when Guzman was secure.

When they got to the hotel, Josef and herself would leave Guzman to them.

There was no other choice. She told herself that. She almost convinced herself.

It was Guzman or her. She would not survive if he existed. She would run again and disappear. She could. But those days were over. Here in this place with these people, she would finish it.

John may not forgive her. She accepted that. That was the risk.

Perez had other motives. Purer, cleaner. The death of his son was the abiding moment that coloured his life. The guilt was too much for him to live with – he believed Guzman's death would make up for the moment when he saw Raul's life bleed out on the street.

Consuela felt sure he was wrong. But when she picked up Jorge's cedula, his ID and touched her brother's photograph, she wasn't sure.

In any event, the decision was made, and she clung to the belief that they would not be carrying out the act. That was for others. It was a belief she knew to be false. But it allowed her some respite.

* * *

Darkness had drawn in. Canary Wharf, the financial centre, never really slept but it did slumber. That was now. Some windows were bright, but most were dark as Tavinor and Lancaster walked into Dan Cooper's boardroom. Lancaster's bulk overshadowed Tavinor's wiry lean muscularity.

Dan Cooper explained that John Doyle had said they might be able to help him.

Tavinor was non-committal. He talked of their respective army careers but was not sure it was what Cooper needed.

Dan Cooper sat alongside Rosa with Tony Tavinor and Ray Lancaster in chairs opposite. He spoke to Tavinor. It was instinctive, Tavinor has assumed command of the situation as soon as he arrived. His placid expression belied a tension that sparked about him, his eyes betraying an intensity which invited attention and caution at the same time.

'So, let me be clear,' said Tavinor after Cooper explained what was happening. 'It is alleged that Guzman owes forty-five million dollars. The caller claimed that there were operators on the way here to kill Guzman as an act of revenge and the killers would likely be drawn from Guzman's ex-colleagues. However, they do not look to Guzman to repay what they owe. That would not satisfy their need for retribution. His betrayal cannot be bought off. It diminished their esprit de corps, or some such bullshit, and cannot be allowed to stand. For the money, they look to you? Have I got it correct?'

Cooper nodded.

'Questions. One, do you know how many operators are coming over? Did he give any indication at all?'

'Only operators, so more than one.'

'OK. Two at least. Can you repay the money?'

'With difficulty, I could.'

'Three, can Guzman repay the money, if he was persuaded?'

'Yes. I know he has more than one hundred million available. We carried out due diligence when he applied for a visa.'

'So, what are *we* doing here. What precisely do you want from us?'

Cooper wanted to think through his answer. The penetrating gaze from Tavinor deterred him from prevarication, but in truth, he was uncertain. To keep Mat and Roisin safe, he would pay the money. Did he want to give them any of the money? No. Were there options?

Before he could say anything, Tavinor spoke quietly, almost too softly to be heard. It was as though he knew what Cooper was thinking.

'You are conflicted. I understand. So I am assuming, in the final analysis, you will pay whatever money is necessary to protect your family?'

Cooper nodded.

'But understandably you would rather not. OK. Guzman wants to stay alive, but what you tell me about him he is likely to resist, and those coming for him will be well trained and equipped and extremely dangerous. There are questions, of course, as to how they know he is here and his precise whereabouts.'

Cooper nodded again.

'But those questions are for another time. So we must get to Guzman before these goons and persuade him to pay what he owes. Whether direct or through you is irrelevant. He can then make his security arrangements after we dump the thugs somewhere a long way off.'

'If Guzman refuses to play ball?'

'We'll make him an offer he can't refuse.'

'What does that mean?'

'It means he gets the good news that we will hand him over and send him on his way with his ex-colleagues. If that happens, you will have to make some important decisions. I don't see that happening though. This bastard doesn't have a death wish whatever crap he comes up with.'

He paused and looked around.

'That is the only option it appears to me. Get to Guzman. Make him safe, at least for a time, and persuade him to pay the money he owes. It may be difficult, but I don't have any other suggestions. Any better ideas?'

He looked around again. Nobody spoke.

'OK.'

He nodded at Ray Lancaster, 'We'll get to work. We must have reinforcements. The two of us can't handle this. We'll get onto the circuit tonight and first thing tomorrow to see if anyone is available for a couple of days work. I'll be offering large bonuses.'

He looked at Cooper, who nodded.

'Whatever you need.'

'Rosa could you get hold of a building we can use to speak with Guzman and house the goons? An unused warehouse would be ideal, secluded if possible. Also, a couple of Transit sized vans and at least ten phones. Burners, untraceable.'

He looked to Ray Lancaster.

'OK. We do this?'

Lancaster nodded. A satisfied smile flickered across his face.

'I suggest we meet here tomorrow at twelve hundred. If anything happens before then, there's nothing to be done. There's no way we'll be ready before then.'

# THIRTY-ONE

Consuela was ready.

She had been ready all day.

Guzman hadn't moved yet.

She stared at Tower Bridge, the sun throwing dramatic shadows across the river as it ambled past, stroked by a warm morning breeze.

The gently flowing water jogged her conscience.

Demanded answers to questions she had given up on asking.

There was no other choice.

The El Salvador team has called Perez – they had arrived and were going to their embassy. There were three of them. They would wait for Perez's call before coming to the hotel.

Her room was already clear, apart from two bags placed by the door.

She checked into the daypack picked up from the church. The iron bar was there and the syringes. It wasn't right. It was inevitable.

She stared through the window.

Lopez didn't move.

* * *

Tavinor and Lancaster arrived at Cooper's office promptly at 12.00. Three tall, solid, and imposing men accompanied them. Tavinor indicated chairs in the empty reception area for them. Rosa came from Cooper's office.

'The office is clear for the moment. We've closed up for a security inspection,' said Rosa.

She looked toward the three figures sitting in the chairs and looked enquiringly at Tavinor. He said nothing. They followed her into the boardroom. Dan Cooper was already seated at one end on the large table. He put the phone down as everyone sat down.

Tavinor started without any introduction.

'When we speak about what is about to happen today, there are certain enforced assumptions we are obliged to make, and that relates to how many we are facing and our own strength. Let us assume there are at least two operators and possibly up to four. Ideally, I would like three on each for pacification, and three to get Guzman clear and of course we may have to take care of Lopez, his driver, who I understand has military experience.'

He gestured toward Lancaster. 'Ray has got three ex-colleagues waiting in your lobby. I've managed to get hold of two. These are capable guys, but we have no idea of their current status. So that's seven of us. We are at least eleven short.

'So another assumption we will make is that when Guzman is in his room, he'll stay there, but we'll keep a watch on hotel exits, and Lopez to make sure, but we can't watch his room until he's under threat, we haven't the capability for that. When the boyos arrive, we deal with them. Subdue them and take them with us to the location Rosa has arranged. However, that decision will depend on circumstances. Remember no plan survives the first contact, and in this case, we're under-resourced so we must be quick on our feet. No proper comms, of course, but Rosa has made available some mobiles.'

Cooper asked, 'What do you mean deal with them?'

'Pacify them. When the money situation is sorted out,

however it's sorted, we let them loose. Guzman must take his chances after. If he doesn't co-operate, they can take him. If he does, we drop them a few hundred miles away. I had in mind Liverpool. They will have no reason to come after you. In any event you should sort out some ongoing security in your operation. But that's for another time.'

Rosa spoke up. 'We have two of our drivers who have volunteered. They're driving the two vans you asked for and are waiting in our basement parking area.'

'Good. The situation has been explained to them?'

'They know roughly. They'll be fine. Young lads, but solid and a big bonus for the day. They have the route to the warehouse.'

'OK. My two guys are currently at the hotel watching the access and exit points of which there are two main ones. The lobby and a rear service bay situated beneath the hotel.'

He produced a sheet of paper.

'Here are the numbers for the phones Rosa got hold of for us. Names are alongside each number. Dan, you said you know the manager, so I want you there to keep him onside if necessary.'

'I've agreed that we will not take any actions in public areas that could alarm the guests.'

Tavinor frowned. He paused.

'That's the aim. We will, however, be attempting to pacify possibly four goons, who could be armed. We may not be making the rules. Are you clear on that? We will do all we can.'

He looked around the boardroom. 'Anything further?'

Rosa spoke, 'The warehouse has been opened and is empty. It's very secluded.'

'Good. OK. So, we get over to the hotel and wait. I'll be in the coffee shop. Dan, I want you with me. Ray will be in command of the rest of the team and will make the calls, as necessary. Ray, where do you want everyone?'

'I'll have five with me. Two are watching the hotel now. That leaves the three in the lobby, outside. We'll get to the hotel as soon as we've finished here. The vans can wait on the road down the side of the hotel. If parking plod comes around, they can go round the block. We always need them on call.

'We'll keep one of the guys with eyes on Lopez. At the right time he needs to be controlled, if necessary. There's no way we want him going crazy if he sees Guzman under attack. We'll have to improvise that situation as it plays out. That leaves five of us and Tony in reserve. The two there now will maintain a watch at both entrances, service and lobby. The service entrance appears to have staff coming and going but nobody of interest as yet. Tony will be in the coffee shop which has eyes on the car park area where Lopez is currently parked. I will be with two guys around the embankment, moving around, so we're not conspicuous but available to move when needed. The two at the entrances will join us as soon as we identify where the threat is coming from.

'Rosa arranged through your man at the hotel to have Guzman's suite checked out. There's no indication he's planning to leave. Also, we've had a chance to check through the guests, and nobody stood out. He's there now. Lopez is sitting in the car. If he leaves, there's nothing we can do but another assumption we have to make is that they will come for him at the hotel. You said the contact said they knew where he was staying?'

Cooper nodded. 'He did say that.'

'So, if he leaves, we just wait on his return. Then we lay up until the action starts.'

Tavinor took over.

'When they get here, we let them get to Guzman's floor and take them there. The advantage we have is surprise. That's the only advantage. So six of us have to take them down, as quietly and quickly as possible. Maximum speed, maximum violence. We put them down, and we do it fast. Weapons – we know they may be armed but let's hope as they're in a hotel and they won't be anticipating opposition until they get to Guzman, any weapons will be concealed and not immediately available. His room is on the fourth floor. There are two ways up. Service stairs, they may get noticed there, so likely will use the lift, but we'll be ready at the stairs. I will advise which route they're taking. If it's the stairs, we take them there. If it's the lift, we hit them as soon as the doors open before they have a chance to organise.'

He leaned into a holdall on the floor.

'These may help.' He pulled up two plastic weapons.

'X26 tasers. One of the guys brought them back from Iraq. The US marines used them over there. Only four cartridges but should be enough.'

Dan Cooper asked. 'Are they legal?'

There was silence. Tavinor's eyes narrowed as he stared at Cooper. He said nothing.

'OK,' Cooper responded. 'I get it. I know what I'm asking you to do, and I appreciate it.'

Ray Lancaster continued. 'When they're subdued, we get them down the service stairs, through the bay into one of the vans. We have to hope there's no-one around. We've got some heavy-duty zip-ties for restraint in the vans. Ankles and wrists and we gag them. Three of our guys will stay with them and get them straight off to the warehouse.'

'The rest of us deal with Guzman. We have a house key, so we get him and persuade him to join us. He's the least of our problems. Once we get in there the game is over. OK. Let's go. We get there and wait. It could be a while until anything happens.'

* * *

Lopez's head occasionally dropped forward in tiredness. He would then open the car door and walk up and down the embankment for a few minutes.

Consuela watched him closely. Her scrutiny suddenly faltered as she was sure she saw Ray Lancaster walking slowly along the embankment. He was distinctive, big, black hair cut short, imposing. He disappeared behind a group of Japanese tourists just as the car door opened. By the time Lopez had lit a cigarette while leaning against the bonnet of the car, the figure she thought was Ray had vanished.

It was late afternoon when Lopez suddenly came alive as he picked up the car telephone and listened. The routine was established; Consuela knew it well by now.

She hurried down the service stairs leading to the rear of the hotel. Pulling on a crash helmet, she kept close behind a couple of housekeeping staff clocking out. Kick-starting the moped, she moved slowly behind a pillar from where she could watch the car.

Guzman emerged from the hotel. He bent down towards the rear door and, without speaking to Lopez, got in the back seat.

Consuela slipped into the line of traffic some fifty yards behind the black limousine as it pulled smoothly up the slope leaving Tower Bridge behind. They skirted City Airport, keeping close to the north bank of the River Thames. Twenty minutes away from the hotel, the traffic became lighter. Consuela fell further back to maintain a safe distance. They kept close to the river. The road was now almost empty. Darkness had crept in almost unnoticed since few of the streetlights were working. They were travelling through an industrial estate, although most of its factories and warehouses were empty and boarded up. Finally, the limousine slowed and came to a halt. Consuela pulled in alongside the porch of a small factory that had once produced T-shirts but was now derelict. She pushed the moped well out of sight and waited.

Climbing out of the car, Lopez leaned back against the bonnet to look up and down the empty roadway. Consuela eased further back behind the corner of the factory. A white van passed along the road before stopping beside the limousine. Footsteps sounded, steel-tipped boots banging on stone slabs. Five of them heads shaved, jeans and braces, swaggered toward the car over a patch of waste ground.

She recognised Brigid Kelly's son, and could just hear the voices as they spoke.

'About time. We want our money.' Kelly looked around at his

friends, legs spread wide, ready for action before moving closer to the car. Intolerant faces, angry voices.

They gathered around Lopez. He remained with his back to the car but didn't move. She strained to hear his voice. 'You didn't get her out of circulation. You didn't scare her off. She just laughed at you.'

Her mouth dropped open.

Kelly's voice didn't waver. He pushed Lopez on the shoulder. 'We trashed the fucking Mission, that was the deal, and we scared the faggot priest.'

'She laughed at you,' retorted Lopez accusingly.

Kelly banged his fist on the vehicle's rear window. 'You said she was an easy target. So where did those two hoods come from? We would have gone equipped.'

He kicked out at the front door panel. Lopez just stood there impassively, eyes showing no emotion.

Kelly shouted, 'We had to get a new windscreen.'

Lopez laughed. Trapped in their inadequacy and sense of corrupt omnipotence they couldn't hear anything above their own words dipped in vitriol, echoing ever to the sound of marching jackboots. Had they looked closely at Lopez their cold straining eyes would not have seen fear but contempt. They didn't look closely enough.

'Fucking give us what you owe us, you fucking spic bastard.' Kelly launched another kick at the car, then pressed closer to Lopez.

The others fell in behind, their faces sneeringly confident that they would soon feel the exquisite relief that came from both inflicting pain and getting what they demanded.

For a moment, Kelly hesitated, but for a split second only. His aroused eyes momentarily detected a coldness that he had not encountered before. Where was the fear he expected? There was nothing, just his shouting voice bouncing back without effect. The pause soon ended because he had nothing with which to understand.

'I said, give us our money.'

He moved closer to the car and kicked again at the rear door. Lopez remained silent. Suddenly that door flew open, catching Kelly in the stomach and doubling him up. Lopez grabbed the boy's drooping head and pulled it violently into his knee. Blood spurted onto the kerb. Lopez released his grip, and the inert body slipped to the pavement. The other four figures moved in to give help. This was new, it had happened too fast; they only had time to see blood start trickling along the pavement.

Guzman hauled himself from the car. The barrel of a 9mm Beretta pointed toward them. He said nothing, they froze. Their glances shifted from the moaning body lying on the ground to the gun, pointing at their heads. It was like a silent film, no words spoken; they were suddenly confronted with the reality of fear instead of the domination they sought, and they had no words to ease the confusion. Lopez stamped on the writhing, helpless figure again as they tried to summon up the courage to help their friend. They barely mustered a movement, however, ending as soon as it began. Kelly tried to rise from the pavement, his friends' scared, shameful eyes meeting his. They retreated transfixed at the sight of the weapon pointing at them. Guzman's laughing eyes derided them, inviting them to stupidity, offering them the path of self-sacrifice. The massive figure suddenly darted forward, the swiftness of the movement was chilling and unexpected. He grabbed the nearest skinhead by the neck, forcing his head back. The barrel of the gun tore teeth apart, forcing its way into the choking mouth. Guzman laughed and dragged the struggling victim closer to his friends as they watched in horror.

Guzman pulled the gun from the skinhead's mouth and then kneed the figure violently in the groin. He fell, screaming to the floor. Eyes were wide, urine leaking onto the pavement. The rolling hum of traffic from a nearby main road was muffled. Tin cans could be heard being kicked along an adjacent street. The soft sound of milk bottles clinking together came from far off. Some distance away, a door slammed.

Darkness now filled the night, silence painting a hesitant

foreboding in fearful minds. It was all anticipation and incipient horror.

Lopez stamped on Kelly's head.

His friends looked, then quickly turned away. The invitation to share the pain still stood, but instead, they ran. Guzman gave an almost silent snort of derision, which subsumed immediately into Kelly's terrified scream.

Lopez walked round to the open driver's door and slipped inside. Guzman did the same through the rear door. He looked ahead, ignoring the writhing, distorted, body lying on the pavement. The car started up and drove away without any urgency. Consuela breathed in deeply and cautiously pulled out behind the vehicle, staying some distance back. A few minutes later they passed an approaching ambulance, its siren blaring, blue lights flashing onto impassive faces.

* * *

Father John Doyle sat in his darkened office. Consuela's absence had given the demand to reconcile his life fresh impetus. She had drifted from him, and he ached for her.

He still recited the words:

*Hail Mary, full of grace.*

*The Lord is with thee.*

*Blessed art thou amongst women,*

*and blessed is the fruit of thy womb, Jesus.*

And so many more. Old friends who had fallen on hard times.

He lowered his head. What had she hidden from him? What words could explain this desolation? All he knew now, in the relentless panic, was that he was losing something too precious and doubted he had the means to survive the loss. There had been no training to cope with this, no warnings given.

What was life? He felt such anger at the deceit. They had sucked out his spirit to feed ageing and penitent hearts.

Wandering deaf and blind, but never without the words that

enticed the innocent toward the darkness. The faithful thought they glimpsed the gateway to salvation, but they only saw his blindness, mistook it for sanctity, and they followed.

Looking over at the bookcase, his expression was calm, belying all the turmoil that raged within, echoing amongst the discordant sounds and voices shrieking in his ear; raging, soaring, crashing. His mouth felt dry. He licked gritted lips.

He swept the books from their shelves. They fell haphazardly across the floor.

All that had gone before had been a charade. Could he now save something, anything, from the wreckage?

John walked over the books scattered about the floor and opened the door. Another door opened along the corridor, but John wasn't listening as he walked into the church.

He took a candle and lit it, its pale glow shining onto the statue of Christ. John whispered Consuela's name as he lit another candle, and then another.

* * *

Guzman's car retraced its route back toward the hotel.

After about ten minutes it pulled over to the side. There were a few pubs and one or two shops scattered along the neglected road that lay only a few minutes' walk from St Mary's.

Cars slowed and waited as mini-skirted prostitutes ran from the shadows and negotiated through open windows. Some got in, others shouted abuse and returned to the shadows as the vehicles accelerated away.

The obese figure clambered out of the rear door when the vehicle stopped. He started walking along the litter-strewn pavement. Lopez continued driving slowly alongside him. The road was quiet, Consuela stayed carefully invisible, her lights extinguished, about a hundred yards behind.

He stumped further along the road, his legs rolling awkwardly.

The car crawled along next to the kerb beside him.

She was blonde, standing in a doorway that she had lingered in for too many nights.

Guzman stopped.

Her smile was nervous.

The car also stopped.

Although she saw a coldness in his eyes, her hand beckoned him nearer. It was a long night without work so far and would be a cold start without money tomorrow.

He came toward her and then turned to his driver with a sharp, persistent pointing of the fingers of his right hand. The driver's door opened as Guzman continued looking her up and down.

A shiver ran down inside her. Cold, hard fear welled up but was pushed aside.

The driver spoke with his mouth almost touching her ear. It was just a whisper. 'Fifty pounds.'

The man had an accent; she remained silent.

Consuela watched the scene, drifting away from the reality of the moment and into a world of remembrance and pain. Indistinct figures were speaking in a far-off place. She waited but knew that the time for waiting was over. She remembered other faces, of the dead, and disappeared. Guzman's face joined the gallery, forever sneering and laughing at her.

The prostitute smiled at Lopez.

Perhaps he thought the smile was a tacit refusal. 'One hundred pounds.'

Looking again at Guzman, she knew that he would hurt her. It was part instinct and part experience.

She also desperately needed the money.

Lopez pulled a roll of notes from his pocket, counted out two fifty-pound notes and then walked away toward the car, stopping only to whisper in Guzman's ear as he approached the frail figure who turned, not willing to face him yet.

* * *

Time passed.

Lopez was slumped in the driver's seat. Smoke filtered through the open window.

Consuela waited beside her moped about a hundred yards back and at the side of a kebab takeaway.

Lopez received a call. He opened the door and ran inside the block of flats. He called out, panic evident in his voice. 'Colonel.'

Consuela phoned Perez.

'He's been warned. They'll be on the way back in a moment.'

'Can you get there before them?'

'Yes. The traffic's backed up. I'll make it easily.'

Guzman stomped from the alley.

The blonde figure followed.

Her blouse was torn, her skirt twisted to one side. She clutched a piece of cloth against an ever, darkening eye.

'Bastard.'

Guzman headed quickly toward the car where Lopez already had the engine running. When he turned back, she stopped following, her legs suddenly weak again. She wanted confrontation but could not face him.

'Bastard.' Her voice was quiet, eyes wide, as he looked her up and down but said nothing. Stooping down, he eased his gross frame through the open rear door and slid into the seat. The door closed behind him.

'Bastard.'

Uncovering her blood-encrusted eye, she aimed a kick at the car door, just far enough away to miss it.

'Bastard.'

The limousine drove away. A few eyes followed her as she stumbled back into the doorway.

'Bastard,' she repeated under her breath, pulling the cardigan closer around her. She wouldn't go back inside there, not yet.

'Patsy, over here.'

Liz was about six feet tall with dyed blonde hair, wearing a black, leather miniskirt and bright-green silk blouse. She held out a tissue and gestured toward Patsy's eye.

'He looked a real creep.'

'Fat fucking, bastard.' Patsy dabbed at the swelling bruise under her right eye. 'I'm going to take a walk, get away from here for a bit.'

'Are you sure you're all right? I could come to the hospital with you.'

'What's the point, Liz? Who gives a shit? The bruises will fade. I just want to get away for a few hours. God, he was disgusting.'

'I'll call in tomorrow, check you're all right,' offered Liz.

As she walked slowly along the street, a car pulled up alongside.

A voice came through the open window, 'Here, darling.'

Her answer hissed from the corner of her mouth. 'Fuck off.'

'Too fucking good for it, eh. You fucking tart.' The vehicle accelerated away.

At the bottom step leading to St Mary's, another car cruised by then halted just along the road beyond the steps. Her eyes followed it.

Give me a break, she thought, and started climbing the steps to St Mary's. It was six years since her marriage which had lasted only two years. He had run off with her sister, who had been her bridesmaid. That was the last time Patsy had been in a church, but at least she would be safe in there, she hoped, from the perverts of her working nights.

The building was quiet and full of shadows, her footsteps echoing on the stone floor. She tiptoed into an empty rear pew. Her keys fell to the floor, the sound reverberating in the empty darkness. There was a movement ahead, in front of a bank of lighted candles where a dark-suited figure, head bowed and immobile, was kneeling. A large, white image of Jesus hung from a cross looking down from the front of the church, beyond the candles. The silence was overwhelming. It was too much; she couldn't bear so much quiet. She suddenly bent over and sighed in pain as one of her ribs dug into a bruise on her chest.

Father John Doyle looked back at her and then stood.

She tried to rise again but grabbed at her stomach again and bent double with the pain.

His voice was concerned as he approached. 'Are you all right?'

'It's OK.' She looked up, grimacing. 'Oh, Father. I'm sorry. I didn't mean to disturb you.'

He shook his head. 'You're obviously hurt. What happened?'

'It's nothing.' She folded her arms across her stomach and bent over again, 'Just nothing, you know ...'

'And your eye,' said Father.

'It's OK. Please, it's OK. What were you doing here?' She pointed to the candles.

'I was praying,' he replied.

She grimaced again. 'What for?'

I was praying for a friend who might be in trouble.'

'Does that do any good, Father?' She paused. 'Would you pray for me too?'

'Of course. What's your name?'

'Patsy.' She smiled. 'I suppose it wouldn't do me any harm, would it? Nobody's prayed for me before.' She suddenly doubled up.

'Patsy, I promise I'll pray for you, but first let me get you to hospital,' said Father Doyle.

'No, no, it doesn't matter.'

'Tell me exactly what happened,' he persisted.

She ignored the question.

'I want to hear you pray for me, please. Would you kneel in front of those candles and pray for me?' She pointed at the candles. 'What are they for?'

Father smiled. 'They're lit for the friend I was talking about. Shall I light a candle for you?'

Patsy smiled through her contorted features. 'A candle ... so, while it burns, it's for me?'

He headed toward the front of the church and then turned. 'Come on.'

Blinking and holding back the pain contorting her bruised

body, Patsy stood up, brushed down her clothes, adjusted her hair and put on some lipstick.

'It's OK. You don't need to do that,' he said.

She frowned. 'I do! Oh, yes, I do. I want to.'

As she slowly approached, he picked a fresh candle, lit it from one of those already alight and then placed it securely amongst the others. They knelt next to each other.

'Father in heaven I pray for your child Patsy. Bring your loving touch into her life, ease her pain, and dispel her sorrow. In the name of Jesus Christ, our saviour, we ask that your arms be placed around her to protect her from danger and bring joy into her life.'

She stared into the flame of the candle and then turned to him. 'That was beautiful, Father.' Patsy pointed and smiled. 'And that's my candle?'

Father John nodded. 'That's your candle. And now I'm taking you to hospital.'

'OK.'

# THIRTY-TWO

The traffic was jammed up solid as Consuela neared Tower Bridge. She skirted around the worst of it, parking the moped behind the hotel.

She called Perez. 'He must be at least twenty minutes away.'

'I'm waiting in the car park. They are at the embassy and will leave when I confirm he is here.'

She made her way up to her room, headed into the bathroom, stripped off and got into a hot shower. The soap had no perfume, and hot water removed all trace of odours leftover from her ride through London. She quickly threw on some loose-fitting clothes and pinned her hair back, before wiping all surfaces, attempting to remove any traces of her presence. All her belongings went into the daypack she had left by the door. Retrieving this, she moved along the corridor to the service stairs and once the door had closed put on a baseball cap and pulled a white disposable forensic suit over her clothes.

Guzman's room was two floors higher. She looked cautiously around the door from the steps into the corridor, and saw it was empty, before walking quickly toward his room. Keeping her head bowed, she removed a key from the daypack and looked carefully at the door. She was pleased to see a "DO NOT DISTURB" notice in place. There was a tiny piece of white tissue inserted between the door itself and the frame. She opened the door to his suite, replacing the tissue as before.

She closed the door very gently and, pausing, scrutinised the living room. A briefcase had been placed carefully on the coffee table. Too carefully? She didn't touch it. A sofa was up against the wall in which a large window overlooked Tower Bridge. His car was not back, and the "NO PARKING" sign was still in place.

She trod carefully through the lounge into a narrow dining area, where a table was set for four guests. This led on to the bedroom. She noticed a thin strip of cotton strung across from one table leg to the skirting board, attached by a small blob of white mastic. She stepped over it warily and moved through into the bedroom itself. A jacket lay at the bottom of the bed, over a grey cover. Just across from the bed, the bathroom door was closed.

She phoned Perez. 'It's clear.'

'I'm here in the car park. Wait. The car's arrived.'

She closed her mobile phone and turned it off.

Her heart was beating faster as she peered around the edges of the curtain again and saw Guzman climbing from the car. He moved out of sight as he headed quickly toward the front entrance of the hotel.

Consuela slipped behind the sofa, drawing the small daypack with her, taking out the iron bar.

The lock opened. The door banged noisily against the wall. Nothing moved. There was silence. Consuela could smell his suspicion. His movements were cautious, treading softly and slowly. Guzman was like an animal, suspicious, wary of predators. He stopped, all was silent. She could feel his caution, his mistrust. The slow, quiet breathing continued. He didn't move. Consuela had known it wouldn't be easy, but this was pure terror. She struggled to remain still, bones aching from fear. Suddenly she understood there was no escape. This wasn't imagination or vengeance; it was horror. Desperate fear clung to the silence; dumb screaming longed to discover freedom away from this dark and sinister prison of her own design. The thought, the planning, had been sterile, but the reality was different, it was heart-pounding horror. She was not equipped.

Little sound came, just slow laboured breathing, wheezing slightly; taking in the air was an effort for him. He moved again, light for his weight and then stopped again … sniffing the air … listening … waiting. Consuela caught her breath. She tried not to swallow, fearing he would sense the movement, even if he didn't hear any noise.

He turned on a cassette player.

Consuela instantly recognised the music. She shivered. Horror and wounded terror again overwhelming her. Elvis Presley – "The Wonder of You." The music the bastard played in the basement. It made her feel sick. It was such a bizarre accompaniment. It had repelled her in those dark, cold nights when the only escape promising relief was death, and she had looked forward to that, prayed for it to come.

He moved more freely. A moment had passed. The wardrobe door opened. He threw two large suitcases on the bed and started grabbing his clothes, placing them into both the cases. Consuela waited, motionless. The bathroom door opened and then closed behind him. The toilet flushed; water ran. She quickly emerged from the tight hiding space behind the sofa and tiptoed through the lounge and into the bedroom, placing a syringe on a shelf beside the bathroom door. Flattening herself against the wall alongside the door, she waited for it to open.

Guzman staggered from the first blow but didn't fall. Consuela pushed him toward the bed and smashed down again with the iron bar. As it caught the side of his head, she felt the impotent resistance of his skull. This time he did fall. She grabbed the syringe. A barbiturate surged into his veins. Her hands shook with fear but also resolve. She fell back onto the sofa, sweating with exertion, eyeing his sweating body, twisted on the floor.

Devoid of consciousness, his power had drained away. Now

he was nothing. An empty sack but consciousness would return soon enough.

She grabbed her phone and called Perez.

The iron bar smashed the tape player to silence.

A few minutes later, there was a gentle knock at the door.

Perez slid through as Consuela looked beyond him into the empty corridor.

Perez whispered. 'We have to keep him here – quiet.'

'He can't hear you.'

'They have just left the embassy. About forty-five minutes and it will be over. We will be out of here.'

He looked through the window at Lopez and saw the driver's head resting on the steering wheel.

They tied Guzman's wrists and ankles with wide leather straps. Black gaffer tape covered his mouth. The barbiturate was slowly wearing off.

His eyes flickered.

As Consuela watched, a terrible understanding began to stir inside her.

Should she release him and let him go? She knew Perez would follow her lead. He hated Guzman, he hated Lopez, but he was weaker than her.

A jury, she thought. A trial. A proper forum, lawyers, a judge. A judge in robes, that's how it is done. To share the responsibility and act in the name of a greater force. It wouldn't be personal then. A meaning above and beyond the merely linguistic power of any words because they would be cloaked in authority. The panoply of justice.

Murder, murder, it's all murder.

However, cloaked in dry words, it was always murder, and Consuela wanted to commit it now. Guzman's eyes opened slightly. They saw nothing, not yet, but soon they would see: they would see Consuela. He would know his fate. His eyes closed again because he still could not see or wished to look no more.

To give or take life?

Not that moment of passion, driving a knife deep into a lover's breast and then weeping on a cold floor while mourning a life cherished so profoundly it could not be let go.

Not through the cacophony of battle: the mind deceived by desperate deeds, and portentous words that inspire bravura and courage in empty landscapes, body piling upon body at the end of exhausting days and fearful nights.

Nor the pulling of a lever in an aircraft, thirty thousand feet above a child suckling at its mother's breast and tasting the warm milk at the last as Enola Gay cuts the cord and kills the earth and all who shelter on it.

Not that.

Not that.

Guzman's eyes flicker beneath his lids. His fat legs move, almost imperceptibly. A shoulder twitches.

The room is dark and still. She smells his fear. His eyes, open now and experiencing what he has visited on so many others.

Now he knows it.

Consuela sat on the sofa.

Perez continued peering from the window.

She looked over at the bound and spread-eagled body. He had recovered consciousness. His eyes didn't waver from hers. His limbs remained limp.

This was not just indiscriminate retribution.

She prayed: this was a moral act.

Closing her eyes, she whispered. 'This is a moral act.' She desperately wanted to believe it.

The windows were shut, the heating on full.

Still looking at her, he struggled to speak. Consuela eyed him quizzically but turned away. She didn't need to hear him. She wouldn't listen to him. His actions defined him. Words were irrelevant.

Guzman suddenly heaved against the straps.

Consuela jumped back in fear as he snarled like an animal. Her heart leapt in terror as one of the straps almost split, promising to open but then, as quickly, holding again. Perez jumped to his feet, motionless, his eyes wide.

Guzman's desperate escape attempt ended, sweat shone on his forehead.

She fell to the sofa, fear and horror exhausting her.

His eyes stayed closed.

Consuela watched him.

He suddenly struggled violently against the restraints again. The strap holding one of his arms snapped, and he ripped his hand free. Consuela jumped to her feet, grabbed for the second syringe, and jabbed it into his leg. He grasped hold of her arm and tugged her, writhing, across his sweating body until her face was next to his. His hot, stagnant breath filled her nostrils. Perez rushed over and pulled her away.

Sliding to the floor, Consuela lay still for a moment. Then clutching the side of the bed, she began hauling herself upright.

Leaning over him, she pressed the tape tighter across his mouth. Her voice was low. 'There may be forgiveness for you, but only in a better place than this.'

Perez's telephone rang out. He listened but said nothing.

'They are ten minutes away. We can get out.'

Carefully moving the blind, she looked through the window. There was a glimpse of a figure moving past the hotel and toward the shadows under Tower Bridge. Ray Lancaster again. She was sure it was him. What was he doing here? She looked again. He was gone.

Perhaps it was a mistake. It can't have been him. Probably imagination.

Consuela looked down at Guzman. His eyes held her. Revulsion ripped through her body, and she almost fell over. Grabbing onto Perez's arm, she steadied herself and whispered, almost inaudibly.

To herself?

To Perez?

She wasn't sure.

'I am not a murderer.'

Perez turned.

Her voice emerged stronger.

'We are not murderers.'

She looked back to the still, silent figure.

'Whatever the past has done to us, however, it has disfigured us, leaving us trying to survive, it's not like this.'

Perez shook his head. Consuela took him in her arms.

'We can't bring Raul back, and it would only spoil his memory. His father is not a murderer.'

She looked again at Guzman and held Perez's hand. 'We're not him.'

Perez touched Consuela's hand. 'We have to go.'

Her voice came out in desperation. 'No. No not like this.'

She grabbed Perez's arm.

'We'll drag him to my room.'

'We don't have time.'

'We have to. They'll kill him. We'll be accomplices. You told them where he was. I put him here.'

She shook her head. 'We are not murderers.'

She cut the binds holding Guzman and stared down at the drugged prone figure lying prostrate on the bed. His eyes flickered open. Disgust coloured her features.

'We'll get you safe in my room.'

She pointed toward the window.

'Your people are here. You betrayed them. You know why they're here. You deserve each other. So help us move you, or you stay here and die. It's your choice.'

Guzman tried to stagger to his feet but dropped back to the floor. The drugs had almost incapacitated him, survival instinct surged through him, and he grabbed at Perez's unwilling hand as it was offered with the greatest reluctance and abhorrence.

Consuela opened the door slightly and checked that the hallway was empty. They dragged Guzman along the corridor and through the service door leading to bare concrete steps. Her room was two floors down. As the three figures staggered down the steps, Guzman fell twice. Still, they just succeeded in dragging him upright again, and resumed their erratic journey, eventually reaching the door to Consuela's room.

Fortunately, the corridor was still empty. They hauled Guzman inside her room, where he fell to the floor again. Consuela closed the door quietly behind them and collapsed onto the sofa, inhaling deeply as she tried to regain her breath. Guzman lay motionless on the carpet.

The car was still in the small car park, but Lopez was motionless.

'What do we do now?'

'Nothing. We just wait, there's nothing we can do.'

She looked to Guzman lying motionless on the floor.

'He's not in any shape to move so we wouldn't get out of the hotel unnoticed. We just wait.'

She shook her head.

'After waiting, I don't know.'

# THIRTY-THREE

Ray Lancaster watched a pleasure boat drift under calm water beneath Tower Bridge. The deck was lined with passengers drinking from champagne glasses; laughter floated across the river. A few stray lights filtered through the evening air from office blocks situated around the riverside.

He turned back to the hotel and thought he saw the blind move in Guzman's bedroom on the fourth floor.

It quickly fell back again.

His glance moved over to the hotel coffee shop.

Tony Tavinor was sitting at a table in the window, opposite Dan Cooper.

Tavinor's return had done more than bring news of Sarah and Tessa. He had reminded Ray of another time. A time when he had not felt obliged to apologise for existing. A time when he had self-worth and not inhabited an empty life. As they had dragged Consuela from the thugs, a shock had passed through him. A strident unspoken demand stemming from Tavinor that Ray face life and stop running from it. Perhaps it was Tavinor, or maybe he was just a catalyst to memories of times past. He didn't care or wish to understand more. It was salvation, and his shoulders straightened, and clarity returned.

He glanced through the window.

Tavinor looked benign. Ray knew the reality was starkly different. He had been by Tavinor's side through desperate times, and the man led not by rank but by example. He had refused a commission, even though it was offered more than once.

His leaving the army was neither expected nor a shock. He just walked away. They were in Belfast, just after the murder of a solicitor.

They were in the canteen having a brew. Ray remembered it to this day, 13th February 1989. It was the day after they had cleared an area in North Belfast and some thugs from the UDA, a loyalist paramilitary group, had carried out the murder.

'I'm done. Didn't join up for this,' said Tavinor.

He had stood up and walked away. It was the last time Ray had seen him until two days ago. Apart from birthday cards for Tessa, his goddaughter, from various overseas locations, Kuala Lumpur, Hong Kong, Luanda and others, not a word.

His phone rang out.

His man on the approach road. Number four. They had all been allocated numbers.

'Brown van. Diplomatic plates ... Wait one. Parked up. Three guys out.'

Lancaster sent a message. 'Four, keep watch on Lopez. Everyone else to positions.'

He turned to the coffee shop. Tavinor was looking at his phone as he stood and moved away from the table.

Three figures appeared at the corner of the hotel. As broad as they were tall, Lancaster knew them. They were trained and primed. Trying to blend in but failing. A crackle of dead flesh walked with them. Orders to follow. Target located. They were focused on Tavinor's limousine.

Ray watched the car as he made his way toward the hotel entrance. Lopez was dozing, as usual, in the reclined driver's seat. Suddenly, as though a sixth sense had kicked in, he jerked upright and looked through the passenger window and toward the three men. He was too late. As he tried to open his door and get out, a powerful arm prevented him. The passenger door opened. Two of the men were situated either side of the car, and the other slipped into the passenger seat. The heavy glass almost absorbed the angry shout and then Lopez slumped back against the reclined seat.

'OK. Speak with the manager. Do it now,' ordered Tavinor looking at Cooper, 'we'll call if we need you.'

Lancaster spoke with Tavinor as he reached the lobby.

'Lopez is out of commission.'

They made their way to the staircase entrance watching the three figures moving toward the lifts. They watched as two of their team moved behind them.'

'Let's go,' said Tavinor and they sprinted up the stairs. As they reached the fourth floor a text came through.

"Right", it said, simply.

Two more of the team were at the entrance to the fourth floor.

'Move,' said Tavinor.

They were met with two more at the lift doors.

A room service trolley stood against the wall.

'Right door. Get the other lift. One of the team pushed the button to summon the left-hand lift.'

'Tasers?' Two of the team held up the tasers.

'OK. We've got three targets. You each take the first two out. The other will be dealt with inside the lift.'

He looked at the lift light.

'Second. Third. OK, make ready. We've done this. Fast and decisive. Don't fuck about.'

Tavinor and Lancaster were talking animatedly as the doors opened, appearing not to notice the lift's arrival and the three figures trying to exit.

'Oh. Sorry,' said Tavinor as they tried to push past.

It was almost slow motion. A choreographed burst of violence which was almost over before it could be noticed.

Tasers took out the first two. They fell to the floor, jerking violently on the thick carpet. A muted shout echoed in the lift as the last man out collapsed when a cosh smashed into the back of his head

He fell and joined his colleagues on the floor.

Tavinor checked their vital signs. 'OK,' he nodded.

One of the men searched through pockets. Three handguns were secured and placed carefully into a backpack which was placed on the room service trolley.

Lancaster texted one of the van drivers.

Thick plastic restraints were clamped to wrists and ankles, and gags wound round mouths.

The left-hand lift arrived; doors opened. It was empty. 'Block it,' said Tavinor.

He pointed to the stair doorway. 'Block that,' he ordered and one the team ran down and stood guard at the entrance.

'Let's tidy them up.'

The three figures were pulled into the lift and laid at the rear. 'You three, as we planned. Service entrance,' he checked with Lancaster who nodded, 'the van is waiting. Get them to the warehouse. Keep them quiet.'

The room service trolley was dragged across the front of the lift blocking the entrance. 'Release that.' He pointed to the left-hand lift. The doors closed as soon as a foot was removed from blocking the door.

'Wait one.' He watched until the lift reached the ground floor.

'OK. Go. We'll be there soon.'

He looked at Lancaster. 'Let's get Guzman.'

# THIRTY-FOUR

'Fresh cartridges,' instructed Tavinor, standing at the doorway of Guzman's suite. 'He may be a handful. If he objects, taser him. I want this done fast and quietly.'

The two men, each carrying a taser, nodded.

Tavinor looked toward Lancaster. 'OK?'

Lancaster held up a key card. 'Ready.'

They looked along the corridor. It was empty.

'Now,' said Tavinor.

Lancaster slipped the key into the door, pushed it open and ran through. He made his way through to the bedroom. Tavinor followed up behind.

'It's empty,' said Lancaster as he stood at the bathroom door.

Tavinor knelt. He picked up two syringes and then some leather straps.

'What the hell has gone on here?'

Lancaster checked out two suitcases on the bed. An open briefcase sat on a pillow.

He picked up Guzman's passport.

'He's not gone far.'

Rifling through the briefcase, he picked up The Mission brochure and threw it back down.

Tavinor called Cooper. 'Guzman's room now please.'

He moved to the door and waited until Dan Cooper came from the lift. Tavinor pointed to the CCTV cameras at each end of the corridor.

'Your manager turned them off when the goons arrived?'

Cooper nodded.

'We need to see what has happened here for the past hour or so. Get your man to give us access please.'

'What's happened?'

'Guzman's not here.'

'We saw him come back about an hour ago. Where the hell could he be?'

'CCTV may help us.'

'I'll go and see Pierre.'

'We'll close up here and then come down to reception.'

Cooper moved to the lift. Tavinor went back inside Guzman's room.

'Anything here that can help?'

Lancaster walked slowly around the bedroom. He shook his head. They started from the room.

As he left Lancaster took a last look beneath the bed. He frowned. He knew what it was. Sarah wore one sometimes when she had her hair done. A hair claw. He had seen one recently but couldn't recall where or on who.

He shoved it into his pocket.

* * *

The reception desk was quiet. The manager looked anxious as Dan Cooper approached.

'It's about finished,' said Cooper.

'I've had a couple of complaints from guests, but I smoothed them over. Are you sure we shouldn't contact the police?'

'I can't prevent you from doing that, Pierre. But we've handled what could have been a disastrous PR situation for the hotel. The publicity would have been unfortunate.'

He paused.

'There is one more thing if possible. We would appreciate a quick look at the CCTV from the corridor on the fourth floor.'

'Is there a problem?'

'No. No. It's a precaution.'

He reached into his pocket. 'You and your staff have been exemplary. Please see to it that this contribution finds its way to their service fund with my compliments.'

He handed over one thousand pounds in notes.

Pierre looked around the desk. A late guest was checking in. He took the money, slipped it into an inside pocket and gestured toward the lifts.

'Security room is in the basement.'

Cooper called Tavinor and told him to meet him downstairs.

There were three monitors in the empty room. They alternated in showing the view from cameras spread through the hotel.

'OK,' said Pierre. 'Firstly, I check who has been in the room so we can confirm timings. It will make it quicker.'

The manager went to a computer and banged out some instructions. A schedule came out of the printer.

'OK. Here we have housekeeping this morning, 10.02. Occupant back in at 10.30. Nothing then until 19.40, housekeeping again.' He shook his head. 'That can't be right. I was asked whether they should go in for a turn-down around that time as there was a *DND* on the door. I said no. Then the occupant is back in at 19.55. Nothing then until 20.30.'

He looked at Cooper. 'That was you?'

Cooper nodded. 'Yes'

Tavinor spoke. 'Could we check out the corridor from 19.20 until now.'

'Who the hell is that?' said Dan Cooper as they saw a slight figure in white overalls come from the service stairs. The face was not visible beneath a baseball cap. Guzman returned ten minutes later.

'And that?' Another figure came from the stairs also with a

baseball cap shielding his face. The door opened. He slipped inside.

Nothing moved for thirty minutes. They stared in astonishment as Guzman was dragged between the two figures who had entered his room. Falling to the floor and almost failing to get to the stairs, the picture ended as the stairwell door closed.

'We have no cameras in the stairs.'

'Who the hell were they?' said Cooper.

Ray Lancaster touched the hair claw in his pocket.

He held up the key from Guzman's room. 'Will this still work?'

The manager confirmed it would.

Lancaster returned. He held The Mission brochure in his hand. He pointed to the picture of Consuela.

'Is she staying here?'

The manager's eyes narrowed. He frowned and gestured toward the stairs.

At the reception desk, he showed the picture to one of the staff.

After a brief discussion, he returned to Cooper.

'Ava Rivera,' he announced before handed over a key and a handwritten note, with a number on it.

'That's her room.' He gripped Cooper's arm, 'and quietly.'

## THIRTY-FIVE

Consuela stared down at the gross inert body, spread-eagled on her hotel room floor.

Guzman had somehow made it to the bedroom and then collapsed.

An occasional jerking of his left shoulder and the rise and fall of his chest was the only sign he was alive.

Part of her hope was that the movements would cease. That the air would escape his putrid body and that would be the end of it. It would be finished.

She would take the consequences. Her conscience could live with an accident.

Perez sat on the bed, facing away from her. He refused to look at Guzman. She felt the tension seeping from the frail body. He was consumed with Guzman, a thick thread of revenge coursing through him, which he believed would bring about redemption for the guilt he felt at watching his son die and feeling responsible.

Consuela felt the same about Manuel, her dead lover, and now the shattering blow that the bastard had dealt her, the knowledge of Jorge's death. So many years hoping, praying and then a few words had crushed the hopes.

The brother whose face had been with her every day since

she had fled El Salvador. The brother who had been by her side through such hard times. No more.

She looked down.

The cause of so much sorrow, so much heartache, lying here beneath her feet, defenceless.

Why not, she thought? Who would care? Who would weep? Who would shed a tear at his passing?

Would the world be a better place?

She put out a hand to touch Perez.

Guzman gave out a sigh, rolled over and banged against the bed.

Perez turned.

Tears were rolling down his face.

Suddenly the door opened.

Ray Lancaster stood in the doorway.

## THIRTY-SIX

Dan Cooper sat in the back seat of the rental Land Rover Discovery that followed the white van in which they had deposited Guzman's motionless body. His wrists and ankles were secured, three of Lancaster's men travelled with him.

It took two hours before they pulled up alongside a warehouse in a rundown industrial estate. Most of the buildings were empty, a sense of decay hanging over the isolated location just off the M20 in Kent.

A "TO LET" sign hung outside the building.

Guzman's death would have set off a storm of investigations which could have led down alleys that Cooper was ashamed to acknowledge and would have posed questions he had long tried to turn his back on

As they pulled up. a large metal shutter at the front of the building opened the sound of rusted chains echoing in the empty darkness. A faint light filtered from the spacious shell of the building.

He heard angry shouts coming from the other white van which stood alone in the empty space.

'Wait,' said Tavinor and jumped from the vehicle.

He marched to the van holding Guzman and spoke to the driver. 'Wait here for a minute.'

Moving inside the building he spoke to the two guards waiting inside.

'Keep a tight hold. Do not release the restraints but let them out.'

The rear door opened of the van opened. A roar of anger came from inside, and three squat figures tumbled onto the concrete floor. Tavinor watched them as they attempted to stand, inhibited by ankle restraints.

He strolled up to them. 'English.'

One of them nodded. A snarling guttural voice demanded. 'Let us go. Now! We have diplomatic immunity.'

Tavinor moved closer. As further words started to emerge, he grabbed the figure by the throat and lifted him off the ground, against the van.

His voice was quiet. 'You have no immunity here. Whether you live or die is my decision. You came to this country to murder, and that is unacceptable.'

He dropped the squirming man to the floor and walked past the other two.

'You will wait here while I decide what to do with you.'

He turned and started to walk away when another angry shout echoed around the building. 'I warn you …'

Tavinor turned back. He moved closer and suddenly stamped on the prone figure. A scream reverberated through the night.

'You do not warn. You stay here, and you wait, and you might survive.'

He walked away and nodded to the guard by Guzman's van. 'He conscious?'

'Groggy but OK.'

'Get him out.'

Guzman emerged. The guard helped as he took a few stuttering steps.

Guzman halted when he saw his three fellow countrymen standing inside.

Cooper walked alongside.

'You know them. Of course you do. Trained them. Put the guns and knives in their hands.'

Tavinor nodded at the guard and pointed toward a flight of steps that led up to a small office overlooking the large, dusty, empty space of the building.

Six furious eyes followed the slow progress as they moved past. A bizarre hissing sound followed them; Guzman struggled up the narrow metal steps.

Cooper followed and turned on a single neon light.

Tavinor and Lancaster stood behind Guzman and pushed him down onto a frail plastic chair.

Cooper remained standing, gazing down from the window.

The silence stretched out, eventually broken by the Salvadorian who gave a tense laugh.

'You saved me for what?'

Cooper ignored the question. He turned to Guzman.

'I said, you know them. Your people. Murderers, killers. You're right. We saved your life. Reluctantly because it's barely worth saving.'

Guzman shrugged and tried to stand, 'So now I go.'

Tavinor and Lancaster each took a shoulder and pushed him down.

Cooper continued. 'You go. You go with them. You know why they came. You betrayed the battalion. That collection of misfits and psychopaths you crafted to carry out your massacres.'

Guzman shook his head.

'And you and the rest of the landowners are innocent. Is that the story you want to tell? I was a soldier. I obeyed orders.'

Tavinor cracked the back of his head. 'You were never a soldier. You were a crook wearing a uniform.'

'I've heard it, Guzman,' shouted Cooper. 'Nobody asked you to massacre, to torture, to rape, to kidnap children. *No. No.* You do not get off by blaming anyone else.'

He waved his hand in front of his face. 'But that's not why you're here.'

He moved to the window again and looked down.

'It's whether we hand you over to your hand-reared murderers. They have orders. You know what they are, I'm sure.'

'I'll take my chances.'

Dan Cooper looked closely at Guzman. The arrogance was undiminished. His resentment at being abused and insulted by this disgusting creature welled up. Why should he keep him from his killers? Was he prepared to pay the price for one death? Death of something that had no value.

He looked up at Tavinor. The eyes were cold, staring beyond him and occasionally darting around the room and then below to the El Salvadorians now silent and cowed. Cooper suddenly felt the focus shift to him. There was just the slightest shake of the head. It said nothing but spoke volumes.

The silence in the room lengthened.

Guzman stirred. He suddenly looked nervous as though a bluff was about to be called.

Tavinor gestured for Cooper to step to the window. He spoke too quietly for Guzman to hear.

'You will regret it.'

Cooper sat down. He stared into Guzman's eyes and then nodded at Tavinor and Lancaster.

'OK. I think we're done here. There's nothing to talk about.'

He stood.

'Leave him, we'll go. Perhaps if he offers them a few million each he might get to live. Not in this country, of course. Not when this comes out. And I doubt they will disobey orders. But let him roll the dice.'

He moved to the door.

Guzman spoke through gritted teeth. 'Why did you bring me here?'

'We made a mistake. Your friends were right. You betrayed them. I will pay them what you owe to keep them from my door.'

'What I owe? I owe them nothing.'

Cooper laughed as he opened the door. 'Forty-five million is what you owe. But they want more than that. They want you. On the slab. Dead.'

'So why stop them?'

Cooper paused. 'You're right. Why? Self-interest. You pay, I save your life. You live another day. You can hide away on the estate you're buying, build big walls, hire guards and live. I have spoken with Sheridan; your residency is approved. They will tire of trying. And I save money. But it's money I can afford.'

'So, they threatened you as well?'

'It's not important. It's done. We're gone. They can have you.'

'They did nothing. I did all the work.'

Cooper ignored the words. He nodded at Tavinor and Lancaster.

'We'll let the guys downstairs loose and get out of here.'

Guzman's head dropped.

Cooper strained to hear.

'OK.'

Cooper turned. 'OK, what?'

Guzman's scorn was dredged from ferocious conceit. He breathed deeply. His voice was frail.

'I'll pay.'

## THIRTY-SEVEN

John was waiting opposite Bush House in Aldwych. Late-night traffic passed by as he stood in a shop doorway. Lights shone from a few scattered windows in the BBC's World Service headquarters.

It was three-thirty when, at last, he saw the stooped figure emerge through the swing doors, looking suspiciously about him before hurrying off toward Waterloo Bridge.

'Senor Perez.'

The man whirled around, looking about him and over John's shoulder. Three taxis sped past them in quick succession. Perez pulled him into a small alley.

'What are you doing here? How do you know where I work? What do you want from me?'

The words spilt out, first in anger and then, with the last sentence, suspicion.

'You know what I want.'

A sharp bony finger pressed against John's chest.

John continued, 'I have to find her.'

The finger pressed harder. Perez looked around again, then came close, his manner suspicious. He turned away after staring intensely into Father John's eyes, then spoke over his shoulder as he walked rapidly away.

'OK, come with me. I won't speak to you here.'

They walked on in silence.

The apartment was dark and silent as they entered. A door leading off the lounge suddenly opened, and a woman put her head round. Perez's hunched figure crept over and whispered to her. The door remained open, and John knew someone was listening behind it.

'What is it you want, Father?'

'I have to see Consuela.'

They sat down facing each other on two large, battered armchairs. A newspaper lay on the table between them.

'And why would you contact me?'

John breathed in deeply, to calm his shattered nerves. 'You *know* why!'

Perez didn't respond.

'Is she in danger?' pressed John.

The thin, drawn face remained expressionless. The voice, when it came, was suddenly animated although Perez tried to disguise his anger.

'Danger is the base currency if you survive.'

John paused as he watched the hooded eyelids flicker and felt the resolution.

'That's meaningless. I have to see her.'

Perez began stroking his throat, pinching the skin between his fingers as he stared down at the table. There was a cough from the open doorway, although the sound was almost lost in the silence. Perez scurried over and listened before returning. John strained to hear what was said but failed.

'Suppose I tell you where she is?'

John began to speak, but Perez removed his hand from his scraggy neck and held it up. He spoke again.

'Let's suppose shall we, Father. You would go to her.'

He fell silent, looked toward the open door and then back to John.

'Be near your telephone tomorrow, midday. I have the number.'

* * *

Dan Cooper sat at the boardroom table.

'So Guzman was taken back to the hotel. Lopez was there?'

'He was sat in the car as if nothing had happened.'

'The goons?'

'Dropped them in Liverpool. Told them to find their own way home.'

Cooper picked up the phone. He dialled. His office in San Salvador had checked the number. It was a prepaid bought from a backstreet.

'Yes.'

The same voice, bristling with authority, whether real or imagined.

'I will transfer your money.'

'Good—'

Cooper interrupted. 'I haven't finished. You will be quiet now. You will have half now, twenty-two million five hundred thousand dollars and seventeen million five hundred thousand in six months assuming I hear no more from you. If I hear from you, or you cause me or anyone or anything associated with me a problem, I will devote the remaining funds to destroying you. Five million I am giving to Carlos Silva's family who your thugs murdered. Do you understand, General?'

There was a long silence.

'That is not the deal.'

'That is the deal. You have the choice of whether to accept it.'

The silence lengthened.

Suddenly the voice barked out an account number.

Cooper looked down at the list of accounts passed over by Perez.

'Your British Virgin Island company?

'That's not your concern.'

The money will be transferred.'

He replaced the phone.

He pointed to Perez's notes.

'He hasn't even bothered to change the company. They think they're above the law.'

Ray Lancaster and Tony Tavinor sat either side of the table.

'He got the message,' said Tavinor.

'That I knew more than he realised? I hope so. I couldn't have handled it without you. I have transferred all the funds to you, but that doesn't come close to the debt I owe. I would have been in serious trouble.'

Tavinor spoke.

'You need to take your security seriously both here and overseas. There are some unstable actors out there.'

Cooper looked between them.

'I realise that. Tony would you be willing to set up a security operation with Ray. I'll give you full authority.'

'Not me, Dan. I'm out of here. I must get to East Timor. I've got a close friend out there and I am anxious to see her again. I only came over to find Ray when Sarah got in touch.'

He looked across at Lancaster.

'There's your answer. You'll find no-one better. You met him at a bad time, but I worked with him for years. He's smart, tough, and loyal. That's if he wants it.'

'Do you?' asked Cooper.

Lancaster smiled. 'What I want right now is to get home and see my wife and daughter. Can you give me a couple of weeks?'

'Where does she live?'

'Woking.'

'I'll get you a car. Take as long as you want. Let me know when you're ready.'

# THIRTY-EIGHT

John didn't sleep.

Instead, he walked the streets he knew so well. Buildings that had framed the backdrop to a life that was sliding from him. The feeling of uncertainty was imbued with exhilaration. Passing Roger and Stuart's house in the early morning, he saw them through the kitchen window, laughing by the sink.

Father Cuff took early morning Mass.

Time passed while John sat in a front pew.

The line waiting outside the small confessional booth started looking surreptitiously at their watches.

Minutes passed.

Father John dropped to his knees. He realised that even as a door was closing, so another opened. The excitement he was feeling, was, nevertheless, coloured with sadness at what he would be leaving. Belief had been the bedrock of his existence. Only slowly, and rarely, had he allowed stray rays of doubt to chip away at his certainty.

Until Consuela. He had suddenly glimpsed a world he had never known. An existence hidden from blinkered eyes and pious complacent hearts.

'Father!'

It was over. The spell was broken.

John turned.

He nodded to the small, concerned face and laid his hand on her arms. 'Your sins will wait another day, Margaret.'

He held out his hands in supplication, as he recited his last words in Holy Orders.

'Hail Mary, full of grace.

The Lord is with thee.

Blessed art thou amongst women,

and blessed is the fruit of thy womb, Jesus.'

Voices joined with him, whispers couched in uncertainty and confusion. They continued as he walked down the nave.

More turmoil awaited him, that was the only certainty, but he had chosen his path and, as he dipped his fingers in the holy water at the door, touching it to his forehead, he closed his eyes and saw Consuela's face.

It was enough. He walked back along the corridor to his office. Books were scattered about the floor but he didn't notice. A cyclist passing along the road threw splashes of water onto the pavement. Three black umbrellas moved across the front of the church; he turned quickly when a red brake light sparked a faint memory. It disappeared.

The next thirty minutes passed slowly.

Eventually, the telephone rang.

He grabbed the receiver, but it was Ray Lancaster. He listened at the story he was told.

He ended the call as soon as he could.

The telephone rang again.

Perez gave him an address and hung up before John could ask any questions.

He remembered the cottage.

* * *

Traffic was gridlocked in London's southern suburbs because of a burst water main. Two hours later John turned off the M23 toward Bolney.

The cottage stood at the end of the track. Slowing down, he could see the front door through the gate hanging off its hinges. He turned in and pulled to the side of the cottage.

John knocked on the door and soon heard footsteps. A shadow appeared behind the small coloured-glass window as the door opened, slowly, cautiously. A chain was pulled tight between door and frame. Consuela's face peered through the narrow gap, her eyes squinting in the sunlight.

She finally opened the door.

Consuela's face alternated between pleasure and fear as she looked directly into John's eyes. Her gaze was defiant.

He reached out to her, but she turned away, pushing a hand through her hair. She led the way back to the kitchen and gestured to a chair.

John sat.

'It felt like it would never end. I felt safe, and then Guzman turned up. I couldn't let it happen again. I couldn't face more years running away.'

John tried to speak. To find some words. None came. Nothing adequate for the moment. He reached out toward her.

Consuela touched his hand and then moved to the window looking over the fields at the back of the cottage.

'How did you know I was here?' She closed her eyes. 'Josef, of course.'

'I had to persuade him.'

She took his head. 'It was Alejandra that you persuaded, even if you didn't see her. I have to tell you what has happened. You need to know. If, afterwards, you want to walk away. If you want to go back to your church, then go you must. With my love, of course, but you must go back to your life if that is your decision.'

He frowned and started to shake his head.

'I left Roger and Stuart's place because I planned to murder Guzman.'

He tried to remain calm.

'I took a hotel room. I had the drug. I, we, Josef, and myself.

We were going to leave him for thugs from El Salvador to finish him off. Josef had told them where to find him. We would keep Guzman there. We would have been responsible for his death.'

She closed her eyes.

'I was willing to commit murder. Which meant I was no better than him. A part of me wanted it so badly. To finish it.'

John remained silent for a moment. 'But?'

'I couldn't.'

John leaned over and took her hand.

She looked at him, 'I could have killed him.'

He nodded. 'But you didn't. You said you were no better than him. But you are. That's the difference.'

He paused. 'Ray Lancaster called.'

Consuela looked surprised. 'He was there.'

'He has been trying to contact you. Guzman is alive. Tony Tavinor and Ray spoke with Guzman. He will not cause you any trouble ever again.'

They sat, in blessed silence. Looking into each other's eyes.

'John, I felt scared before and never wanted to be touched again, not by anyone. It's different now.'

Nothing else was said as they held each other, engrossed in their own thoughts, each trying to make sense of their own feelings.

Consuela stood and led John to the narrow stairs. He was trembling with tension.

They lay together on Consuela's small bed. His slow, sensuous, tender fingers stroked across her smooth dark body, knowing her excitement, feeling her rise, and fall to his touch. Her hands held him, touching him, roaming his pure virginal body. Flesh of all flesh. He touched with wonder and felt a stirring that was mystery and desire previously hidden from him. Fingers traced across her silken stomach, soft, yielding and giving all that he wanted. Her eyes followed his expression, so absorbed, a strange journey for him; beyond temptation. This was different. Consuela couldn't take her eyes from his face. She took hold of his hands, slowly stroking, kissing each finger, taking them one by one between her soft lips. This was fresh, new, a guileless wonder at sensation that had not been spoken of. His face was serious. This was experience beyond words, reality beyond existence. She kissed his eyelids, reverence and passion mixed in a prayer of craving which absorbed the words and filled the soft, dark, scented evening with desire.

Hands touched, bodies enfolded into each other, she knowing and feeling what she had felt before. But never like this, all supposition shattered and irrelevant. They touched with such care. At the end of each exploration, the discovery of self; at the tips of fingers, fulfilment. Her hair so soft and gentle. His arms pulled her to him, and their bodies touched, breath came quickly, eyes looking and enchanted by beauty and knowledge. She looked again at his soft, caring eyes. He wept to the heavens that this was not temptation; this was realisation, a slow intensity heightened as he gazed at her closed eyes, her face straining for another source of understanding. She had nothing with which to understand this perfection.

Slowly their bodies were consumed in passion; they touched and understood the fragile beauty of devoted intimacy. She wrapped herself around him, and she knew all she ever wanted to know of love. He knew all he had ever craved to know of life. My body given for you, they rode their knowledge until stirrings of mortality brought them to another place, beyond explanation and beyond all experience.

# POSTSCRIPT

## Easter 1997
## Antigua Guatemala

It was Good Friday, just after five thirty. The sun was emerging behind one of the volcanic peaks overlooking Guatemala's one-time capital.

The town hadn't slept during the night. Roads were covered in diverse patterns of brightly coloured flowers and sawdust and were already lined with men and boys wearing purple cassocks and distinctive white headdresses.

John and Consuela walked from their hotel, the Convento Santa Catalina.

As they walked through a large arch topped with an ornamented clock tower, Consuela pointed out a large church highlighted with delicate stucco decorations depicting vines, geometric patterns, and graceful figures.

'That is Iglesia y Convento de Nuestra Señora de La Merced or simply La Merced to an Irish peasant like you, Doyle,' said Consuela.

He smiled. '*Gracias, Señora,* and as you know I am Scottish if you don't mind.'

'The procession starts from La Merced at seven.'

She gestured to the painted colourful, carpets on the road, 'These are called *alfombras.*'

She grabbed John's arm and guided him through narrow-crowded cobblestone streets, alongside beautifully preserved houses, still displaying a style of architecture brought from Spain hundreds of years before.

'This is wonderful.' Consuela's smile was irrepressible. 'I've always wanted to be here at Easter. I don't know how Flavio managed it; hotels are booked months in advance, especially on the processional route, like ours. You've still no idea why he wanted to meet up?'

Doyle shook his head.

They waited amid the crowd until just before seven o'clock. Trumpets suddenly started to sound, incense burners appeared from the doors of the church, after which many in the crowd knelt on cobbled streets as a priest wearing a white habit emerged and stood outside the magnificent building. He intoned a prayer into a microphone and then led a procession down the steps.

The air was soon filled with a musky fragrance of flower petals and incense.

A massive, carved wooden-litter was borne from the church, bearing a cedarwood image of Christ carrying his cross. It was borne by about one hundred purple-robed "penitents", marching slowly in time to the grave beat of a marching band, accompanied in the background by the solemn lament of a choir.

Consuela shouted in John's ear, 'It's now taken around the town and only the litter-carriers – cucuruchas - can set foot on the alfombras. It weighs about three and a half tons, so they have to keep changing the bearers.'

The procession continued down the steps, winding slowly and carefully through streets and plazas past the colonial-style homes with ornate, metal-studded doorways, whitewashed walls, and red-tiled roofs.

After an hour had passed, John turned to Consuela.

'Let's go back to our hotel. We'll watch from there. You shouldn't stand any longer.'

More processions continued through the day as the alfombras were restored and watered to stop them wilting in the sun. As the afternoon wore on the litter-bearers' robes changed from purple to black, their faces concealed under black pointed hoods and similar processions continued into the atmospheric darkness of the night.

* * *

John and Consuela checked out early the next morning as yet more festivities were being prepared. They took a detour off the Pan-American Highway through the lower highlands and past Lake Atitlan, surrounded by the three mountainous volcanoes which guard its deep, dark waters. The waters reflected a rich mauve as the sun rose over the hills and complemented the dramatic colours and weaves of native dress that varied as they passed through Indian villages lining the shore of the thirty-kilometre-wide lake.

Consuela glanced across. 'Where are we meeting Flavio?'

'He said that we should make our way to the church of Santo Tomás and he would find us.'

They passed the town of Solola; the roads crowded with Mayan Indians loaded down with fabrics and fruit.

Consuela pointed to the bat symbol embroidered on men's shirts, 'The bat emblem wards off evil spirits in Mayan Indian mythology.'

Thirty minutes later, they drove into Chichicastenango, isolated amongst the Guatemalan highlands. Surrounded by looming mountains and deep valleys, it was enveloped in mist, bringing a magical detachment to the small Mayan town of narrow cobbled streets and red-tiled roofs.

John managed to park beside Santa Tomas. They wandered toward the front of the church. Market stalls, selling brightly coloured clothing, foodstuffs, hats and flowers filled the crowded marketplace in good-natured chaos. The steps up to the church were spread with flowers and groups of people talking and laughing.

Incense wafted from censers swung by Indian priests at the door to the church, intoning prayers to their ancestors.

Thick clouds of aromatic incense obscured the dim light inside the church. Groups of Indian worshippers knelt around collections of lighted candles, throwing rose petals onto the flames. Smoke drifted upward into the ceiling, its fragrance permeating the still air.

Consuela leaned across to John.

'They are Mayan pagan altars; the church has allowed them in for hundreds of years.'

John breathed in the scent and looked toward an altar at one end of the large church. A statue of the Madonna hung amongst figures on a dramatic wooden Reredos behind the altar.

As Consuela wandered away through the nave, John walked toward the Madonna, crossed himself, knelt and prayed. After a few minutes, he felt a hand touch his shoulder.

He looked around and stood up. 'Flavio!'

Flavio wore a long, white habit tied at the waist with a black rope. His grin stretched from ear to ear. 'John. John, you look younger than ever. What do you think?' He ran his hand over his head and then pulled John, holding him tightly.

'It looks very distinguished, Flavio, the red cap will fit better.'

'Slip off easier I think you mean.'

'Why did you come here?' asked John looking around.

'Rome was suffocating me. I told you when we met that I was hoping to get out of Rome. I've been here for two years, part of the Pontifical Council for Interreligious Dialogue. Can you believe it? A report requested on Mayan culture. So I came.'

He looked carefully at John, 'But you, Father Doyle. A married man. I wasn't surprised when I heard it. Not after what you told me. How long now?'

'Almost two years. Our first child due in three months.'

John put his hand on the priest's arm, 'How did you know where we were?'

'Brother Roger at your last church, told me. And Consuela is with you.'

John looked around the building and spotted Consuela sitting in a pew. A little Mayan girl was smiling and touching her swollen stomach. He pointed out his wife.

Flavio took John's arm and guided him to a quiet corner.

'You are happy?'

John smiled.

'OK, OK. There's no need to answer that. I can see.'

Flavio sighed.

'I remembered all that you told me about Consuela. How she was treated, the murder of the Jesuits, her poor brother—'

John interrupted. 'We have found out his brother died. He was killed in an ambush on the Honduras border.'

'John. Please ...'

He gripped John's arm.

'Tell me, was Jorge, that was his name I believe, a medical student?'

John nodded.

'And Consuela witnessed the murder of the Jesuits and then had to leave El Salvador.'

'She has only returned once since we were married, and of course, she has a different name now.'

'It would be best if you sat down.' They found an empty pew.

Flavio leaned close to John. 'I was at a conference in Rome two months ago. A gathering of Salesian brothers from across the world. A Brother sought me out when he knew I was in Central America. He is based in East Timor, a Mission at Lospalos. I confess, at that time, I knew little of East Timor, but I have since discovered that it has suffered terribly from occupation by the Indonesia Army. Hundreds of thousands killed. There is brutal oppression. The Brother told me of a young doctor. A hero amongst the indigenous people for helping them, despite threats and harassment from the Indonesian army. This doctor is from El Salvador. His name is Roberto Garcia.'

John looked across at Consuela. She smiled and waved.

Flavio paused and, also, hesitantly, waved a hand in greeting.

He continued. 'Garcia told of his sister, who he believed had been killed, or had "disappeared" after she witnessed the murder of the six Jesuit priests in San Salvador in '89.'

He looked from John and then back to Consuela.

'Her name was Coretta Delgado.'

# EPILOGUE

**Ex-Salvadoran colonel to be tried over murder of six priests in 1989**

*The Guardian* 7 June 2020

**Inocente Orlando Montano accused of planning atrocity aimed at stopping peace talks**

A former Salvadoran army colonel who served as a government security minister will appear in court in Madrid on Monday to face trial over the murders of six Jesuit priests, a woman and her teenage daughter in 1989.

The attack, at the Central American University (UCA) in San Salvador, was planned and authorised by senior military commanders and was an attempt to derail peace talks aimed at ending the country's civil war.

But the atrocity backfired spectacularly, provoking international outrage and contributing to the US's decision to pull its support for El Salvador's military regime.

Five of the murdered priests were Spaniards, and the trial is taking place in Madrid under the principle of universal jurisdiction, which allows human rights crimes committed in one country to be investigated and tried in another.

**Ex-Salvadoran colonel jailed for 1989 murder of Spanish Jesuits**

*The Guardian* 7 June 2020

A former Salvadoran army colonel who served as a government security minister has been sentenced to 133 years in prison after being found guilty of the murder of five Spanish Jesuits who died in one of the infamous atrocities of El Salvador's 12-year civil war.

Judges at Spain's highest criminal court, the Audiencia Nacional, on Friday convicted Inocente Orlando Montano, 77, of the "terrorist murders" of the five Spaniards, who were killed along with a Salvadoran Jesuit and two Salvadoran women 31 years ago.

**US deports El Salvador ex-general Casanova over abuses**

*BBC News* 9 April 2015

The US has deported a former general during El Salvador's civil war after a court ruled he was responsible for torture and killings while in command.

Eugenio Vides Casanova, once El Salvador's defence minister and head of the National Guard, arrived at the country's main airport with more than 100 other deportees, reports say.

**Spain pushes El Salvador Jesuit murders case**

*BBC News* 25 August 2011

Spain has asked El Salvador for information on the legal status of nine Salvadoran ex-soldiers charged with the 1989 murder of six priests, five Spanish and one Salvadoran.

The killing became one of the most infamous of El Salvador's civil war.

The nine were indicted by Spanish judge Eloy Velasco in May under Spain's universal jurisdiction law, which holds that some crimes are so grave that they can be tried anywhere.

Judge Velasco also issued arrest warrants through Interpol for the former soldiers.

Judge Velasco indicted a total of 20 former soldiers, including two former defence ministers.

The man accused of ordering the killings, Gen Rene Emilio Ponce, died in May.

**'I knew in my heart she was alive': Families in El Salvador are finally reunited with children abducted during the country's civil war**

*Independent Nina Lakhani* 19 January 2014

During El Salvador's merciless 12-year civil war, hundreds of children were forcibly taken by the military and illegally put up for adoption, many overseas. Only now, more than three decades since the hostilities began, are some of those children finally finding their families again.

Josefina Flores was given two choices: give up her one-and-a-half-year-old daughter – her youngest child – for adoption by a childless couple ... or risk all three of her children being shot dead.

It was a decision no mother should have to make, but this was El Salvador in 1984, during one of the bloodiest periods of the tiny Central American nation's brutal 12-year civil war – and Josefina was one among hundreds whose children were forcibly taken and illegitimately put up for adoption after being snatched by the armed forces, which carried out massacre after massacre in rural villages suspected to be supportive of the leftist guerrillas.

THE END

Thank you for reading *A Candle for Consuela.*

If you enjoyed this book, I'd like to hear from you and hope that you could take some time to post a review on Amazon.

Contact Mike@Mitrepublishing.com for any further information and prepublication discount on *A Flyblown Solution* due in 2022.

## ACKNOWLEDGEMENTS

My thanks to Peter Lavery for his superb editing and advice. To David Benjamin and Hugh Burnett, together with Jane and Peter Jukes for their enthusiastic support, and to Michelle Emerson for her patient and expert guidance in bringing the book to publication. To Margaret, my dear wife, I give my eternal thanks for the love, support and companionship we have shared through the years.

Finally, I am in debt to so many people in El Salvador for their courage and the inspiration that inspired this work.

# ABOUT THE AUTHOR

Mike Kingston has spent much of his career carrying out investigations throughout the world for many organisations – from worldwide media companies to multi-national corporations and global law firms. He has been reporting on and investigating corruption, espionage and conspiracy for more than 30 years.

His books reflect events he has encountered and the amazing characters, both courageous and depraved he has met along the way.

Underlying his words is an enormous respect for the resilience of the human spirit in surviving heartbreaking situations and managing to live meaningful and fulfilling lives, often in desperate circumstances.

## COMING 2022...

*A Flyblown Solution*

**November 1989**

Jorge Delgado ran from San Salvador University.

Pushed out by his sister, Coretta, he dashed from the scene of horror that he glimpsed when he saw the bodies of the six Jesuit priests lying on the grass outside their house. Coretta wanted him a long way from the crime. A long way from the trigger-happy soldiers guarding the site of their atrocity and looking to eliminate any witnesses.

Coretta had seen everything. She had shoved Jorge away from the window as shots rang out, realising that what he saw would mark him, as over the coming years it marked her.

They agreed to meet in a few days, back in their hometown Aguilares about twenty miles from San Salvador.

Coretta hid until it was safe to emerge, and then a couple of days later revealed what she had seen in a statement to a Judge. Supporters had persuaded him to meet her in an office in the Government Centre.

The army came for her as soon as they read her statement. A copy had quickly found its way to the Defence Ministry. She hid in friends' houses until it became too dangerous. Doors were kicked in. Heads were broken. After assurances were received from Paris and a junior French minister, Bernard Kouchner, who was visiting El Salvador, Coretta was dropped at the French Embassy, where she was kept hidden and safe. Two days later, she was smuggled out of the building and escorted by French soldiers and Kouchner to the airport and flown out of her homeland for her own safety.

She never made it to Aguilares.

Separation was beyond pain for Jorge and Coretta. They had survived together since their father's death in 1980. This was the first time they had been separated since then, apart from Coretta's time in the tortured confines of the basement of the National Guards Headquarters, after which Jorge learned to nurse his sister back from her horror.

Each day apart now, for both of them, left an empty space in their lives. Fear gave no time for grief. Hope had little foundation but was, however, a dream they both clung to, even at the worst of times.

Jorge waited for a week. He then went back, briefly, to San Salvador and talked to friends who sheltered him. They told him of Coretta. Her statement and escape.

The army wanted to silence her. They knew she had a brother. Colonel Adolfo Guzman wanted the brother. His capture would ensure Coretta's return and silence.

At one of the houses he sheltered for a night, he was handed a letter from Coretta.

*I have to get out. I made a mistake telling what I saw. It won't be safe for you either. Get out. I don't know where I'm going but we'll find each other one day xxxxxx.*

He grew a beard. He shaved off his long hair. He fashioned some wire glasses. He hoped it was enough.

Jorge escaped from the capital, but only just. Guzman and his fellow psychopaths were always just behind him. He took a bus toward the border with Honduras. The journey along the Pan-American Highway had been uneventful. As they passed San

Alejo, he began to relax for the first time since leaving San Salvador. There were only a few miles left until the border.

The army checkpoint was on an isolated spot beside a steep hillside. A gasp of fear ran through the vehicle as it came to a halt. Couples grabbed at each other. Children began to cry.

Women and children were separated from the men who were lined up on the ridge of the hill behind the bus. An officer walked slowly along the line, smoking a cheroot, looking carefully into each terrified face. He paused at Jorge. The scrutiny was intense; Jorge inhaled the aroma of stale smoke and tried to hold the eyes scrutinising him before dropping his glance in apparent submission. Suddenly the officer moved on to the end of the line. He snapped an order. The soldiers raised their guns and started firing.

Jorge felt a sharp pain in his leg. He fell, a body crashed on top of him. The firing continued, sharp staccato gunfire overwhelming the injured's short-lived screams and the yells of horror from women and children gathered in front of the bus. Suddenly the firing stopped. The body lying across Jorge was still. He surreptitiously felt for a pulse, there was none, as he was doing so the dead man's *cedula* – ID card - fell from his pocket. Jorge carefully eased it to himself and replaced it with his own. The soldiers were nearly all occupied at the front of the bus, trying to hold back the mass of desperate, screaming wives, mothers and children of the dead men.

Jorge eased his way from under the body and then inched agonisingly slowly to the edge of the hillside. He crawled over the slight ridge and dropped about ten yards, crashing into a thick tree root. Stifling a cry of pain, he moved beneath heavy, gnarled roots. His leg was wet with blood from the bullet, which luckily had only grazed his calf. There were more shouts from above and further gunshots. He forced his way deeper into the fresh lichen-packed twisted roots. He could sense eyes looking down from the road, a cigarette end fell just beyond his arm, a shout of laughter came, and then he heard the engine of the bus fire up. It moved away. The officer's voice rang out again and then, risking a careful glance through the roots, Jorge saw soldiers snatching up documents before throwing the dead bodies into an unholy mound. He smelled gasoline. Suddenly an enormous pyre reached toward the sky. Feeling the heat, he pushed his head into the fresh earth. The laughter he heard felt like an assault. The smell of burning flesh dragging him to a horror he didn't want to understand.

The time passed, somehow. Sounds ceased. The engines of lorries and the jeep roared into life. He waited and waited and only eventually emerged after what seemed a lifetime of panic and terror. Dragging himself to the top of the hill, he clasped his hands together, fell to his knees and wept.

Three months later, he found himself in Rio de Janeiro.

A year later, he married Rosita.

A year into their marriage, Jorge had completed his medical training.

Six months later, Doctor Roberto Garcia travelled with Rosita back to her homeland, East Timor.

Printed in Great Britain
by Amazon

21032237R00169